Incognito

**Center Point
Large Print**

**This Large Print Book carries the
Seal of Approval of N.A.V.H.**

Incognito

Gregory Murphy

CENTER POINT PUBLISHING
THORNDIKE, MAINE

This Center Point Large Print edition
is published in the year 2012 by arrangement with
The Berkley Publishing Group,
a member of Penguin Group (USA) Inc.

The text of this Large Print edition is unabridged.
In other aspects, this book may vary
from the original edition.
Printed in the United States of America
on permanent paper.
Set in 16-point Times New Roman type.

ISBN: 978-1-61173-277-1

Library of Congress Cataloging-in-Publication Data

Murphy, Gregory.
Incognito / Gregory Murphy.
p. cm.
ISBN 978-1-61173-277-1 (library binding : alk. paper)
1. Widows—Fiction. 2. Real property—Fiction.
3. Long Island (N.Y.)—History—20th century—Fiction.
4. Large type books. I. Title.
PS3563.U7298I53 2012
813′.54—dc23
2011033699

For Ludovica

Acknowledgments

I would first like to thank my agent, Judith Ehrlich, for her supreme patience, encouragement, humor, and unstinting support—for, in short, being the kind of agent every writer dreams of, but so rarely finds. Special gratitude must also go to my editor at Berkley Books, Jackie Cantor, for her professionalism, knowledge, and meticulous work that improved this book in countless ways. I am indebted as well to Sally Arteseros and Karen Hollenbeck for their passion, expertise, and editorial input. There are so many people without whose generosity and encouragement this novel might never have been completed. They are, in no particular order, but with the greatest gratitude: Peter and Renate Nahum, Richard and Joanna Balding, Henry Buhl, Antonia von Salm, Richard D. Kaplan and Edwina Sandys, Otho and Therese Eskin, Marnee May, Joyce Cecelia and J. Seward Johnson, Jana Brockman Seitz, Joan Kedziora, Helen Merrill, Huon Mallalieu, Nicholas and Virginia Finegold, Lima Addy, William and Julie Sargent, Paul Leyden, Beth Adler, Judy Wenning, Chris Lione and Tom Leonard, Vivian Bullaudy, George Weinhouse, George Elmer, and Yona Zeldis McDonough. I would like to thank my father, James Murphy, Sr., for providing a perfect template of a gentleman of the old school and my mother, Helen Glasco Murphy, for showing me that intelligence, kindness, strength, and wit are what make a woman truly irresistible. I would also like to thank Veronica Glasco, Virginia Curran, Kathleen Mencher, James Murphy, Kevin Murphy, Curtis Murphy, Paul Murphy, Donald Murphy, Maryellen Peck, Sheila Murphy, Elizabeth Murphy, and Margaret DeAngelis for their friendship and love and for contributing to the spirit of this novel in a thousand ways. I am grateful to the staff of New York Society Library for their enthusiastic assistance in my research into the details of New York life *circa* 19ll. Finally, to Ludovica Villar-Hauser—who found the money, time, and courage when I had none, and who never expressed anything but delight in having to live in a tiny one-room apartment for years so that I could write—goes my astonishment, my love, and my deepest gratitude.

Perhaps the most difficult heroism is that which consists in the daily conquests of our private demons, not in the slaying of world-notorious dragons.

—GEORGE ELIOT

Chapter 1

October 1911

William Dysart entered the small breakfast room of his brownstone and found his wife, Arabella, reading *Town Topics*.

"Good morning." William kissed the top of her head, recognizing the subtle floral scent of her perfume. "You're up early today."

"I heard you in the bath." She put down her magazine and poured his coffee. "Rather casual this morning," she said, fingering the lapel of his brown twill jacket.

"I have to go out to Long Island." William slid into the white wooden banquette next to her. "To see about purchasing some property for Lydia Billings."

"I thought she owned Long Island." Arabella smiled, reaching to rearrange one of the red tea roses in the small crystal vase on the table. The roses perfectly matched those on the Meissen breakfast service that had arrived for her from Tiffany's earlier that week. "Is it a large piece of property?"

"Just a few acres." The dishes irritated William more than he cared to admit, since they had been a gift from his father after Arabella had complained that William had put them on a horrible budget. "Probably owned by some tough old farmer's widow, who'll drive a hard bargain." He took a sip of his coffee.

"A perfect match for Mrs. Billings." Arabella stretched out her slender arms. The late October sun streaming in through the beveled glass windows turned her red-gold hair to fire, accentuating the delicacy of her exquisite features and dispelling William's annoyance about the dishes.

"Yes." William picked up the *New York Tribune* folded by his plate and snapped it open. "Unfortunately, I have to deal with them both."

"Anything interesting?" Arabella leaned against her husband's shoulder, glancing at the paper.

William kissed her cheek, then scanned the front page. "Just the usual mayhem."

Mary, the young kitchen maid, entered through a swinging door and placed a toast caddy before them.

"Good morning, Mary." William reached for a piece of toast. "How are you today?"

"Very well, sir," Mary said, but she scurried back to the kitchen more briskly than usual.

"Something the matter with Mary?" William buttered his toast as he peered through the etched panels of the swinging door.

"Not feeling well, perhaps. I hear the Goelets' entire staff is down with something." Arabella sank into the green velvet pillows of the banquette. "I had the most delightful time with your father last night at Delmonico's. I'm so looking forward to dinner at their house tomorrow."

"Are you?" William was surprised; he knew his wife and his stepmother did not care much for one another.

"Yes, I think it should be very interesting."

"Why?"

"Just a feeling," she said.

"You're being rather mysterious this morning." William glanced at the curve of his wife's white shoulders beneath the linen wrapper she'd draped over her silk nightgown. She tucked a curl of reddish blond hair away from her sleepy green eyes and yawned. William wondered if she could feel his eyes on her.

"I had a port." She leaned very close to William. "Two, in fact," she said like a young girl confessing to a crime. She raised her hands to her cheeks.

He felt a sudden urge to take her in his arms, but Mary entered and placed a covered silver dish on the table. He lifted the cover. "Stewed tomatoes! Lovely," he said. He tried to meet Mary's gaze, but she kept her eyes on the floor.

"I must look a perfect hag this morning," Arabella said after Mary had left the room.

"You know you look beautiful," he whispered.

"Darling," Arabella said, taking his arm, "I want to move."

"Yes." William sighed. "I know."

"I can't abide living in this house any longer."

"It's a lovely house."

"It isn't." She fingered the scalloped rim of her delicate coffee cup unhappily. "It's a warren of little rooms. You don't feel it, because you're at work all day."

"Belle"—William took a breath—"I know you would like a different kind of house. Something grander, but we—"

"Can't . . . afford . . . it."

"Precisely," William replied.

"But this house makes me feel as if I'm suffocating," said Arabella. "Your father would help us, I'm sure he would. All you need to do is ask."

"I'm not asking my father for anything."

"No. You're too proud."

"Pride has nothing to do with it. He tries to tell us how to live now. Can you imagine what it would be like if we were in debt to him?"

"It *is* your pride."

"Belle, please don't be unreasonable, I—"

"Unreasonable? I am miserable here." Tears sprang to her eyes. She threw down her napkin, rose from the banquette, and left the room. William sighed and picked up her napkin, then called for Mary.

She appeared at the edge of the door. "Yes, sir."

"I'm afraid we won't be having breakfast after all. Would you call the garage and have them bring my motorcar round?"

Upstairs, he found Arabella reclining on the chaise longue in her bedroom. "Let's not quarrel, Belle," he said, bending to kiss her.

She turned her head away. "I cannot abide living here, William. You don't know what it's doing to me."

"You would think we lived in a tenement."

"I feel trapped."

"Then we'll find another house." William sat down next to her. "There's a town house on East Sixty-ninth Street I think you might like. Larger than this. It went on the market last week."

"I don't want a town house. I want a proper house."

"A house with rooms we'll never use, staffed by people we hardly know. That's not a home."

"I want a place where I can entertain properly."

"So we can get our names in the papers like the Vanderbilts, the Astors, and all the others drunk on newspaper ink and a warped sense of their own importance in the grand scheme of things?"

"Oh, William, you would be happy to live out your life in this little house, when the whole world is yours for the asking."

"The whole world? A bunch of stuffed shirts and their overdressed wives."

"It is like talking to a wall!" She stood. "If you will excuse me, I have to bathe." She undid her wrapper and dropped it onto the chaise longue, then let her silk nightgown fall from her shoulders.

This sudden unexpected display of her naked shoulders and breasts caught William by surprise; he looked at her transfixed.

She pulled her wrapper to her. "You, Mr. Stuffed Shirt"—she pushed him into the sitting room separating their bedrooms—"have an appointment on Long Island." She shut the door. "We have the opera tonight with the Bradley-Martins."

"I thought that was tomorrow."

"Tonight! At seven."

He sighed. "I'll be home in plenty of time." He rested his hand on the knob, with an almost overwhelming urge to throw open the door, but hearing the key in the lock, he turned and hurried down the stairs.

William found his black Lozier touring car waiting for him at the curb, the man from the garage having cranked it to start and given its brass headlamps a final polish with a chammy. William jumped in the car and drove off, trying to quell a rising feeling of despair. He and Arabella had every reason on earth to be happy, but it was rare now that their conversations did not end in a quarrel. Perhaps he needed to make more of an effort to see things from her point of view, he thought as he waited for a pedestrian to cross Park Avenue. She had not been born to money, so it was understandable that things like houses and society meant more to her than they did to him.

He recalled when they were first engaged, how happy she had been to receive her first invitation to Mrs. Livingston's ball. Now she was invited everywhere, but it was still not enough. He put his car in gear and drove off.

He had hoped to make it out to Lloyd Neck, Long Island, in less than two hours, but a horse had pulled in front of a motorcar on the Queensboro Bridge, leaving a wagon overturned across two lanes of traffic, and it ended up taking him an hour just to cross the East River.

Fortunately, he had no appointment with Mrs. Curtis, the woman whose five-acre property he wanted to buy for Lydia Billings. Mrs. Curtis had no telephone, and Philipse Havering, the managing partner at his law firm, had asked William to call in person. Now he was regretting his acquiescence. Lydia Billings wanted to annex the woman's property to her two-thousand-acre estate, Bagatelle, which she planned to endow to the State as a park in her husband's memory. "She wants to build a pavilion on the Curtis property," Havering had told William. "The views across the Sound there are magnificent."

Havering, William knew, had already sent two letters to Mrs. Curtis inquiring about the property, which had gone unanswered. Of course, Lydia Billings could not approach the owner directly. Once it was known she had an interest in anything, the price would triple. But why, William wondered, had she specifically asked Havering to give him the job? Havering had authorized William to go as high as ten thousand dollars for the property, almost double what it was worth, but his advice to proceed cautiously so as not to arouse any suspicion left William feeling uneasy.

Bright orange and yellow leaves clung to the birch and maple trees lining the road to the front gate of Bagatelle, two simple square columns of brick, six feet high, topped by ivy-filled planters. The driveway ascended gradually through sloping meadows, then leveled and turned sharply by an ancient elm tree. William passed a large dairy barn, then farther on an imposing red brick and limestone stable with an enclosed courtyard. In the courtyard, a groom was brushing down the coat of a magnificent horse. Moments later, William could see the slate roof of Bagatelle, high above the treetops, hovering like some colossal bird, a sight that reminded him of childhood visits there. As a boy he would walk to Bagatelle almost every day from the Holborns', with whom he had stayed during the summer of his father's honeymoon in Italy. The memory of those long-ago days at Bagatelle, the feel of cool fields under his bare feet, and of sailing in Mr.

Billings's great yacht, lifted his spirits. But then something dark seemed to seep into the brightly woven threads of his childhood memories, like a pinprick of blood suddenly appearing and overspreading everything, a feeling that vanished as mysteriously as it had come, leaving him baffled.

William shook his head as if doing so might free him of even the memory of this disturbing feeling and pulled into a small gravel lot at the front of the house, an enormous red brick Georgian pile with unending wings and chimneys. He thought of all the times he had played tag with the children of the Billingses' chauffeur, once hanging out of one of the mansion's second-story windows, then dropping more than fifteen feet to the ground so he wouldn't be caught, but breaking his arm. For all his mischief, Mr. and Mrs. Billings were always happy to see him. They never had any children, but loved having them about, especially Mr. Billings, who was always ready to organize a game of blind man's bluff or hide and seek for them.

After asking the butler if he could leave his car, William began to walk to the Curtis property. He thought it would be better if he didn't arrive at Mrs. Curtis's door in his sleek motorcar, which might make his interest in her small farmhouse seem rather incongruous. He crossed the lawn to the back of the house and gazed at Long Island

Sound in the distance, remembering how Henry Billings had told him that the large rock just offshore was called "Target Rock" because the British had used it for target practice during the American Revolution. Mr. Billings had guided him around the property, relating the area's history and legends, his arm resting easily on William's shoulder, an expression of affection William had never received from his own father. Billings had given William a flint arrowhead from the grounds, which he said had been made by the Matinecock Indians, the original inhabitants of that part of Long Island.

He followed the slope of the property down toward the Sound, then walked along the sandy beach until he reached a path that wound its way up through a stretch of jagged bluffs. At the top, he paused to catch his breath, then took off his jacket and rolled up his shirtsleeves as he walked across a flat plain toward a large, old maple tree. Its orange, leafy fire was scarcely dimmed by the leaves it had strewn over the ground around it. He stared at the solitary maple framed by the waters of the Sound, and noticed a young woman reading on a bench beneath it. She looked up from her book and met his gaze.

"Hello," he said.

She smiled and returned to her book.

He walked on until he came to a small white clapboard house. Its green enameled screen door matched the trim on the screens of its shutterless windows. He stepped up on its porch and knocked at the door.

"Hello," he called. After waiting a moment, he knocked again, then stepped down from the porch and went around to the back of the house, where he found a bicycle with a sweater thrown over the handlebars. He returned to the front porch and fumbled through his jacket until he found the envelope with the letter he had written for Mrs. Curtis briefly discussing his interest in her property and giving the telephone exchange where she might reach him. As he bent to slide the envelope under the screen door, he heard footsteps behind him.

"Is that for me?"

William turned, surprised to see the young woman who had been reading under the tree. "You live here?"

She nodded.

"I'm looking for a Mrs. Curtis."

"I am Miss Curtis. Miss Sybil Curtis."

"I see. Well, I have some business I'd like to discuss with your mother."

"Mr. . . ." she inquired.

"Dysart."

"Mr. Dysart, my mother has been dead many years. I live by myself."

William flushed. "I'm sorry." He wondered why Havering hadn't told him she was a young, unmarried woman. "Have you a moment, Miss Curtis?"

"Yes, I think so."

William noticed her book—George Eliot's *Middlemarch*. "Enjoying your book?"

"Very much." She smiled politely.

"I think it's her best."

"Would you like some tea, Mr. Dysart?"

"I'd love some, if it's no trouble."

"Dysart." She paused at the screen door. "Scottish?"

"Yes, it is."

"I knew a family named Dysart when I was a girl. They were from Perth."

"Distant relatives, perhaps."

"Perhaps." Miss Curtis opened the screen door.

At the far end of the front room—the largest in the cottage—William saw an open door, leading to what he supposed was a bedroom. Directly in front of him another door led into a small bathroom, a modern convenience that surprised him. The only other room appeared to be the kitchen, its small entryway at a diagonal to the front door. It was a sturdy, well-built little house, more rustic hideaway—with its beamed ceilings, whitewashed pine paneling, and indoor plumbing—than farmer's cottage. Odd, he thought. Not at all what he had expected.

Miss Curtis turned to him, smoothing down loose strands of hair at the back of her neck.

"Please sit, I won't be a moment." She turned toward the kitchen. She was rather plain, he thought as he watched her walk away, but she had a trim, attractive figure.

William sat on the flowered-chintz sofa and looked around the room, which was quite pleasant and neat. The comfortable sofa was offset by two wooden chairs of monastic aspect with barley twist legs; a matched pair of blue-flowered ginger jars on the mantel glowed against the whitewashed pine. There was an artfulness in the placement of the furniture, rugs, and other objects that indicated a sophisticated aesthetic sense. Books were scattered on shelves, on the mantel of the fireplace, and in piles on the floor. Many had to do with the study and cultivation of plants and flowers. William picked a book from a shelf for a closer inspection. Miss Curtis entered with a tray and placed it on a low rosewood table before the sofa. "You have a great interest in gardening," he observed, holding up the book.

"Those were my father's."

William put the book back on the shelf, hoping he hadn't offended her.

"I hope you like your tea black, Mr. Dysart," she said as she poured him a cup. "I'm afraid I haven't any lemon or cream."

"I always take mine black," said William, returning to the sofa.

As she handed him his tea, William thought he saw a flicker of apprehension in her eyes, and it occurred to him that she might suddenly feel uncomfortable with a strange man in her house. "Would you prefer we sit outside?" he asked.

"Not unless you would," she replied, offering him a plate with a muffin. "I was just in town this morning and bought these from a woman who bakes them fresh every day. They're quite good."

William shook his head and took a sip of his tea. "Just the tea is fine, thank you."

She nodded.

"Miss Curtis, if you wouldn't mind, I'd like to get right to the point."

"Of course."

"I'd like to buy this house," he said, feeling guilty at the pretense, "and the surrounding property. About five acres in all, I believe."

She stared at him silently. "Yes, that's right," she said at last.

"I'd be willing to pay you a good price for it."

"I'm sorry, Mr. Dysart."

"A very good price."

She shook her head.

"Perhaps once you've heard my terms, you might reconsider."

"I'm sorry. It's not for sale—at any price."

William sipped his tea. "Well," he said at last, "if for some reason you should change your mind about selling, you will let me know?"

"Frankly, Mr. Dysart, I'm not going to change my mind."

"I see." William set his cup on the table. "Might I leave you my card, in any case?"

"If you like." She stood and smoothed out her dress.

William handed her his card.

She looked at it a moment. "Mr. Dysart, may I ask you something?"

"Certainly."

"Did you want to buy my property for yourself or for someone else?"

"Myself, of course," he said.

"I see."

"Well, thank you for the tea." He pushed open her screen door. "Good-bye then."

"Good-bye, Mr. Dysart."

William, distracted by his certainty that she knew he was lying, stumbled as he descended her porch steps.

"Are you all right?" she called.

"Yes—fine—thank you," said William. He tipped his hat, then walked off with the feeling that Miss Curtis was watching him with a very skeptical eye.

Chapter 2

When William came down to breakfast early the next morning, he was relieved to find that Arabella was not there. Her chatter with the Bradley-Martins over dinner and in the motorcar to and from the opera had left him feeling distant and cold. She hadn't touched him the whole evening—hadn't even let her gaze flicker over him—in what he knew was meant as a sign of her continuing displeasure with him. And as soon as the Bradley-Martins had dropped them off, she had darted up the stairs, complaining of exhaustion and a headache from "that dreadful soprano."

He ate his breakfast, then left the house and walked the four miles to his office on Wall Street. He walked every day to work, a fact he never confided to anyone—even when someone in his office would comment on the poor state of the trains or streetcars on a particular morning.

But as William paused to let a motorcar pass, he felt a sense of darkness begin to envelop him again, as it had at Bagatelle. He caught his breath and walked on with greater urgency through the borderless neighborhoods of New York, past red brick and gleaming limestone; over granite, slate, and cobblestone; through the smell of fallen leaves and horse manure, oil and gasoline; past glittering store windows and hovels. And amid these turbulent and ever-crowding city streets, William walked faster and faster as he tried to shake off the black, inexplicable feelings that pursued him.

When he reached his office, there was a message on his desk from Philipse Havering about a three o'clock appointment regarding the Curtis property. William was still troubled by his lie to Miss Curtis, however regrettable a necessity it might have been. It was certainly reasonable for Mrs. Billings to wish to maintain her anonymity in the case, and the price she was willing to pay for the property was more than generous. Still, the look in Sybil Curtis's eyes when he had lied to her haunted him.

He was thinking of that look as he sat across from Havering later in the dark sanctuary of his office with its view of New York Harbor.

"She won't sell then?" Havering asked.

William shook his head.

Havering glanced away. "We didn't think she would."

"Why?"

Havering shrugged. "Wait a few days, then go back to her."

"Phil, she's not going to sell for any price. She couldn't have been clearer."

"Then we'll have the State condemn the place.

It's what I recommended to Lydia from the first, but she has such a fear of the press and the circus they might make of it."

"You really think the press would pick it up?"

"In a minute," Havering huffed. "The widow of the infamous Henry Billings—all those thousands of acres—using her influence to swallow up a few more against the objections of its owner?"

"But having the place condemned seems rather excessive. There must be other areas on the Sound that would do as well as the Curtis property."

"That is not for us to decide."

"But if Lydia is wary of the press, wouldn't it be worth her while to consider an alternative?"

"She's never in her life had to consider an alternative, and you can be sure she's not going to start now."

Havering shuffled the papers on his desk and put them in a folder. "In any case," he continued, "the young woman who owns the property is a hermit, a recluse. She hasn't anything but that bit of property—no family, no income, nothing. She hasn't the ability to raise much of a fuss."

Havering seemed to know quite a bit about Miss Curtis, William thought. Why, he wondered, hadn't Havering shared any of that information with him? And why did he speak about her in such an odd way? William would never have thought to describe her as a hermit or recluse. He glanced out the window and saw a large luxury liner pulling into New York Bay and watched as two small tugboats struggled to keep the great ship on course.

"But . . ." Havering paused. "It will be easier all around if you can convince her to sell."

"Phil, I don't know that I'm the right person for this."

"Nonsense." Havering pushed his chair away from his desk. "Lydia specifically asked for you. I understand your families go back quite a way." Havering smiled. "The Dysarts and the Romneys, of course," he said, using Lydia Billings's maiden name, pointedly excluding the déclassé Billingses. "Your Great-Uncle Isaiah and Lydia's cousin Cornelia were, I believe, married."

William smiled wanly, wondering how Havering could possibly know such a thing, or even care.

"Give this Miss Curtis another call. We can't give up after only one attempt."

Perhaps, William thought, if he stayed with the case, he could at least make sure that Miss Curtis got the best possible price for her cottage. "When does Lydia need the property?" he asked.

"I'm sure she would be happy if Miss Curtis is gone by January." Havering stood, ending their meeting.

On his way back to his office, William stopped at his secretary's desk and asked her to send a wire to Miss Curtis requesting a two o'clock meeting at her home on Thursday.

Back in his office, William returned to work on the Consolidated Ironworks case, which his meeting with Havering had interrupted. The case had, up until this business with the Curtis property, engaged all his attention, and he hoped it would burnish his reputation among the senior partners at his firm.

He was writing at his desk when Theodore Parrish, a colleague at the firm and a friend from his days at boarding school, walked in.

"I didn't see you yesterday. Were you out?" Theodore asked.

"Yes," said William, "Lloyd Neck, trying to buy some property for Lydia Billings." He motioned for Theodore to close the door.

"Why the mystery, Billy?"

"You've done some work on the Billings account. Do you know about the plans for her place on Long Island?"

"Bagatelle?" asked Theodore, adding a facetious long "e" to the end of the word. "Of course, part of her campaign to salvage old Billings's reputation—you know *Satan's Banker*." Theodore sat down. "Your best chum and horse's ass *extraordinaire*, P. Havering, is handling the whole thing, and the little social climber couldn't be happier to be rubbing shoulders with the Baroness."

William nodded. "There's a small piece of land Havering wants me to buy in connection with it."

William got up and sat on his desk by Theodore. "It's owned by a young woman—a Miss Curtis—about whom I think Havering knows a lot more than he's letting on."

"Such as?"

"I don't know. He authorized me to make a fantastic offer to her, and she wouldn't even hear it. I think if I'd offered her a million dollars, she wouldn't have taken it."

"Maybe she's just very attached to the old place."

William walked to the window and looked at all the people passing by below. "One thing's for sure, Lydia Billings wants this young woman's property, and because she's rich and powerful, she's going to get it."

"Gee, that's really shocking, Will." Theo leaned back and folded his hands behind his head. "This young woman, is she pretty?"

"Pretty enough." William glanced at him. "Why do you ask?"

"If the place were owned by some old farmer, would you be as concerned?"

"I'm not one of those idiots that falls for a pretty face."

"Right. That's why you're married to one of the most beautiful women in New York." Theo brushed something from his pant leg. "In any case, Will, I don't think there's much you can do."

"They're planning on having the State condemn

the place if we can't come to an agreement. Perhaps if this young woman understands that she's going to lose her property no matter what, and would be far better off accepting the offer I was authorized to make her, she will—"

"Mrs. Billings's solicitor seems to be placing himself in an ambiguous position."

"Possibly," William admitted.

Theo shook his head. "Don't be an ass, Will." He took out his pocket watch. "I'm leaving in about an hour, care to join me for a drink?"

"I can't—have to catch up on the Consolidated case. This Billings mess has put me behind."

"It's not your mess, Will. Do whatever you have to do to make Havering and Billings happy, then go home to your lovely wife and forget all about it."

Chapter 3

As William dressed for dinner at his father's house, he thought about the Curtis property. At their initial meeting, Havering had told him that the property sloped down naturally to the Sound, providing easy access to the beach for future visitors to Bagatelle. Yet try as he might, William could not recall any slope to the land surrounding Miss Curtis's property. He fiddled with one of the silver cufflinks his father had given him for his birthday, but the clasp wouldn't hold and he tossed it on his dresser. He would have to forgo this token of filial devotion, however much he might feel the need for it that evening.

He went downstairs and began pacing in the front hall, waiting for Arabella. He glanced at his pocket watch. He did not want to irritate his father by being late for dinner. When Arabella finally came down the stairs in an elaborately pleated Fortuny tunic, she paused before the front hall mirror to study her appearance. Her eyes drifted to her turban with its stiff green and white feathers. Suddenly she turned without a word and began walking back up the stairs.

"We're going to be late," William called after her.

She did not respond, but called for Fanny Holland, the upstairs maid. "How is it my turban has a crease in it?" he heard her ask Fanny.

William leaned against the staircase and sighed.

"I don't know, ma'am."

"Is it that you don't know, Fanny, or that you don't care?" Arabella closed the door to her room.

Ten minutes later, Arabella descended the stairs in an unblemished hat, followed by a red-eyed Fanny.

Arabella sat brooding in the cab on their way to dinner. "I want Fanny dismissed."

"Because your hat had a crease in it?" Their cab moved past Central Park down Fifth Avenue toward his father's house on Fifty-seventh Street.

"Turban—not a hat—and it is ruined. I've told her time and again she's to wrap my hats in tissue paper before putting them away. Now I'm forced to go to your father's wearing a hat with grosgrain, when no one wears hats with ribbons after five anymore."

"You have dozens of hats with feathers."

"None I can wear with my hair in a Psyche knot."

"A what?"

"Oh, never mind. We're getting rid of Fanny and that's all there is to it."

"We're lucky to have Fanny. She is unfailingly polite and works hard. But you get her in such a state with your unceasing demands that—"

"I refuse to put up with her incompetence any longer," Arabella cut in, "but as you're so attached to her, she can work in the kitchen. I'm sure she has a genius for chopping and stirring things. I'm going to employ a real lady's maid."

"And where will we put this lady's maid? On the roof?"

"You're determined to vex me, aren't you, William?" Arabella lowered her voice. "When we might have room for all the servants we need. You don't care how unhappy it makes me living in that narrow, old-fashioned brownstone. Your father told me the other night he is embarrassed by the way we live—that horrible little house with no staff to speak of."

William heaved a frustrated sigh and watched the rain pelt against the window of the cab, the drops splitting and vibrating as they trickled down the side of the glass. He turned back to Arabella, but her eyes were shut, her fingers pressed to her lips as if she might cry.

"The beautiful Arabella Dysart," the papers called her, or "the devastating Mrs. D." She had been christened "The Gibson Girl Incarnate" by the *Times*, while the *New York Tribune* declared that she and the actress Maxine Elliott were the two most beautiful women in New York. She kept a scrapbook of all these clippings, which William had discovered on her dressing table two years after they were married. "What do you think you're doing?" she had demanded when she saw him flipping through the pages.

Such a fuss over a scrapbook, William had thought then, but he had since come to realize that it was a small clue to the much larger puzzle of his wife, for it directly challenged what was considered to be a complete lack of vanity in her nature—an attribute especially compelling and forever commented upon in one so exquisite. After the incident with the scrapbook, William had come to realize that most of the virtues he had originally admired in his wife were merely the result of a strenuous pretense. At first, he had pitied her and done everything he could to make her feel protected and loved, but the greater his efforts, the more firmly she seemed to resist him.

William turned from his wife and stared out into the night. He saw the gates of the Vanderbilt mansion on Fifty-eighth Street come into view, and beyond the gates, the great dark windows of the house, like the eyes of a corpse, and he thought of himself and Arabella adrift in a cold limestone mansion with endless halls opening into empty rooms.

Their cab pulled to the curb in front of his father's house. Rogers, his father's butler, stood in the columned doorway framed in a rectangle of light. A footman ran down the steep steps with an umbrella. William and Arabella entered the house and saw his father and stepmother descending the oak staircase in their evening clothes, his father holding solicitously on to his stepmother's arm.

"William, you will write to us often while we're away?" William's stepmother, Cady Dysart, asked him over their first course of oysters in his father's dining room. Its red Italian damask walls and deeply carved wooden ceiling were lit up by a fire from the room's great stone fireplace, which had been imported from a fifteenth-century French manor house. Cady and Charles would be leaving after Thanksgiving for Europe, traveling with the Livingstons to visit the de la Noyes at their seaside villa in Amalfi, before driving up to Cortina d'Ampezzo in the mountains.

"Of course, Cady," said William, smiling with

affection at his stepmother. Cady had come into his life when he was still very young and she had always been very kind to him. The former Esther Hathorne of Hartford, Connecticut, she had an impeccable New England lineage stretching back hundreds of years with nothing less than a college professor to boast of, though nothing more in a material way than Old Mill, the family farm of about seventy acres on the Connecticut River. William looked at Cady and thought how alike she and Arabella must appear to the world, both beautiful elegant women, but he could not imagine Cady humiliating anyone, least of all a poor servant girl.

Now, in her fifties, Cady was as lovely as she had ever been, but William noticed that her wineglass at dinner was emptied more quickly and filled more often than in the past, and that she could be almost short with his father. He remembered his own surprise a month earlier when he had heard her say absently, as she stood staring out the drawing room window after Sunday breakfast, "I'm so tired of it all."

William had hesitated. "Tired of what, Cady?"

She turned to him and he could see that she had not meant for him to hear, and the question weighed heavily upon her. She had hesitated, and then thrown his question off with a graceful smile. "Nothing. Mornings tire me, that's all."

A servant moved to take William's plate as

another placed a bowl of consommé before him. William looked over and saw Arabella talking quietly with his father. How beautiful she looked, he thought—like a goddess—dressed in the pleated white tunic that exposed her lovely shoulders. Her hair swirled up in layers, ending in a graceful twist. Ah, the Psyche knot, he thought. Over her tunic she had draped a sheer green shawl shot through with silver braid and beads, and at her throat hung a delicate web of platinum set with a single pear-shaped emerald, a gift William had given her for their first wedding anniversary.

His eyes drifted over the black-and-white diamond pattern of the dining room's marble floor and then to the ancient Gobelins tapestries hanging on either side of the fireplace—"The Hunt for the Unicorn" and "The Unicorn in Captivity." His great-grandfather, the Revolutionary War hero Colonel Charles Forrest Goodhue, glared down at William from his portrait over the fireplace with implacable determination, making him wonder how he might measure up against his courageous ancestor. Silently, he questioned if something had been lost to all the cosseted, privileged generations that had followed the colonel.

Arabella threw back her head and laughed at something her father-in-law had said. William sipped his consommé, remembering how as a child he would creep into the dining room when no one was there and climb up on this table to reach for the crystal ball hanging from the great chandelier. He used to imagine that it might reveal a picture of his future, like the magic globe in the tale of the witch and the prince his Scottish governess had read to him. As he gazed now at the firelight glinting off the smooth crystal, he mused that his wish would be to peer into the past, to unlock the mysteries of his childhood for which he still had no proper answers. The disappearance of his mother, who had gone away one October morning when he was a young boy promising to return, but she never had. Was it her death, not long after, that made his father such a puzzle to him—sometimes loving, sometimes inexplicably cruel? Finishing his consommé, he turned to Cady, who was toying with her wineglass. "You return in May?" he asked.

"Yes, we'll be sailing from Italy on the Livingstons' yacht."

"I'm told it has a ballroom!" Arabella exclaimed from the other end of the table.

"Cady insists," Charles added, "that we be back in time for spring at Old Mill."

"Why spring especially?" Arabella leaned toward Cady, her eyes sparkling.

William glanced at his stepmother, who looked uncharacteristically ill at ease. She had never invited Arabella to Old Mill, something William knew Arabella resented. "I—I'm not sure really . . ." she stammered.

39

"I think," said William, "the best thing about Old Mill in the spring is that old apple orchard. White blossoms everywhere—the smell of it."

"It is lovely," Cady agreed, "isn't it?"

William's father beamed at Arabella. "You must come see it. Captain Kidd's gold is supposedly buried beneath one of the floorboards there," he continued. "Isn't that right, dear?"

"That's the legend." Cady smiled uneasily.

"How picturesque." Arabella set her consommé spoon to the side of her plate and dabbed her lips with a white damask napkin. "I fancy it all wide planks and open hearths reaching to the ceiling." Arabella's smile drifted from William's father to Cady. Cady brushed the rim of her wineglass with her finger. Arabella cleared her throat. "In *Town Topics* today, it said that Consuelo Vanderbilt and the Duke of Marlborough are reconciling."

"Really?" asked Cady, signaling the butler for more wine.

"But it isn't true." Arabella shook her head. "Consuelo's mother, Alva Belmont, rang this morning that she won't be attending the Settlement House Ball, and everyone knows it's because the Duke is going to be there with his mistress, Gladys Deacon. Of course, now every ticket has been sold, thanks to Sunny"—she used the Duke's familiar name—"and Gladys."

Cady nodded.

"We're all just as happy Alva isn't coming,"

Arabella continued. "Do you know she was arrested two weeks ago for picketing the White House? Some women's rights affair. She and Edith Bradford."

William glanced at his father, who stared grimly down at the table. Edith Bradford was his mother's aunt, from whom his father was estranged.

"William," Charles spoke up, "I ran into Lydia Billings at the opera the other night and she mentioned her plans for Bagatelle, said you're trying to pick up some property for her." His father smiled at him. "She said she's counting on your tact and discretion. Bit of a sticky situation?"

"Only in that the owner doesn't want to sell." William shrugged. "Such a small piece of property. Frankly, I can't understand why Lydia needs it." He took the tongs from the silver tray held before him by his father's footman and placed several slices of roast duck with apples on his plate.

"Sometimes I think having so much makes people sick for things," said Cady. "Just the asparagus vinaigrette," she murmured to the young housemaid assisting the footman. William had never seen this housemaid before, and wondered what had happened to the stern-looking Nancy, who had served at his father's table for the past twenty years.

"My wife has become a socialist," his father

said, accepting the poached salmon with mousseline sauce.

"Not a very good one, I'm afraid—unless you count my support of half the milliners and dressmakers in Paris."

Three more courses followed, during which Arabella offered a recap from the latest *Town Topics*, while William and Cady silently picked at their food and William's father ate generous portions of everything served. William felt sick at the waste as the servants cleared platters heaped with food he knew would be dumped in the streets to feed the pigs.

"If we had your cook," said Arabella, "I would be so fat that cabmen would refuse to take me as a single fare. The only thing our cook makes well is stews. Thankfully, William has decided to put one of our housemaids to work in the kitchen, so perhaps the situation will improve." Arabella glanced at William, her lips pressed together in a pout.

"I have a bit of a surprise for you both," Charles said, putting down his dessert spoon. "William, I have decided I'm going to give you those two lots I own uptown."

"What?" William was caught completely off guard. His father owned two prime lots on Fifth Avenue near Ninetieth Street, on which he had always planned to build a house for himself and Cady one day.

"Yes, and . . ." He looked from William to Arabella with a great smile. "I'm going to build a house there for you."

William looked at Arabella. Her carefully composed features hid everything but her formidable resolve.

"But what about the house for you and Cady?" asked William.

"We're happy here and we don't want all the fuss and bother."

Arabella clapped her hands. "How perfectly marvelous, I—"

"I am sorry, Father, we can't accept it."

Arabella flashed William a look of fury.

"Why is that?" his father asked coldly.

"Arabella," said Cady, "why don't we have our coffee in the drawing room?" There followed an awkward silence, broken only by the rustle of the two women getting up to leave the room.

"William," said Charles, the instant the dining room door was closed, "why must you always be so obstinate?"

"Father, please listen to me. I appreciate the offer, but—"

"Don't patronize me."

"Very well, the answer is thank you, but no."

"How is it that I never have the benefit of the tact and discretion Lydia Billings praised in you? Or is that something you reserve only for your clients?"

"Is it rude for me to think I might choose where and how to live?"

"Are you offering that choice to Arabella?"

"I always believed, because it is what she told me before we were married, that she wanted to live a simple life."

"Simple life," his father said scornfully. "Hiding her away in that narrow little house on Seventieth Street."

"The newspapermen always seem to know where to find her."

"Of course they do—a woman like that—though you have her living little better than a clerk's wife."

"They must be paying clerks extraordinarily well these days."

His father sighed. A footman entered and took a silver coffee service from a dumbwaiter and poured them coffee.

Rogers entered and signaled for the footman to leave. "A cognac, sir?" His father nodded. "Mr. William?"

"Nothing, thank you, Rogers."

"Thank you," Charles said when his cognac was set before him. "That will be all, Rogers." His father stared at his drink. "You are just like your mother," he murmured. "She always had to have her way and didn't care who she hurt to get it."

"Maybe she just wanted to have a . . . a . . . way," William stuttered, amazed to hear his father mention his mother, "that was not always your way."

His father swirled his cognac in one hand. "You are"—he sniffed the amber liquid—"all I have left of her." He closed his eyes and drained the glass. "You needn't worry. I won't *burden* you about the house again."

How old his father had gotten, thought William, observing him. His life, which must have seemed so full of promise early on, had dwindled now to mere things—houses, furniture, his rare collection of Chinese porcelain—all to be dispersed at his death. His father's dreams had slipped from his grasp with the early death of William's mother, and William realized that he himself was a bitter reminder of the life that might have been.

William glanced up at the portrait of Colonel Goodhue. "Why are there no pictures of her?" he asked suddenly.

His father looked surprised. "They were lost."

"All of them?"

"Yes," his father said flatly. "In a fire." Then he stood. "Now, shall I have the motorcar brought around, or will you be taking a cab?"

"The motorcar, I think." William folded his hands. Then he called, "Father."

His father turned, his hand resting on the brass doorknob.

"I . . ." He shook his head. "Perhaps a cab—it will be easier."

Chapter 4

On Tuesday afternoon, William returned to the office from lunch and found a wire from Sybil Curtis in response to his, saying that she could not meet with him on Thursday, but could arrange to see him on Wednesday afternoon if that would do. He hastily rearranged his Wednesday schedule in order to accommodate her.

When he arrived at her cottage the next day, she was standing outside, just beside her screen door, talking to a handsome woman who looked to be in her thirties.

Sybil waved to William. He was surprised to hear her speaking French as he approached. "*Notre prochaine leçon. Est-il vendredi?*" she asked the woman.

"*Oui,*" the woman replied.

Sybil turned to William. "Caroline, this is Mr. Dysart, a gentleman who is interested in buying my property."

"Very happy to meet you." The woman held out her hand to him. "Caroline Jameson." She turned to Sybil. "You're not thinking of selling, are you? Not that I wouldn't like to have you as a neighbor, Mr. Dysart, but I would be lost without my friend."

"Now you've heard it yourself, Mr. Dysart. I'm

obliged to stay on here." She leaned toward Caroline and kissed her cheek, handing her a small, neatly wrapped package. "Shall I come on Sunday for tea?"

"I think you'd better—the children had an absolute fit this morning when they discovered I would be seeing you without them." She bent to start her motorcar.

"Here, let me do that for you," William said, reaching for the starting crank.

"Why, thank you," said Caroline Jameson. "I like to play the modern woman as well as the next one, but last week that thing almost sent me flying into a tree."

William gave the starting crank three fast spins until the motor turned over. He helped Caroline into the motorcar, then waved as she drove off.

"She's French?" William asked.

"No, but she used to live in France. She teaches me French, and in exchange, I watch her children. We barter to get by out here in the country, Mr. Dysart." Sybil held open her screen door. "Won't you come in? I can offer you tea. Or since it's rather warm for October, perhaps you'd like a cold sarsaparilla?"

"I haven't had a sarsaparilla since I was a child."

"All the more reason to have one."

In the kitchen, Sybil opened a wooden icebox, its nickel trim sparkling, and took out a brown bottle, then poured the sarsaparilla into a glass. "I keep it on hand for Caroline's children." She handed the glass to William. "I must say, I was rather surprised to get your wire," she said as they walked from the kitchen. "It's such a lovely day, why don't we sit on the porch?"

William sat in a wicker chair, noticing her copy of *Middlemarch* on the glass-topped table between them. "Very nice," he said, sipping his sarsaparilla. "Still enjoying your book?"

She nodded. "I like to read her when I find it difficult to . . ." She trailed off, then said, reluctantly it seemed to William, "Believe."

"Believe?" asked William.

She laughed. "I don't know why I said that."

Odd, he thought, as he watched her, that he had at first thought her plain. She had a beautiful, pale complexion that was set off by the deep color of her lips, and the lovely almond shape of her eyes imparted a liveliness to her expression when she smiled—a smile that seemed to overturn completely her look in repose of a kind of melancholy. She's probably a great favorite of the local boys, he thought as he took another sip of his sarsaparilla.

"Miss Curtis," he said, glancing away, "I'm afraid I have a confession to make. I wasn't being completely honest with you the last time we met. I am a lawyer and I was making the offer for your property on behalf of a client."

"I had wondered."

William hesitated. She would find out eventually in any case, he thought. Better to let her know what she was up against now than have her facing an order of condemnation by the State in a few months' time. "For your neighbor—Mrs. Billings."

She nodded.

"As you probably know, Mrs. Billings is a very powerful figure in New York. In the past she has given vast amounts of money to different charities. And now, in what is perhaps her most generous undertaking . . ." William paused as Sybil's eyes strayed off the porch.

"Yes?" She looked back at him. " 'Her most generous undertaking'?" The words sounded strangely hollow to him.

"Yes." He sipped the sweet sarsaparilla. "She is willing her property to the State to be developed as a public park and nature preserve."

"I see."

"Designers and architects have already drawn up plans, which they intend to begin working on this spring."

Sybil twisted a long loop of her dark chestnut hair around her finger, her thoughts obviously elsewhere.

"Naturally, the Sound and the surrounding beaches are important to those plans." William began to feel like a child's wind-up toy, bouncing into a wall, a painted smile on its face. "From what I gather, Mrs. Billings's property has no natural access to the Sound." He gulped the cold sarsaparilla. "But your property does, which makes it important to her."

"Does it?" Sybil got up from her chair and looked out over the porch railing. "Mr. Dysart, you must know that Mrs. Billings's property covers thousands of acres, many of them on the water, and that there is virtually no difference between my property and hers in what you call natural access to the Sound."

"It had occurred to me," William admitted, a trifle uneasily.

"And if her property were, in fact, so unsuitable to her plans, she could have her engineers bring the Sound to her front door if she wished. Please, Mr. Dysart, you insult me when you speak of the importance of my property to Mrs. Billings's plans."

"Why does she want your property, then?"

"I suggest you ask your client."

William felt his face flush. "Miss Curtis, I strongly advise you to get a lawyer, if you don't already have one." He stood. "Lydia Billings is determined to have your property at any cost."

She studied him, the hint of a smile playing at the corners of her mouth. "You're not at all what I expected, Mr. Dysart. You seem to be an honest man, even a kind one, but do you really think that one lawyer or a thousand would make a difference?"

William was caught off guard by her frankness.

"I did think you would want to do everything you could to hold on to your property."

"I'm going to lose my property to Mrs. Billings no matter what I do. The only thing I can do—which I intend to—is to make it as difficult as possible for her."

William tried to think of something further to say, but every possibility seemed insipid. There was a history here, something personal, familial perhaps, a grudge, a need for revenge or vindication of some kind. "Well, thank you for the sarsaparilla," he said, stepping down from the porch. When he had reached his car, he turned to wave good-bye, but Miss Curtis had already gone inside and closed the door behind her.

Chapter 5

During his meeting with Havering the next morning, after being pressed repeatedly about his failure to convince Miss Curtis to sell, William finally said in exasperation, "Miss Curtis seems to think—no, she is convinced—that Lydia Billings has some personal reason for wanting to purchase her modest property."

"How does she know it's Lydia?"

William felt his face flush.

Havering glanced out a nearby window. "I suppose she was bound to figure it out."

William breathed easily.

"A personal reason," Havering snapped. "Been living by herself too long. She's probably a bit off."

"She seemed perfectly sane to me."

Havering frowned and drummed his fingers on the gleaming surface of his mahogany desk. "We tried repeatedly to settle," he said finally. "We were prepared to make an extremely generous offer on behalf of our client and she wouldn't even consider it. If there is a problem at some future date, that will all be in our favor."

It had all been a charade, William realized. Havering and Lydia Billings had known all along Miss Curtis was not going to sell her property to Lydia, and they knew why, too. Now, if Miss Curtis managed to raise a fuss—which was doubtful—William would make a credible witness to her obstinacy, and his discretion could be relied on in view of the long-standing ties between his father's family and Lydia's family, a relationship that Havering—and no doubt Lydia—assumed William would take great pains to protect.

William returned to his office, angry at being used as a pawn in some bizarre game. He wondered for a moment if Miss Curtis might not be a love child of Henry Billings's. Probably just a poor relation, he thought as he made a quick note in the file he had started for the case, marking it closed. He then took a walk outside to clear his head.

When he returned from his walk, he found a message from Havering on his desk. "Lydia Billings wants to see you. She's not happy," Havering had scrawled on his monogrammed stationery.

"Damn it," William whispered as he pushed down the phone hook several times to put through a call to Lydia. Her private secretary answered and canceled a previous engagement so that William could meet with Lydia at two thirty that afternoon at her home on East Fifty-fourth Street. As William put down the receiver, he thought again of Sybil Curtis, and of her suggestion that he ask Lydia why she was so determined to have her property. He decided he would do just that.

It had been some time since William had last seen Lydia Billings. She had been considered quite a beauty in her youth, so when she entered her drawing room, he was surprised to see that age had given a sharper line to her chin and greater prominence to her nose, imparting a certain severity to her face.

"William"—she held out her hand as her maid closed the door—"thank you for coming by today. I hope I'm not taking you away from anything too important."

"Nothing more important than this, Lydia." He took her hand.

"How kind of you to say so. Would you like a drink?"

"No, thank you."

"So, William," she began, and sat across from him on a delicate sofa upholstered in yellow silk, "how can we solve this little problem of ours?"

"Frankly, I don't know. As you are aware, I have spoken to the owner—twice now—and she is not willing to sell, whatever the price. Your only recourse, as I believe you have already discussed with Philipse Havering, is to have the property condemned."

"I really would like to avoid any unpleasantness." Lydia toyed with an amethyst ring on her finger. "Such a bore." She laid her hand against the smooth yellow fabric of the sofa and studied the deep purple of her ring against the bright silk. "I can wait until late spring, if that will help. Perhaps, by then, you might find a way to convince the owner to sell."

William hesitated for a moment. "The owner—Miss Curtis—is aware that it's you who wants to buy her property."

Lydia sighed. "These things have a way of getting around, don't they, William?"

"And my impression is that she has some personal reason for not wanting to sell it to you in particular."

"A lot of people have something against me simply because my name is Billings." She clasped her hands together. "But there is nothing I can do about that, is there?"

"Perhaps," he pressed, "but Miss Curtis seems to think you have something against her."

"How ridiculous!" She made a sweeping gesture. "I don't even know who she is." She leaned forward. "What could I possibly have against her?"

"She said I should ask you."

"How extraordinary!" She laughed. "It seems the moment people hear the Billings name, they go mad. You know, of course, that Mr. Billings was responsible for the Civil War, the Johnstown Flood and . . . the Blizzard of '88. I shouldn't wonder." She shook her head. "So I have some ulterior motive for wanting this woman's property? Well, I would like very much to hear it. But you can tell her that she had better be willing to repeat it, whatever it is, in court." She sighed.

William waited a moment. "Lydia," he said finally, "since the owner is determined not to sell—whatever the reason—and you wish to avoid a struggle, which could bring negative publicity, what about an alternative site for your pavilion? Have you considered that rise of land not far from your dock—"

"William," Lydia cut in, "it is not for me to consider alternatives. This Miss Curtis can either accept my offer now or the State's later, and you may assure her that the State's will not be nearly so satisfactory as mine. Now, she has until the end of May to be off the property. How this is accomplished, I don't care, but it will be accomplished."

"I see," said William.

"I do so hate to be harsh." Her large gray eyes, which had a keenness undimmed by age, burrowed into him. "Now, I am sure you think me a perfect monster," she said, her voice suddenly smooth, her smile almost flirtatious.

"Not at all."

"Well, it's kind of you to say so. You must realize how important this is, not only to me, but to all those who will enjoy the park for generations. You will try one last time, William? Please."

William nodded, and as their conversation continued, he felt that each word he spoke was false, his every smile a small lie.

When he stood to leave, William could see that Lydia was pleased, certain he would be a useful tool in her attempt to wrest Sybil Curtis's property from her without any negative publicity. He glanced around her drawing room with its soaring arched windows, Flemish and Italian paintings, and silk-hung walls, and it oppressed him as no wanton display of poverty or ignorance could. He said good-bye to Lydia and her butler showed him out. As he made his way home up Fifth Avenue, his black leather shoes scuffing against the pavement, a sense of apprehension began to grow in him that this battle over a small piece of property on Long Island might somehow, before it was over, cause him to forfeit either his self-respect or the slow, steady rhythm of his uneventful life, and he was desperate to lose neither.

Chapter 6

On Friday, William spent a long yet unproductive day at the office, filing briefs all morning and wasting an entire afternoon in the firm's library, reading volume after volume of fine-print case histories referencing the rule of reason as enunciated by William Howard Taft in *Addyston Pipe and Steel Company v. United States*. Irritated with his secretary, Miss Leary, for being home with a cold, and with both Miss Curtis and Lydia Billings for distracting him from the Consolidated case, he rushed home, taking the Lexington Avenue subway to its terminus at Forty-second Street and Fourth Avenue. From there he ran to Third Avenue to catch the elevated line to Sixty-seventh Street. Arriving home finally, he hurried to get ready for a formal reception for his friends, the Lyalls, who were visiting from England. He was in no mood for yet another social function, nor for being harangued by Arabella for arriving home late, so he was pleasantly surprised when he entered his bed-room to find a fire in the fireplace and his evening clothes laid out with a note.

Meet me in the library. I have champagne chilling.
—A

She hasn't given up on the idea of a new house, he thought as he rushed to take his bath. A house, a goddamn house! He scrubbed his neck with a washcloth and considered every way he might find a compromise with her. It was more than a house she wanted, it was a way of life—with concomitant expectations, obligations, and pressures. He imagined himself in middle age, a prisoner to his evening clothes, master of the witty retort and the smallest of small talk—probably a glassy-eyed boozer, for how else could one tolerate such a life? Still, he thought as he dressed quickly, he would continue with the social whirl he detested and she craved and hope that she would grow tired of it all. Perhaps, he reflected, after they had a child or two, or after she was superseded as the girl of the moment in the news magazines, she might see the pointlessness in such a life.

Winding a white silk bow tie around his neck, he smiled wearily at his reflection in the mirror. Two difficult women, Arabella and Lydia, both used to getting what they wanted and both wanting houses from him. He had always been good at finding ways of meeting expectations and not disappointing others, but now he was stumped. He sighed, pulling the ends of the tie tautly. Why did his father have to offer to build them a house in the first place? William opened a drawer and put a clean handkerchief in his breast pocket. But then his father had always seemed competitive with him about Arabella— indeed, about every woman who had ever come into William's life. He frowned and gave a few final brushstrokes to the cowlick at the back of his head and rushed from the room.

"My, don't you look handsome," Arabella said, sitting with her arms draped over the back of the sofa when he entered the library. She took a bottle of champagne from a silver ice bucket.

"And don't you look beautiful." She was wearing feathers in her hair, and around her neck were several ropes of pearls. Her silk dress of green and yellow stripes was cut low, the stripes emphasizing the curve of her breasts and narrowness of her waist. She leaned forward to pour the champagne and William could see the naked arch of her back. Despite all their difficulties, he could still feel the same desire he had felt for her six years earlier when they had married. He bent to kiss her, but she offered him her cheek. Only her cheek, until she's certain I'll yield, he thought, sitting down across from her. "Thank you, Bella," he said, accepting the glass of champagne, "this is a nice surprise."

Smiling, she sipped her champagne. "I saw Laura Lyall this afternoon. Apparently they're going out West before returning to London."

"Really?" He had spent a summer in Maine with cousins of Laura Woodward, now Lady Lyall, after his graduation from college. Laura had lived just across the road in a large old clapboard house overlooking the sea.

"It seems Andrew wants to buy a horse." She reached for her silver cigarette case. "Frankly, I think he's an imbecile." Opening the clasp, she drew out a cigarette. "I spoke to Lucie Parrish today. She invited me to one of her women's rights events next week."

"Yes, I know." He leaned forward to light her cigarette. "I promised Theo I would go."

"How ghastly. You are a better friend than I. If you ask me, Lucie wears the pants in that family."

"The meeting might be interesting."

"No thank you." Suddenly Arabella's tone changed. "I really don't care about any of that. I suppose I could make myself care if it became important."

"You can't make yourself care."

She looked at him, then glanced away. "I can," she said quietly.

Watching his wife silently slip on her green

velvet gloves, William felt there was something rather tragic about her at that moment.

"Dorothea Biddle will be there tonight," she said, studying her reflection in the tiny mirror tucked inside her cigarette case. "Do you think she's prettier than I?"

"No one's prettier than you." William put down his champagne glass and stood. "And you know it."

She lowered her eyes, the hint of a smile playing at her lips.

"Shall we walk?" he asked.

She shook her head. "A cab."

"It's three short blocks. By the time we get into and out of a—"

"I'm not going to walk up to their door like some farmer from the place down the road."

"Can't anything ever be easy?"

"Only for you, darling," she said, picking up her purse.

When they arrived at the newly renovated home of Albert and Julia Hamilton, Laura Lyall's mother and stepfather, a footman rushed to open their cab door.

Light blazed through the many shimmering windows, and the freshly washed marble and limestone glinted in the night. Julia Hamilton, Arabella told William as they stood before the house, had eliminated the 1890s vulgarity of the original steeply pitched slate mansard roof, balustraded cornice, and stone urns, replacing them with a sheer wall of limestone embellished by a simple frieze. "I heard her husband wanted to install a glass and copper canopy over the front door," said Arabella. "Can you imagine? Thankfully Julia was able to restrain him."

Inside, in the front hall, the Hamiltons stood with Laura and her husband, Lord Lyall, in a small semicircle that echoed the curve of the circular marble staircase rising in a great spiral behind them. The knot of people surrounding them gradually unwound itself into the drawing room. William could smell the odor of fresh concrete, new wood, varnish, and paint.

"Ah, the Dysarts," said Albert Hamilton, taking Arabella's hand. "I'm so glad you were able to come."

"The house looks lovely," Arabella remarked.

Mrs. Hamilton turned from her last guest and smiled graciously. "Thank you, my dear. Actually, I think I would have preferred something with old-fashioned red bricks, but ever since Albert's been to Paris, he's had his heart set on something grand like this. I'm afraid I'm going to have to put on my jewels first thing in the morning and traipse about all the rest of the day carrying a large fan or something just to make certain I don't disappear."

"I think we'll always be able to find you, my dear," said her husband. He turned to William and Arabella. "Have you met Lord and Lady Lyall?"

"Of course." Julia Hamilton placed her hand on Arabella's arm, directing her toward her daughter and son-in-law. "William and Arabella know Laura, but I don't believe they've met Andrew yet."

If Julia Hamilton was embarrassed by these not infrequent blunders made by her rich husband, who had begun life in the slums of Chicago, she never gave the slightest indication. William had seen other marriages like this, of people with unimagined new wealth wed to members of old New York society living in straitened circumstances. Inevitably the patrician eye would wink in acknowledgment that the best was being made of an unfortunate situation. Julia Hamilton, a Halcombe from one of New York's oldest families, never betrayed her husband, and William wondered if Albert Hamilton knew how rare his wife was in the world into which he had married.

"Why, yes, we met in London two years ago," William heard Arabella say to Lord Lyall. "I think it was at the Wilbrahams'. I don't suppose you remember."

"As if anyone could forget you, Mrs. Dysart," said Lord Lyall, a tall, fair man of about thirty.

William turned to Laura Lyall. "It's wonderful to see you. How long do you plan to be in New York?"

"We'll be staying here with Mother through

Christmas, then we're going on to Chicago," Laura answered.

"I was always afraid you were going to marry that little brown sparrow," William's father had joked about Laura in front of Arabella more than a year after William and Arabella were married. William had smiled as they laughed, but the thought of Laura pained him—the memory of August days spent talking with her by the ocean, the heat of the summer sun tempered by breezes skimming across the sea, up the rocky cliffs, over stone walls, caught in the embrace of wild roses.

As Laura spoke to him now, he could not help recalling the moment he first took her hand, their first tentative kisses, the stolen embraces, and the night before Laura left for Europe, the tears she cried at leaving him. How close William had felt to her then, closer than he had ever thought possible. Then the fear began. That something terrible would happen to Laura and it would be because of something he had done or had failed to do. A fear that only grew stronger as his feelings for her grew, until the anxiety became almost more than he could bear, and he felt he had to give her up. And when it was over, she had never really known why.

"From Chicago," Laura continued, "we're going out to the Far West, which Andrew has wanted to do since he was a boy. I'm afraid he wants to be a cowboy." Arabella put her arm through William's.

Laura lowered her voice and asked very seriously, "Where can I find some cowboys, William? Real cowboys."

"Hoboken, Laura."

"William." Laura hit his arm as she laughed.

"I'll look for you both next spring . . ." William felt the gentle pressure of Arabella's hand and turned to accompany her into the drawing room. "In a covered wagon on Fifth."

"Yes, do," Laura called after him, "pursued by Indians."

William and Arabella entered the Hamiltons' drawing room, a high-ceilinged, airy rectangle running almost the entire length of the house. He looked around the newly refurbished room. French doors at the front opened onto two small wrought iron balconies, while doors at the back led to a small conservatory. The room was painted in various shades of light brown and gilt, which set off the bright white ceiling festooned at its corners with plaster fruits, vines, and flowers. Fragile-looking gilt chairs filled the center of the room's highly polished parquet floor, while upholstered chairs and settees were placed among potted palms at the perimeter. William watched servants glide with silver trays among the hundred or so guests, who were clustering together and drifting apart like bits of glass in a kaleidoscope.

Arabella stopped to say hello to Eugenia

Beckwith, a society matron, as William went to speak with David Isaacson from his firm.

"You could at least be pretending to have a good time, David."

Isaacson looked out at the crowded room. "I was just thinking how happy my parents would be to see me here. And all I can think is *so what?* It's the same at work—they were so proud when I started at the firm. But what are we really doing? Making rich men richer—not to mention ourselves. Law should be art, philosophy; your heart should pound with it!"

"Maybe someone should tell Phil Havering that."

"In thirty years we're all going to be Phil Haverings, Will, and wondering how it happened."

"Is that your greatest fear?"

"My greatest fear is that by then we won't care."

William heard his name being called and turned to see his friend Theodore Parrish.

"Lucie said you were coming," Theo told him, "but I was sure you'd find some excuse for hiding away in your library with a whiskey and a book."

Before William could respond, Eugenia Beckwith bustled over with Arabella.

"Theodore, is Lucie here?" Eugenia asked.

"Over there, Mrs. Beckwith"—Theodore turned his head—"talking to Grace Newington and Theodate Rutherfurd."

"If you'll excuse us," said Arabella, "we have to

speak to her about the Settlement House Ball." Arabella and Mrs. Beckwith hurried away.

Theodore looked around the room. "I suppose this is Al Hamilton's formal debut in society— rather too old and a bit too bald for a debutante, if you ask me. I'm getting a drink. Do you want one?"

William shook his head, but regretted it when Philipse Havering suddenly appeared at his elbow.

"How did you make out with Lydia yesterday?" he asked.

"I promised her I would make one last attempt. I've already wired Miss Curtis."

"Very gracious of Lydia, if you ask me. Now this young woman will have no one to blame but herself if she loses her property."

"Phil, she was always going to lose her property, no matter what she did."

"You know what I mean." Havering smiled, patted William's back, and moved on.

Theodore Parrish returned with a drink in his hand. "I've been circling the room waiting for the old mastodon to leave. What did he want to know? Why you weren't at your desk?"

"About that bit of property Lydia Billings wants on Long Island," William said, turning when he heard someone calling his name. He was surprised to see a frail-looking older man approaching, whom he didn't recognize.

"Christ, Thomas Holborn," Theodore whispered,

"and three sheets to the wind. I'm going to see if Lucie needs a drink or something. Hello, Mr. Holborn," Theodore called before dashing off.

"It's been so long since I've seen you, William." Holborn's voice was thin, and his eyes filmy. "I was sitting over there, and I thought, well, if it isn't . . ." Holborn slurred. "Yes, Willy Dysart. Remember the summer you stayed with us at Lloyd Neck?" His hands were shaking. William helped him into a nearby chair. "You were a boy when Mrs. Holborn, my . . . Lottie . . ." The tremor in Holborn's hands spread to his arms.

"Of course I remember, Mr. Holborn. It was one of the happiest times of my life. If not for Mrs. Holborn's kindness, I would have had to spend the entire summer with that sharp old governess of mine, Mrs. MacKenzie."

"The tartan tigress."

"Yes." William smiled. He sat down and ran his hand gently over Thomas Holborn's trembling forearm. "I was just out that way yesterday—at Bagatelle."

Holborn glanced at William furtively. "Oh," he whispered. "Terrible."

"Terrible?" asked William.

"Lottie . . ." He looked into William's eyes. "It was my fault, of course. She was so good." His shoulders began to shake, and William was afraid he might cry.

"Yes, she was," said William, scanning the room

for Theo, wondering what had happened to the dignified Mr. Holborn he remembered from his childhood.

Holborn's body began to sway in the chair.

"Why don't I get you a cab, Mr. Holborn?" William helped Holborn up, guiding him by the arm to keep him steady. He passed Arabella. "I'll be back in a moment," he called to her. In the front hall, he saw Julia Hamilton, who volunteered one of her footmen to accompany Holborn home.

When William returned to the reception, Arabella strolled over to him. "I don't know why they bother to invite him," she said. "He always drinks too much."

"He's very lonely, misses his wife."

"Then he might have been kinder to her when she was alive."

"What do you mean?"

Lucie Parrish came over to them and put her hand on William's arm. "Shall we sit back here?" she whispered. "I think we'll be able to hear very nicely from here."

At the front of the room, musicians were perched at their chairs, instruments poised. "Who cares if we can hear," muttered Theodore. "I just hope it's short."

Riding home in a cab after the party, William asked Arabella to explain her comment about Thomas Holborn.

"He had a mistress. Isobel Rhinelander told me."

"But he adored his wife."

"Apparently he adored his mistress more."

"I don't believe it."

Arabella sighed. "According to Isobel Rhinelander, there was a large party at the Newingtons' house in Rhinebeck. Charlotte Holborn got drunk. Mrs. Newington came to Isobel and asked for help and they hurried Charlotte off to a bedroom. While they were trying to put her to bed, she kept saying something about her husband and some girl. They tried to quiet her, but it only made things worse. Finally she fell asleep. That was the last anybody saw her. She died not long after—drank herself to death." They had arrived at their door, and the cabman opened the motorcar door for Arabella.

"It wasn't always like that." William paused on the sidewalk. "I stayed with them one summer. I never knew a happier couple. He wasn't interested in other women. They used to row out almost every day to a small island near their place to picnic by themselves."

"Really, William. An island"—she laughed— "and probably where he kept his mistress hidden all along."

William stared at his wife. An incomparable beauty—flawless complexion, fine cheekbones, full lips—but how little empathy lay behind those lovely eyes.

"You are such an innocent," Arabella said as William opened their front door for her. He watched her enter the house, her opera cloak adjusted carefully to expose her bare white shoulders. How different Laura Lyall's reaction would have been to Holborn's situation, he thought, then pictured Sybil Curtis's guileless expression when she had asked him if he would like a sarsaparilla. How syrupy and sweet it had been, but he'd drunk the entire glass because she had seemed to be so happy to have it to offer him. He cringed, recalling the taste.

"Would you mind?" Arabella asked. "I'm freezing."

"I was just thinking of something," he said, closing the door behind them.

Chapter 7

Monday morning, as William was working on the Consolidated Ironworks case, challenging the assertions of the plaintiff, Kelmscott Coke & Petroleum, a return wire arrived from Sybil Curtis confirming their meeting on Wednesday. He was surprised that she had agreed to meet him—how many times, after all, had she to tell him she would not sell? But perhaps she realized he was being pressed to it by Lydia Billings and took pity on him.

Two days later they sat across from one another in her comfortable front room, the long shadows of the November afternoon falling across the floor.

"Mrs. Billings doesn't understand the meaning of the word 'no,' does she?" Sybil smiled. "I don't suppose she hears it often."

"You know her well."

"Well enough."

"She says she doesn't know who you are."

Sybil shrugged.

"If you think you're going to have your day in court with Mrs. Billings, or embarrass her in some way, there is not a chance in the world of that happening. The condemnation proceedings will all be executed with such brutal precision, you'll hardly know what's happened until you're on the street somewhere."

"Do I seem so very naive?"

"Just young and idealistic."

"I might say the same of you."

"I merely expect people to act in their own best interest."

"Perhaps I am acting in my own best interest."

"Not from where I sit." He sighed. "I must say I admire your fortitude. You're certainly going to need it." He reached for his coffee cup and took a sip. "Now, Miss Curtis, before I go, I have one last question for you."

She looked at him.

"What exactly is it that George Eliot helps you to believe?"

She laughed. "I'm flattered you have given such thought to my little remark." She paused. "I'm not sure what I meant exactly." She hesitated. "My father used to say that everyone is sacred. I think it's important to believe that."

"Why?"

"Because if it's not true, nothing else matters."

"Maybe nothing does."

"Sometimes I believe that, too."

"Well, then." He set down his coffee. "Do you see Mrs. Billings as sacred?"

Sybil reached for the coffeepot and refilled his cup, then leaned back in her chair and looked out the window. William followed her gaze to the fields of brown grass and the naked branches of trees in the distance, an otherwise somber view made majestic by the slanting golden light. "Is there anything more beautiful . . . or sad . . . than an autumn afternoon?" she asked.

"And Lydia Billings?" he repeated.

She looked into his eyes. "I suppose . . . yes, I do think she's sacred." She turned to glance out the window again. "Though sometimes I forget, and just think she's holy hell."

William laughed and she turned to him with a surprised smile as if she'd just been told a bit of happy news.

"If I see her as sacred," she continued, "if that's even the right word, then I'm able to have some compassion for her. And if I don't, I am filled with hatred for her. On the one hand, I see God in her. On the other, I see the devil in us both." She flushed. "I'm sure, Mr. Dysart, that you're now thinking I've been out in the country too long."

"On the contrary, I was thinking perhaps I've been in the city too long." William sipped his coffee. "I hope you will reconsider, Miss Curtis. Frankly, I don't like the idea of you being at the mercy of someone like Lydia Billings."

"Who is your client."

William looked down. "Yes, of course." He stood and noticed a small set of binoculars. "Keeping an eye out for Mrs. Billings?" he asked.

"No." She smiled and stood. "I'm taking up birdwatching." She picked up the binoculars. "A bit of an extravagance, but I got them secondhand." She reached for a library book, *The Birds of Long Island*, and leafed through it. "Isn't this beautiful?" She held the book up for William to see.

The Blackburnian Warbler, William read, and beneath it a drawing of a bird with a yellow face, a black mask around its eyes, and a splash of red at its throat. "Interesting. I've spent a good part of my life on Long Island and have never seen one."

"You have to look very carefully." She raised the binoculars to her eyes. "They're very shy."

He looked at her with the binoculars held up to her eyes as she spoke. What lovely lips, he thought, delicate, finely etched.

"Besides, they're only here in the spring." She lowered the binoculars and looked at William. "Oh, dear," she quipped, trying not to laugh, "you look embarrassed for me—the dotty country spinster."

William was charmed. He noticed another library book—Melville's *Typee*—and picked it up.

"I just started it," she said. "I loved *Redburn*, but have to confess, I could not get through *Moby-Dick*. I know it's supposed to be his masterpiece, but . . ."

"I think you have to be in just the right mood for it," said William.

"Thank you for not saying it's because I'm a woman."

"And thank you for agreeing to see me yet again, Miss Curtis." He extended his hand. "I'm sorry for taking so much of your time with this unpleasant business."

Sybil shook his hand. "Will I be seeing you in court, then?"

"No, this is the end of my involvement. I imagine the next thing you'll be getting is a letter from the State."

"I see," she said. "Well, it was a pleasure to have met you, Mr. Dysart."

"And you," said William.

He opened the screen door and stood on her porch for a moment. Then he turned back. "It just occurred to me, do you think you might show me some of those places at Bagatelle you spoke of—locations similar to yours?"

She looked surprised. "If you like."

"Maybe I can still convince Mrs. Billings to consider an alternative."

"I'm happy to show you, but I'm afraid it won't make any difference."

"Try to be more optimistic." William stood in the doorway as she went to get her coat. He noticed a small package wrapped in brown paper, with "Caroline" written on it.

"I'm afraid I'm a bit gloomy by nature, Mr. Dysart. My mother was Irish."

"I didn't know the Irish were gloomy; I just thought they drank too much." William could feel his face flush, and he hoped he had not offended her.

"Really?" She stood by her closet. "Well, perhaps before all this is over, so will I." She put on her coat, wrapping a scarf around her head. "But I was always told it was the Scots who drank."

"Were you?" William raised an eyebrow. "Well, whoever told you that lied."

"A Scotsman, I'm afraid." She paused. "I hope it's the last time I'm lied to by one."

They walked out onto the porch. She looked up

at the darkening sky and the late afternoon sun just beginning to sink into the west. "How beautiful," she said, then rushed down the steps as William raced to keep up with her.

Tramping across a wide, flat field, he said, more boldly than he'd intended, "I imagine it can get a bit lonely living out here by yourself." A strong wind blew in off the water.

"At times." She looked out toward the Sound, which was cresting with waves in the wind. "It looks like a great monster now, doesn't it? As if it could swallow up everything."

"Yes," he agreed, taking a deep breath and smelling the salty sea air. "So, how do you pass the time?"

"Other than birdwatching, you mean?" She cast him a wry sideways glance. "Well, reading, I suppose, walking, thinking."

He searched the autumn sky. "And what do you think about, if you don't mind my asking?"

"How can there be a God in a world where there is so much suffering? Where will I go after Lydia Billings takes my property? Who is Mr. Dysart?"

He laughed. "And have you come to any conclusions with all your thinking?"

"Only about the last," she said as they descended into a shallow ravine leading through a stand of pines.

"And?"

"My guess is you're from one of those old New

York families, who believe the world began with the American Revolution."

"Anything else?"

She hesitated. "I think you're a bit of a snob."

"I think you're a bit blunt."

"Oh, dear. I've been too personal and given you the perfect opportunity to look down your nose at me."

"I think you're too proud, Miss Curtis, to give anyone the opportunity to look down his nose at you, though I expect you'd consider it a good joke to give some snob from New York the idea he's had the chance."

She laughed.

"I have been making my own observations," he said.

"So I see." She glanced at him. "You remind me of Percy."

"Who is Percy?"

William could see she regretted having mentioned Percy at all.

"Someone." She gave a quick shake of her head.

William nodded and they walked on for some time in silence. They came to a broad clearing of land, which sloped gently toward a wide beach.

"Here is a lovely spot for Mrs. Billings's refreshment stand, string of seesaws, or whatever it is she wants to build near the water," Sybil said.

"Are you sure this is her property?"

She nodded. "Over those trees you can see the roof of her house. Besides, just about everything on this side of the main road belongs to her."

He looked around. "It looks ideal. Just the thing"—he turned to her—"for a string of seesaws."

"Would you like to see more? I know of at least two more spots that are as good, if not better, than this one."

"No, you've made your point. Besides"—he looked up at the sky, which had begun to grow darker—"I really should be on my way."

She nodded, then turned to walk back in the direction from which they had come. He stood and watched her walk away, then hurried to catch up.

"I hope you don't have a difficult drive back," she said, looking at the clouds gathering overhead. At the top of the ravine, they gazed out over a broad expanse of russet fields bending at the horizon into the low November sky. "It looks rather bleak," she said, "but I think I prefer a landscape like this to any other."

He felt a drop of rain on his face. "Maybe we'd better run," he said, but it was too late, and the rain began to pour down. They ran the rest of the way back to the cottage and stood, soaking and panting, on her porch.

"Thank goodness we weren't far away," she said breathlessly.

He shook his coat. "Do you remember the *General Slocum*, Miss Curtis?"

"The boat that caught fire some years ago?"

Nodding, he gazed out at the rain. "I was sailing on the East River that day with friends when it passed by—mothers and children on their way to a picnic somewhere, working people, a holiday for them, all dressed in their very best. They laughed and waved to us as their boat passed. I remember one little girl in a blue neckerchief, giggling as she waved." He hesitated. "I don't know why I brought it up."

"What happened?"

He looked at her, then glanced away. "Shortly after their boat passed, someone next to me shouted. I turned and saw a great cloud of black smoke rising over the *Slocum*. And for a moment, there was absolute quiet—then screaming like I've never heard before. Our boat turned around at once to try to help. Flames shot up from the *Slocum*, hundreds of feet into the air. Women and children on fire, throwing themselves into the river. I watched them drown."

"How awful."

He took a deep breath. "We pulled people onto the boat—saved as many as we could—but some were already dead. The little girl with the blue neckerchief was lying on the deck. So happy only moments before. Her life over. Was that little girl sacred, Miss Curtis?"

She looked down. "Do you ever think there might be some purpose, even in something so terrible?" she asked.

"No." He shook his head.

"Or a reason why you witnessed it?"

"If it was to confirm my belief in the utter pointlessness of life, yes, I suppose that might be a reason."

She watched the pouring rain. "I would not have taken you for a cynical person."

He looked at her. "No? I'm glad—I don't know why, but I'm glad." He held out his hand. "Well, thank you for showing me around, Miss Curtis."

"It was a pleasure." She pushed the wet strands of hair from her forehead and shivered. "I hope you don't get ill, driving home in those wet clothes. Do you want to dry off by the fire?"

"I've taken enough of your time already." He started down the stairs. "I hope . . ." He tripped and grasped the rail.

"Be careful, Mr. Dysart," Sybil said, reaching out to steady him.

"You might want to fix that." He pointed to a board in the stairs. "Just the sort of thing Mrs. Billings's attorneys will drudge up to support the condemnation proceedings."

Sybil peered down at the steps. William laughed. "There's nothing the matter with your stairs, Miss Curtis—just the clumsy Scotsman who keeps tramping up and down them." He stepped into the pouring rain and called out, "I'll speak to Mrs. Billings and see if there isn't something I can do," then ran to his car.

Pulling away from her cottage, William glanced back and saw her watching him. He tapped his horn, and she raised her hand and waved.

Chapter 8

William sat in his robe drinking coffee in his library on Saturday morning as he read the newspaper. Arabella and Eugenia Beckwith had gone to a breakfast at Sherry's for The Ladies' Society for the Beautification of New York.

As William read, he was distracted by thoughts of his discussion with Havering following his meeting with Sybil Curtis on Wednesday.

"Strike three," said Havering.

"She did show me a place on Lydia's property that was every bit as—"

"She's out," Havering interrupted and returned to a file open on his desk.

William looked up from his paper. She had said she would not have taken him for a cynical person. But he was—bitter, even—however much he might try to hide it. Was it disappointment in his marriage? Or something else? Perhaps it had to do with his mother's disappearance, though he hardly remembered her. He thought back to the

October morning when he had last seen her, when she had swept into his room, out at the house on Long Island.

He had been reading a book she had just given him for his sixth birthday.

William could still remember the book, a collection of Currier & Ives lithographs called *The Life of a Fireman*. It was probably still at his father's house, if it hadn't been lost in "a fire" or boxed up and given away like so much else from his childhood.

He remembered one picture that had particularly intrigued him. Two groups of firemen stood before a flaming building, working furiously at a hand pump as black smoke poured into the night sky. Red and yellow flames exploded out of windows. People stood in the streets screaming. On a ladder raised to the third story of the building, a fireman stood with one foot on the ladder and one foot still in the burning building; in his arms he held a young girl. In a house next door, a man and woman stood watching the whole spectacle with blank expressions on their faces. William had asked his mother why they didn't seem to care about the fire, or the little girl. And she had told him that they did care, but they were frightened their own house might catch fire and they would lose everything they owned.

His mother had seemed in a great hurry that day.

She had been crying, he remembered, as she bent to kiss him. He remembered squirming as she held him tightly—too tightly. Remembered the rain pelting against the window of his room and wondering where she could be going on such a day. She had made him promise that he would wait in his room until she returned for him. It was a game, she said, but he mustn't tell anyone. He did wait, and he had never told anyone, but she had never returned.

William heard a cab pull up in front of the house. He glanced out the window and saw Arabella and Alice Bourden, a powerful society dowager, get out. Arabella and her Settlement House Ball, no doubt, William mused. He turned to look at the clock on the mantel and was surprised to see it was already half past eleven. He put his paper aside and went to get dressed.

Afterward, coming down the stairs and walking past the partially closed doors to the drawing room, he heard Mrs. Bourden murmur, "Oh, I'm so sorry." He stopped at the half-closed door. "Knowing how fond of children you both are," she continued, "it must be a terrible burden."

"Yes," said Arabella in a hushed voice, "but we try not to dwell on it."

William coughed.

"Hello, darling," Arabella stood.

"Mr. William Dysart," said Alice Bourden. "Do come in and say hello to an old friend."

William entered the drawing room and listened politely to Alice Bourden's words, bore the sympathy in her eyes, and endured Arabella's soft-voiced remarks before excusing himself.

"Now promise me, darling," Arabella said as she accompanied him to the drawing room door, "not to forget we're dining at eight tonight with the Rutherfurds." She leaned up on her tiptoes to kiss him, bringing a look of romantic satisfaction to Alice Bourden's face.

William waited in the library until he heard Arabella see Alice Bourden out. "I'd like to speak to you," he told her, pulling the drawing room doors closed. "You're telling people we can't have children, aren't you?"

"No," she said stiffly, "and I'll thank you not to use that tone with me."

"Then what was all that about her knowing how fond we are of children and what a burden it must be?"

"She merely misinterpreted what I said. But you, with your listening at drawing room doors, only heard part of our conversation, and have apparently invented the rest."

William struggled to maintain his composure. "Before we were married, you told me you loved children, that you wanted children."

Arabella wheeled around. "The servants will hear you!" she whispered fiercely.

"For once, I want you to acknowledge your true

feelings. You don't like children. It's obvious. At best you're indifferent to them."

"I'm tired of these attacks, William." She stood at a nearby window, her back rigid.

"I'm not trying to attack you." William sighed. He went and sat in a chair near her. "Bella, we have been married for over six years. You used to tell me you longed to be a mother. We both looked forward to having a family. Yet ever since you"—he paused—"we have done everything possible to make sure we wouldn't have children. What is it, Bella? Are you frightened for some reason?"

"How tiresome you can be! There will be plenty of time for children." She went to the door. "I don't wish to discuss this again. It always ends in our bickering." She slid the door open and walked out, shutting it noiselessly behind her.

William sat in the drawing room for some time, then got up and left the house. He began walking blindly down Fifth Avenue, past all the majestic, turreted limestone mansions and elegant broad-stooped brownstones, and farther downtown, past the imposing hotels and high windows of the polished commercial establishments. All he could think of was how tenderly Arabella must have related her tale to Alice Bourden—and to how many others? What a shame, and she loves children so, he imagined them confiding among themselves. He thought of the change to separate bedrooms, of the many nights when her door had been locked to him, the excuses, pleadings, and humiliations. She had never wanted children. She had lied about that from the first.

William felt desperate, angry, and tired. When he saw the arch in Washington Square, he realized with a start that he'd been walking for well over an hour. He went and sat on a bench in the park. A few leaves held fast to the trees, but most were scattered on the ground, giving a sweet pungency to the brisk air.

Two young men walked swiftly past him, smiling and chatting. They looked very much alike. William imagined they were brothers. He wondered where they were going as he watched them disappear into the crowd at the southern end of the park. He turned and looked up at the sky. Soon it would be dark and most of these people would be in their homes eating dinner. He imagined them sitting in warm, well-lit kitchens in railroad flats and small apartments. He had seen such a kitchen once. When he was about ten, Mary Conran, their cook, had taken him to the flat of a friend she was visiting in Greenpoint, Brooklyn. He remembered walking up the three flights of narrow, dark stairs, with their smell of cooking onions, and waiting in the hallway with Mary for a door to open, the sound of children laughing and talking within. Once inside, William saw five children sitting at a table not far from the front door. Their father sat in his undershirt at the head of the table, and their mother, after taking off her apron, walked her visitors, to William's profound disappointment, into the front room. William turned and stared back down the long, dark hallway to the kitchen. The one boy in the family, about William's age, got up from the table and peered through the darkness at him. In a moment he was joined by two of his sisters.

"If you children don't sit down at once, you'll be put to bed early," William heard the father say, and they scattered. Long after, William wondered what it would have been like to eat in that kitchen every night with a brother and sisters, a mother and father.

William's thoughts returned to Arabella. Should he divorce her? After all the acrimony and bitterness, he would still be alone. He thought of all the lovely women, like Laura Lyall, who would have loved him had he allowed it—women he had rejected to avoid that moment when love came to feel like terror. He realized that he had never had to face that moment with Arabella.

Sitting in the park, he was ready finally to admit what he had always known to be true, that he did not love his wife. That he had willed his feelings to match her beautiful face and body, willed desire into love and infatuation into tenderness and affection.

He stood finally to return home, but something pressed him back down onto the bench again. A deeper sense of hopelessness—the realization that if given the chance, he would make the same choice—that he would do anything rather than face the horrible fear of loving and being loved, a fear that seemed to spring from nowhere, to be everywhere at once, and to vanish only when he retreated once more into a terrible isolation.

Chapter 9

William was so absorbed in responding to a brief filed on behalf of Kelmscott Coke & Petroleum, the plaintiff in the Consolidated Ironworks case, that he jumped when Phil Havering rang late Monday morning, wanting to see him right away.

When William entered Havering's office, he was surprised to see Lydia Billings sitting there, with a well-dressed young woman at her side.

"My secretary, Olivia," said Lydia.

"How do you do?" William said to the young woman, who smiled at him politely.

"William," Havering began, "Mrs. Billings has decided to move ahead with the Order of Condemnation on the Curtis property. She spoke to the Governor last night. It's to be filed in January."

"I think if we wait," said Lydia, "this small problem will grow into a larger one. And frankly, there is too much that needs my attention right now. Mountains to be moved—literally." She spoke pleasantly, but a glint of something hard in her eyes belied her easy tone. "We're going to begin work in March. I'm going to make that property the focal point for the entire preserve."

"The Curtis property?" William asked.

"Of course," said Lydia matter-of-factly.

William thought of the formal gardens at Bagatelle, the copse of old white birch trees running down to the Sound, the waterfall by a hidden pond. And the focal point was to be a flat stretch of land traversed by a dirt road? "They'll be doing a lot of work to it then," he said.

"Only tearing down that little house and putting up a rustic pavilion," Lydia replied. "Enchanting— all made out of branches—out near the water. I want to keep it as natural as possible. The views are the thing. Sublime."

Not nearly so sublime, thought William, as the view from the back of the main house at Bagatelle and from many other points on the property.

"So, William," Havering said, "Lydia would like you to be her liaison with the State on this."

"Just to keep things moving along," Lydia said. "You know the State. Such a muddle. Do you mind, William?" Lydia looked at him and smiled.

Feeling bewildered by this sudden turn of events, William shook his head. "No, of course not." Olivia gave him a piece of paper with the names of different people at the Statehouse in Albany. William scanned the list. "How much is the State assessing Miss Curtis's property for?" he asked.

"Three thousand dollars," Lydia said.

William shifted his weight. Little more than half its worth.

Lydia fingered the strand of pearls at her neck. "It was her choice, William."

"Yes, of course," he said, then excused himself, citing the pressing demands of the Consolidated case.

"I wish I had more like him," William heard Havering say as he was leaving.

William spent the rest of the afternoon in an agitated state. The more he tried to lose himself in the Consolidated case, the more the unpleasant business with Lydia Billings and Sybil Curtis nagged at him. His duty to Lydia was clear, but Sybil Curtis was going to be cheated out of her property, and William was now to be an accomplice to it. The three thousand dollars was vindictive—Lydia's retaliation for Sybil's obstinacy. All afternoon, he tried to think of a way he could make Sybil Curtis aware of the consequences of her decision without further compromising his professional commitment to Lydia Billings. The fact that he had revealed Lydia's identity to Sybil, whatever his justification at the time, struck him now as

91

indefensible, especially in light of the evident acrimony between the two women.

Walking through Greenwich Village on his way home from work, he decided to stop at a small secondhand bookshop he knew of on MacDougal Street. He was weary of his own thoughts; perhaps the shop had an out-of-print book of essays on the English Industrial Revolution that might offer an interesting sidelight to his pleadings in the Consolidated case. At the very least the book might provide a distraction for him.

As he approached MacDougal Street, he saw Albert Penniman, a man he had known from his college days, pass within a few feet of him. William paused, relieved that Albert had not seen him. He was not in the mood to engage in idle conversation with an acquaintance like Bertie Penniman, who boasted as his antecedents a prominent Dutch shipping family that had settled lower Manhattan in the mid-sixteen-hundreds. To William, Albert represented all the worst aspects of New York society—its arrogance and belief in its own superiority, based on nothing more than money and a shared history.

Albert Penniman was handsome and powerfully built, but his face and body had recently begun to take on a formless aspect. He had a fair, ruddy complexion with thick blond hair and large, deep blue eyes that seemed almost opaque when he smiled. William knew that many people found

Bertie charming, but those who did always fell somewhat in his estimation.

William ducked into Llewellyn's bookshop on MacDougal Street and climbed the stairs to the second floor. He found a copy of the book he was looking for, Richard Hastings's *The Advent of Industrialism in Rural England*, but it was in poor condition. Taking it to a nearby window to examine it in the light, he glimpsed Bertie Penniman standing outside a restaurant smoking. William watched a young woman approach him, then saw Albert take her by the arm and pull her into an embrace.

William had known for years that Albert was unfaithful to his wife, Vivian, and had even heard recently that Vivian herself had taken a lover, with whom she was living in Biarritz. As he watched Albert and the young woman, William frowned. His frown quickly turned to a feeling of unease as the sight of Albert and the young woman forced him to recall the dimly lit sitting room of a country house outside Philadelphia, where he had sat before a fire with Alice Haviland, a woman he barely knew from Washington.

It was only last spring. William remembered the muted sounds of people laughing and talking somewhere in another part of the house as Alice told him how unhappy her marriage was; he remembered the tentative, warm light of the fire as it flickered over Alice's slim body and lit up her hazel eyes. Her lips parted, revealing even white teeth as she began to say something, then stopped and placed a hand on William's leg. A current shot through his body. He had by this time taken sufficient measure of Alice to know that he could ignore the overture without recrimination, or respond to it with equal impunity. For once in his life, he did not hesitate. He was too lonely and unhappy, and in the presence of such generosity, with Arabella back at home with the flu, all his intricate, artificial constraints fell away.

William reached over and placed his hand on Alice's waist. Her mouth on his was sweet, soft, and supple. She took his face in her hands as her fingers played over his ears. His hand caressed her throat and shoulders, dropping slowly to her breasts as she leaned back against the sofa. William felt her hand press insistently against his inner thigh. Suddenly there was a clicking sound and a turn of the knob at the door. Alice shot up and stood before the fire as William sat up on the sofa. Two men and a woman walked in, insisting their hostess wanted them to come to the drawing room to play charades.

Alice's husband had arrived later that night, and William never had another moment alone with her. When he had returned home, he felt furious with himself for violating the harsh code of conduct by which he tried so hard to live.

Now William watched Albert take the woman

by the arm as they turned to walk into the restaurant. He probably doesn't expect to see anyone he knows down here, William thought.

Running his finger over the frayed binding of the book, William caught sight of the young woman's profile as she turned toward Albert—the delicate chin, the lovely almond eyes. It was Sybil Curtis. William stood for a moment, too stunned to move. Sybil Curtis with Albert Penniman? How could that be? Perhaps he was mistaken. No, he shook his head. He took a deep breath and went to buy the book.

Chapter 10

For the next few weeks, no matter how William tried, he was unable to put Sybil Curtis completely from his mind. How could a woman like that ever become involved with someone like Albert Penniman? How, in fact, had she even come to know Albert?

He continued to work tirelessly on the Consolidated Ironworks case, but every now and then he would pick up the telephone with the intention of calling Penniman, only to drop the phone receiver back onto its hook after an uneasy moment or two.

Thanksgiving was spent as usual at his father's country house, Tekahoka, in Oyster Bay. After dinner, William went for a solitary walk along the Sound, whose waters lapped at the front lawn of his father's property. The property had been in the family from the time of William's great-great-grandfather Talbot Dysart. Its original house, Mulberry Farm, a humble, early-eighteenth-century farmhouse, had been stripped of its clapboard siding, reclad in the weathered brown shingles of the house William's father had built, and swallowed up in one of the mansion's many wings. The house was then rechristened Tekahoka, an Indian word meaning "light at the top of the hill." Viewed from the road that ran past its main gate, it appeared on the rise of a hill like some great ship, its high chimneys belching out smoke as if to power it over the crest of a sweeping green wave surging up from the Sound far below.

The sky over the Sound had begun to change in the cool, receding November light. Brushes of pink and orange appeared on the horizon. William's eyes turned from the sky to the lengthening shadows cast by the four tall brick chimneys peering up from behind the gables of the house. As a small boy, William had been afraid that one of the chimneys would one day topple over. Sometimes he would stand on the lawn and force himself to stare up at one of them, until he was certain he had seen it sway, then turn and run away, exhilarated and dizzy with fear.

William saw a woman come from the French doors of the dining room, although he was too far from the house to see her clearly. She began walking down toward the Sound, pulling on a heavy sweater. Arabella, he thought at first, but as she drew closer, he realized it was Cady.

"Is this a private party?" she asked, buttoning her sweater.

William shook his head.

"Why your father feels he has to entertain seventy-five people at Thanksgiving every year is beyond me." She sighed. "I know they're your relatives, but frankly, the Goodhues bore me senseless."

"You, too?" William asked.

Cady reached for a cigarette case in the pocket of her sweater and offered one to William. He shook his head. He took her lighter and lit her cigarette. Cady took a long puff. "What's wrong, William?" she said, exhaling. "You seem so distracted today."

William shrugged. "A lot of things, I suppose. I'm sure I'll have forgotten them all by Christmas."

"I noticed from the dining room you staring out toward Lloyd Neck and wondered if that Billings business was troubling you." She paused, but William remained silent. "Well, if you ever want to talk about anything." She kissed his cheek, then turned back toward the house.

"Why hasn't he ever invited the Bradfords?" William asked suddenly.

"Your mother's family?" Cady looked away. "Well . . . they live mostly abroad now, and . . ." She shivered. "He was too hurt by it all, William."

"By what?"

"I don't know. He never talks about it."

"Not even to you?"

She shook her head. "I am everything your father wants me to be. No more, no less. And the last thing he wants is difficult questions." She put out her cigarette. "I go along, William. I always have."

"But I don't remember her at all. I vaguely remember a funeral. Can there really be no pictures of her? Is it possible they were all burned in a fire?"

"He went almost mad with grief when she died. There was a fire. I don't know anything else." She pressed his arm gently, then walked toward the house. At the driveway, she stopped and turned. "There is a portrait of your mother painted by Sargent. It's hanging in your Aunt Edith's house in Gramercy Park."

William looked at Cady, deeply touched that she had told him, knowing she must be acting against his father's wishes. "Thank you," he said, watching her step elegantly along the path until she reached the house. So there was a painting of his mother, and his father had kept its existence hidden from him for all these years.

On the first of December, William and Arabella accompanied his stepmother and father in his father's Delaunay-Belleville limousine to the Livingstons' yacht, *Cygnet*, at the New York Yacht Club's pier at the foot of East Twenty-third Street. They then went to a dinner at the Pall Mall room of the Ritz-Carlton Hotel at Forty-sixth Street and Madison Avenue given by the Bradley-Martins.

Later that night, he sat in his library trying to read Hastings's book on the English Industrial Revolution. The unending round of social obligations had left him little time for the quiet preparation he needed for the Consolidated case, further irritating him. As the clock on the mantle struck nine, Arabella entered quietly. She lay on the sofa and began reading Katherine Cecil Thurston's *Max*. In a plain white dressing gown, her hair tied behind her with a simple ribbon, William thought she looked more alluring than ever. Glancing up from his book a moment later, he was surprised to see tears in her eyes and wondered what in the novel could have moved her.

"How is the book?" he asked.

"I love it, but I don't think you would."

"I was thinking about going out to Long Island tomorrow."

"But we just got back."

"I know, but I promised Father I would look over the property. See how the new caretaker is managing everything. He meant to take a look for himself, but never got the chance."

Arabella nodded without comment and returned to her book.

"Maybe cut down a Christmas tree for us." William coughed. "Care to join me?"

She looked up, her eyebrows raised, then shook her head. "I find the country depressing at this time of year."

"I . . ." He hesitated. "I might even pay a visit to that young woman whose property Lydia Billings is so keen to have."

"I thought that was all settled."

He shook his head. "Lydia wants me to run her off the place in January." He closed his book. "And frankly it's not something I want to do."

"Why is she being so obstinate?"

"Lydia?"

"This young woman."

"It's her property. She doesn't want to sell. I don't know that I'd call that obstinate." He tossed his book on a table and stood. "I'm hoping I can still work out some sort of compromise." Putting aside the fireplace grate, he stirred the embers and added another log. "There is something else, rather strange," he said, gazing at the log as it caught fire. "I saw Miss Curtis—the young woman—down on MacDougal Street a few weeks ago with Albert Penniman, of all people."

Arabella put down her book. "In a romantic way?"

"It seemed."

"Is she one of the Boston Curtises?"

William shook his head. "I think she's English, has a bit of an accent."

"Is she beautiful?"

"Pretty. Nothing more."

"She must have something if Bertie Penniman's interested in her."

"Intelligent—a certain charm, I suppose."

"Probably a fling—a distraction."

"Do you think so?" William recoiled inwardly to hear Sybil described in such a way and realized he had been hoping Arabella would discount the possibility of an affair between the two.

"What else could it be?"

He shrugged and Arabella returned to her book. She reached up and gracefully placed a tendril of hair behind her ear.

"Would you like a nightcap?" he asked. "I could make us something called the *velvet glove*. Just invented by the bartender at the Savoy. Theo and Lucie swear by them."

Arabella shook her head and continued to read. "No, thank you."

William sighed quietly. "How about a fast game of Parcheesi?"

"Pardon me?" Arabella looked up.

"Nothing." William stood. "I think I'll go to bed."

"Good night," said Arabella into her book.

• • •

William set out the next afternoon for his father's country house. It was raining so hard that as he threaded his way through the stanchions of the elevated tracks along Third Avenue, he narrowly missed hitting one. Once he swung his motorcar onto the Queensboro Bridge, unencumbered by stanchions, slow-moving horse-drawn wagons, and people running into Saturday traffic, he was able to pick up speed. By the time he exited the bridge in Long Island City, the weather began to clear, and when he pulled onto Jackson Avenue, traversing the North Shore of Long Island, the sun was shining. He drove along the avenue, recently paved with asphaltic concrete macadam, through an industrial area of Queens, until he came to the small village of Flushing, where he stopped at Bohlen's Feed and Supply for gasoline.

"Hello, Mr. Dysart. Fill 'er up?" an elderly man called from a small shed. A potbellied stove glowed just inside its narrow door. "Heading out to Oyster Bay?" he asked as he pumped gas into William's car, his breath forming small white clouds in the rapidly chilling air. "Now, you be sure to tell old Teddy Roosevelt that old Joe Randall sends his regards."

"Sure will, Joe," said William, as he always did when Joe made this same request about President Roosevelt, whose house was in Oyster Bay not far from his father's.

After leaving the filling station, William drove for another hour through the main streets and broadways of the small villages and farms of Nassau County that formed the northern boulevard running along the North Shore of Long Island. After he left the city line in the town of Douglaston, the dirt roads became more rutted and treacherous, the high, four-tiered power lines leaning this way and that, marking the direction for him.

William turned at last onto the unmarked road leading to his father's property and drove along it until he could see Long Island Sound and his father's house in the distance.

Pulling through the front gate, he looked toward the window of the room that had been his when he was a child. It was in the oldest part of the house. He pulled his car beneath the porte cochere at the front of the house.

"Hello, Henry," William said to the old houseman who opened the front door, "how are you, you old thing?"

"Fine, you young thing. Good to have you back again so soon."

"You're looking a little peaked about the eyes, I think." William entered the house and put down his satchel.

"Just got over a terrible cold, Master William. How is it," Henry asked, gesturing with William's coat in one hand and his hat in the other, "an autumn that starts out so mild can turn so bitter? What a winter we're going to have. Did you see how the sky has changed?" He paused dramatically. "Snow!"

William nodded in agreement. "How's the new caretaker?"

"Good man." Henry put William's things away in the front closet. "Staying long?"

"A day or two. Tomorrow I'm going to cut down the second best Christmas tree on the place."

"Second best?"

"I know you, Henry, you'll make sure I don't see the best. You're keeping that for you and Mary."

Henry's old face creased into a broad smile. "Now would old Henry do such a thing to his boy?"

"Now I'm your boy. I'll be lucky to get back to New York with a half-dead sapling."

"Go on. Though I will tell you, there's nothing so much as worth your notice out by the old back road."

"Oh, I'll bet you've got a little beauty hidden there, haven't you, Henry?"

"Fancy that." Henry laughed.

"All fresh and green, shaped like a pharaoh's pyramid."

William followed Henry toward the back of the house. "Mary, come see who's here," Henry called to the kitchen. "And nasty as he ever was."

That night William decided to stay in his old room. After he had gotten ready for bed, he sat in the window seat where he had spent so many hours of his early life. How cramped it seemed now. Looking out the window, he could see only patches of the dark waters of the Sound through the bare branches of the trees, which had grown so tall and wide. He leaned his head against the cold, dark windowpane, remembering sitting there as a child, waiting and watching for his mother's return.

He went to the blue painted bookshelves surrounding the small fireplace in the room and scanned the book titles. At last he found it. *The Life of a Fireman.* He took down the book and began leafing through it. He could still remember some of the pictures. An inscription flashed before him, taking him by surprise:

For my Will on his sixth birthday.

All my love always,
  Mother

He had never, so long as he could remember, seen his mother's handwriting, and it shocked him to look at it now. She had existed, and was not just a hazy memory from his long-ago childhood. He ran his finger over the script and looked around the room. He remembered now the darkness outside seeping over the windowsill onto the wide planks of the floor in the room, the padding steps of a servant moving quietly along the narrow hall turning up the gas lamps, the golden thread of light appearing under his door. There had been a quarrel. His mother had left that morning and then his father was gone. Where had they gone and would they ever be coming back?

William stared out at the Sound. An unhappy memory from childhood, he thought. That was all. His parents had fought, as married couples will; his child's mind had just made more of it than that. Through the branches of the trees he saw the lights of a large, solitary boat gliding across the still water, with people on its deck. He went to the window and opened it. The faint sounds of music, voices, and laughter could be heard. He watched until the boat was out of sight, then he closed the window and left to sleep in another part of the house.

Chapter 11

The next morning William covered the more than three hundred acres of his father's property on horseback in the company of the new caretaker and was as satisfied with the man's competence and the condition of the property as Henry said he would be. After breakfast, he and Henry set out to find a Christmas tree, which, as Henry was almost crippled with arthritis, William had to insist on cutting down himself.

When they returned to the house, William asked Henry to tell what little staff there was still on for the winter that he would be staying until Monday morning. He then went to the small sitting room at the back of the house to read. Henry had one of the servants light a fire in the stone fireplace, and his father's old mastiff, Keeper, snored quietly before it. Looking out the room's mullioned windows, William saw snow beginning to fall.

"Keeper," William called to the dog.

Keeper raised his head.

"How about a walk later? Would you like that?"

Keeper's tail slapped the floor rhythmically. He slowly raised himself up and walked over to William.

"Good boy." William rubbed Keeper's neck and back briskly as the dog lay down beside his chair. William settled into the chair and opened a newspaper. He began to read, but was unable to concentrate, reading only a sentence or two under each headline before moving quickly on to the next. He could not get out of his mind the thought of Sybil's face as she turned to Albert Penniman. Soon he began scanning the pages more rapidly, until finally he pushed them together in disgust and threw the paper down. Why had he come out to Long Island? Did he really have anything further to say to her? She seemed to have a very good idea of what to expect from Lydia Billings. Hadn't he really come to find out how she could possibly be having anything to do with someone like Albert Penniman? He sighed. I should be writing for *Town Topics*, he thought. The very idea of his seeing her tomorrow—weeks after he had last spoken to her—struck him now as an embarrassment.

He rang for Henry.

"I'm sorry, Henry, I've decided to return to town."

"Such a short stay." Henry seemed genuinely disappointed.

"Yes . . . well, I just remembered something."

"I'll have Mrs. C. pack your things."

"Don't bother her, Henry, I can do that," said William, putting on Keeper's leash to take him for a walk. "If you would just have the Willets boy tie up the Christmas tree and bring the car around."

His motorcar was packed, and in less than an hour he was on his way back to New York. He drove down the narrow dirt lane and reached the main road, where a right turn would take him back to New York City. Idling, he heaved a sigh, then turned left and drove on until he crossed the slender strip of land bordered by the vast Sound. He passed the gate to Bagatelle and drove on until he came at last to the unmarked byway leading to her cottage. There he pulled his motorcar over to the side and stopped. He got out of the car and looked around, then began walking up the road. Snow fell noiselessly through the bare branches of the trees on either side of the road, screening the surrounding meadows in whiteness. He walked for some time and was just about to return to his car when he saw smoke from a chimney. He picked up his step, and a moment later he was knocking at her door. No one answered. He knocked again and waited; still nothing.

At last he had turned to leave when he heard the door opening behind him. "Hello?" he heard her ask and he turned back around. She was wearing a sweater that circled her neck and clung to her body, its deep brown color making her pale skin look almost white; but for the energy in her dark eyes, he might have thought her unwell. He could not help but notice the way the sweater accentuated the roundness of her breasts and the slenderness of her waist. What an unusual looking, very pretty creature she is, he thought.

"Mr. Dysart."

"You remember."

"Of course."

"Yes. Well . . . I don't suppose you expected to see me again," William said, a bit too brightly.

She gave a brief smile and shook her head.

"You know, Miss Curtis, you're making my life very difficult."

"Am I?" She smiled. Her eyes strayed off the

porch to the falling snow. "I hope you didn't drive all the way out from New York in this weather just to tell me that." She glanced inside the cottage. "Would you like to come in? You must be cold standing out there." William entered the cottage. A fire was burning in the fireplace. Sybil began picking up papers that were scattered on the sofa, papers with scrawls and crossings out.

"Writing a book?" asked William.

"Poetry. Very bad poetry. All these pages will be condensed into about four lines."

"I'd love to read them."

"Thank you, but I never show my poetry to anyone. *Anyone.* Can I get you some tea or something?" she asked.

William shook his head. "I'll only be a moment. I probably shouldn't be telling you this, but you'll find out about it soon enough anyway, so I don't really know that it makes any difference. They're going to start condemnation proceedings in January and you're to be off the property by March. The worst is you're only going to get three thousand dollars for the place."

She nodded.

"What are you going to do about it?"

"Nothing."

"This is not a joke, Miss Curtis."

"Yes, I know."

"Are you going to fight the order of condemnation?"

"Now that would be a joke."

"I can still get you ten thousand for the place."

She shook her head.

He sighed. "Well, I tried."

"You did, and I appreciate it."

"You know I'm the one who's going to have to handle this for Mrs. Billings."

"I promise not to hold it against you."

He frowned. "Why are you doing this?"

"Mrs. Billings can't buy a clear conscience."

"She doesn't care."

"I do."

"Well, I suppose there's nothing more to be said, then." He walked to the door and paused. "Might I ask you a rather personal question?"

She hesitated. "Very well."

"Are you related to Mrs. Billings?"

She shook her head.

"The Curtises of Boston?"

"No." She laughed. "Whoever they are."

"It's just that several weeks ago, I . . . Never mind. It's not important." Feeling a bit out of his depth, William glanced away and saw a large book covered in green leather open to a drawing of a pinkish-white snapdragon. The drawing was exquisitely done. "That's remarkable," he said.

"My father did it."

"Really?"

She nodded and turned to the next page and picked up a piece of onionskin. Beneath it,

William saw a drawing of a purple and white tulip.

"Your father was very talented."

She smiled. "He always thought of himself as more of a botanist or naturalist than an artist. I have two more books just like this one. I wrote to the library in New York to see if they might be interested in them. A Mr. Fiske wrote back that—"

"Arthur Fiske?"

"Yes, that's right," she said, surprised. "Mr. Fiske asked me to bring in one of the books, so he could see it." She paused. "I'm so nervous that he won't like them."

"If he doesn't, he's a fool, which he is not. I went to school with his son. When are you seeing him?"

"Next Thursday, the fourteenth."

"What time?"

"Two thirty."

"I'm doing research at the library for a case I'm working on. I usually go every Tuesday and Thursday. I could meet you on the fourteenth. Put in a word with Arthur. Not that you really need one. But maybe I could smooth the way a little. Only if you'd like, of course."

"I wouldn't want to impose."

"I'll be there anyway."

"Thank you. I don't know why I'm so nervous. I suppose it's because I want to know that the books will be safe." She looked down at the delicately drawn tulip. "I wish I could draw."

"I used to when I was a child, but my father said it wasn't a fitting thing for a boy to do."

"How sad." She picked up the book and placed it with two others on a long table at the side of the room.

William heard an odd scratching at the door and opened it to see what could be causing it. He was surprised to see a boy of about eight years old standing on the porch.

"Hello there," William said as the boy backed away.

"Hello, Walter," Sybil called over William's shoulder. "Come in and meet my friend, Mr. Dysart." Walter entered shyly, handing Sybil a textbook with the words *Pas à Pas* emblazoned on the cover.

William held out his hand to Walter, who stared up at him. "Mister," he whispered, "is that your motor down the road? The Lozier. Six cylinders!"

"You know your motorcars, Walter." said William.

"Is the Lozier a thrilling motorcar, Walter?" Sybil asked.

William smiled at the serious expression on her face.

"I'll say!" Walter exclaimed. "It went almost two thousand miles in the AAA's twenty-four-hour race, and they never had to raise the hood.

Ralph Mulford just drove one in the Vanderbilt Cup race."

"Did you see the race?" William asked.

"Oh, no, sir," said Walter, as if such a thing were beyond imagining.

"I was there—quite a showdown. Mulford came in only minutes after the winner."

"Harry Grant."

"Right you are, Walter."

"Gosh!" He stared up at William as if he had won the race rather than Harry Grant.

William looked out the window. It had stopped snowing. "Walter, would you like to go for a short ride?"

"Do you mean it?!"

"Of course." William turned to Sybil. "Care to join us?"

"Sounds wonderful," said Sybil, walking into the kitchen. She returned with a small, neatly wrapped package. "Walter, would you give this to your mother?"

She put on a coat and together the three of them walked down the road toward William's motorcar.

"I wondered how you got here," Sybil said.

"Did you think it was by aeroplane?"

"Something like that, yes. As I recall you came on foot the first time as well."

"Then I thought my car might give the wrong impression. Today I left it down the road because I wanted to be able to turn and bolt if I changed my mind. I wasn't sure how you'd feel about my barging in."

"I'm glad you stopped by." Sybil saw the Christmas tree strapped to the back of the car. "And you got yourself a tree already. I think you must be very efficient, Mr. Dysart."

William opened the passenger door for Sybil, and Walter jumped in the backseat.

He drove down the road, then along the lagoon. Sybil seemed to take almost as much delight in the excursion as Walter. When they came to the point in the road where the Sound cut in opposite the lagoon, William pulled over to turn around, only to see a chauffeured Daimler limousine speed by on the opposite side of the road. William saw Lydia Billings in the backseat, and he turned away, wondering if she had seen him. He looked at Sybil, but she stared ahead with seeming indifference. Was it possible she had not seen the limousine?

"Would you mind if we stopped and looked at the water a moment?" she asked.

"Not at all," said William, and let the car idle. They stared at the choppy waters of the Sound slapping against the beach by the side of the road.

"I saw a shark once," Walter piped up from the backseat. "Not here. At the ocean."

"Did you pop by, Walter, just to deliver my book, or was there something your mother wanted?"

"Oh, I forgot—she wants you to come over for dinner."

"I suppose we should be getting back, then," Sybil said.

William put the motorcar in gear and turned it around. He drove Walter to his home, an old farmhouse at the end of a long driveway. Caroline Jameson, the woman William had met at Sybil's a few weeks earlier, came to the door and waved. "Please let your mother know I'll be over in about an hour," Sybil told Walter as he slipped out of the backseat.

"Okay." Walter sprang out of the car and slammed the door. "Thank you, mister!" he called over his shoulder.

As they were driving back to her cottage, William suddenly spoke. "Miss Curtis," he stammered, "a few weeks ago I . . ." He glanced quickly at her profile; she was watching the snow, which had begun to fall again. "I was in Greenwich Village and saw you with a friend—an acquaintance really—Albert Penniman." He cleared his throat. "I don't know how well you know Mr. Penniman," he said at last, "but I've known him for years, and . . ." He put the car in gear in front of her cottage. "Please . . . be careful."

She looked at him, then turned and began to fumble with the latch of the car door. "Here, let me help you with that." He jumped from the car,

116

but she had opened the door and let herself out before he reached her.

"Good-bye, Mr. Dysart," she whispered as she rushed up the snowy stairs to her cottage.

"Can I drive you back to the Jamesons'?"

"No, thank you," she said abruptly. "I prefer to walk."

William returned to his motorcar, regretting having said anything, and angry with himself for having come to see Miss Curtis. Her reaction to his warning about Albert Penniman left him feeling more discouraged than he cared to admit.

Chapter 12

Two days later, William found himself in Theodore Parrish's old-fashioned double parlor on West Tenth Street, waiting with more than seventy others to hear Carrie Huffam, a disciple of Emmeline Pankhurst, speak on women's suffrage. William was still haunted by the memory of Sybil Curtis's reaction when he had mentioned Albert Penniman.

"Is Arabella coming?" Theo asked.

"Pardon me?" William responded distractedly. He was reading the words on a blue and gold banner: WE DEMAND AN AMENDMENT TO THE UNITED STATES CONSTITUTION ENFRANCHISING WOMEN!

"Arabella," Theo repeated. "Is she coming?"

"She said she had better things to do than to listen to some humorless woman from Boston in broken-down shoes talk nonsense." William shifted on the wooden folding chair, trying to stretch his cramped legs.

"She's probably right." Theo laughed. "About the shoes, at any rate." He glanced around the room. "Same old crowd," he said, waving to Lucie, his wife, who was standing at the door with two other women, greeting and directing people to seats. "Lucie is so passionate about all this. If anyone had told me five years ago that I'd be attending a meeting of suffragettes in my own house, I would have told them they were mad. The vote! Women's rights. What happened to my rights? I'm sick of the whole thing."

"Would you be happier if Lucie's interests began and ended with who's wearing what hat, with whom, and to where?" William studied the crowd of mostly women.

"No, I suppose not." Theo gave a quick pat to William's arm. "I'm really glad you came tonight."

"I had to see Mrs. Huffam's shoes. Ever since Arabella mentioned them, I can't get them out of my head."

"I was sure you weren't going to come, that you would make up some excuse. I know I would have." Theodore looked over his shoulder. "Well, this should make Lucie's night. Edith Bradford's here. Isn't she a relative of yours?"

"My aunt, or rather, my mother's aunt."

"I can't say I see a family resemblance. Though it looks like we're going to have a family reunion. She's headed this way."

"Is she?" William took a deep breath.

"No, Lucie is dragging her to another seat. 'You'll be more comfortable on one of the parlor chairs here, Edie,' she's probably telling her. 'Better view and all that. No wooden chairs for you, you old bat.' So, what's the old firebrand like?"

"I've never met her."

"What?"

William nodded toward the front of the room as Carrie Huffam, a trim, middle-aged woman, took her place at the podium.

Mrs. Huffam smiled at the enthusiastic applause, then paused theatrically, adjusted her glasses, and began to speak about the injustice of women not having the vote. Her voice, unfortunately, seemed to waver over several octaves.

William glanced furtively at Edith Bradford, remembering an incident from childhood. When he was a young boy walking with his father through Madison Square Park, a woman in her sixties rushed up to him, tears welling in her eyes. As his father grabbed his arm and pushed him past her, the woman flung a look of scorn at his father. His mother's Aunt Edith, his father had told him later—"a vicious and unnatural woman. You must never have anything to do with her," he had warned. "But for her, your mother would be alive today."

"That voice," Theo whispered to William, glancing up at Mrs. Huffam, "I tell you, the room's beginning to spin."

"Nice shoes, Huffam," William whispered back. "What did you do, walk all the way here from Boston?"

"Now I know why they call it *suffrage*," Theodore retorted.

Lucie Parrish leaned forward in her chair and stared at them, her eyes alive with silent reproach.

"Trouble," Theodore murmured, and he and William listened with greater deference to what Mrs. Huffam had to say. Her deep conviction to the cause lent some life to her protracted speech, but not enough to provoke more than a few polite remarks when it was over. There seemed to be no further questions and Mrs. Huffam was about to thank her audience when someone spoke up.

"I'd like to say something." William heard an older woman speaking with a tremor.

"Auntie," Theodore nudged him.

"Your speech was all very nice as far as it went, but I can't say as I haven't heard much the same before."

There was a low murmur in the room as Mrs. Huffam smiled with more stoic grace than seemed warranted.

"One issue I never hear discussed at these gatherings is what I find to be the resistance of my sister females to our having the vote," said Edith Bradford. "Now I've been at this a long time, and I've never seen a man get as angry at the prospect of women having the vote as I've seen a lot of women. And do you know why? Because we're asking a lot more of women than we are of men. We're only asking men to give up some power—unpleasant, I am sure—but we are asking women to take real power into their own hands for the first time *ever* and it terrifies them."

There was some indignant shifting and squeaking of chairs.

"I'm sorry, ladies, but it's true. There is nothing so frightening to people as change. Well, I say don't worry so much about those men in the statehouse or down in Washington. What we have to do is give them wives, daughters, sisters, and aunts with a will to change, and we will see a revolution. And if we don't—well, then, I'm afraid, ladies, we'll be jackassing around with all this well into the next century."

Several women rose at once and bustled toward the door.

"That's all I have to say." Edith Bradford sat down.

There was a moment of complete silence. Carrie Huffam looked down from her podium with a patronizing expression that William found irritating.

Suddenly Lucie Parrish began to clap vigorously. Theodore smiled and quickly joined her, followed by William and several others. Lucie beamed at them from across the room. Carrie Huffam thanked her audience and stepped down from the podium.

"Your aunt's a real ball of fire," said Theodore. "And apparently she's struck a nerve." He nodded toward a crowd gathering around Edith Bradford on the other side of the room.

Lucie, in the middle of the crowd, waved for them to join the group.

"Come on"—Theodore squeezed William's shoulder—"let's jackass over there and say hello."

"Sorry, Theo." William picked up his coat from the back of his chair. "I really have to go. Please say good night to Lucie for me."

"All right," said Theodore, fixing him with a curious stare.

William made his way toward the parlor door, but was momentarily blocked by two women speaking to Edith Bradford. His aunt turned to one of the women to say something and saw William. Their eyes locked for an instant. "Pardon me," William said to the two women, and as they parted to let him pass, he glimpsed his aunt's piercing blue eyes once more, now shaded with pain. "Vicious . . . unnatural," he heard his father's words. Was it possible? he wondered, as the Parrishes' maid opened the front door for him and he made his way back into the night.

Chapter 13

William spent most of Wednesday working on the Consolidated case, but early in the evening, when the office was empty, he let himself into Phil Havering's office, dug out the maps of Bagatelle, and studied them. On one, he retraced the path that he and Sybil had walked in early November and found the spot she had shown to him. He searched the map for other areas that might also serve Lydia Billings's purpose. Lydia had said she would not compromise on her vision, but William thought he might still be able to convince her that finding an alternative location was the only sensible course to take. Lydia had bullied him when they had met the first time and he was determined not to let her bully him again.

He rolled up all the maps, except for the one detailing Bagatelle's coastline, and returned them to the slot in Havering's cabinet. He would replace the missing map after he'd had a chance to talk to Lydia. Havering would probably not even notice it was gone—as far as he was concerned, the State was going to condemn Sybil's cottage, and that would be the end of it—but if he missed it, William would just explain that he had been working after hours on Lydia's case and had needed it for reference. Havering would applaud his enterprise, he was sure.

As he was walking home, an easy solution to the whole problem suddenly occurred to him. Lydia Billings could move Sybil Curtis's cottage to a site nearby, perhaps to a site superior to the one she currently occupied. The more he thought about the idea, the more excited he became. He stopped at the Western Union Telegraph office at 195 Broadway to send a wire to Sybil Curtis.

HAVE A SOLUTION I THINK WILL BE AGREEABLE TO ALL, he wrote.

He stood for a moment with his pen poised. Should he say anything about his remark to her about Albert Penniman? A quick apology? No, he would keep it very businesslike—as he should have all along. When he saw her in person, he could say something if necessary. He quickly finished:

CAN WE MEET FRIDAY?
  WD

He handed the sheet to the clerk, paying for the wire and for a return response, then left the

Western Union office and quickly walked the more than eighty blocks home.

The next morning, when he came down to breakfast, Arabella told him there was a wire for him. "From Long Island," she added as William hurried to the tray in the front hall to pick it up. He opened it:

NO THANK YOU.

He stared at the smudged letters of type. "No, thank you. I prefer to walk," he heard her words again in his head. He took a breath and tucked the wire into the pocket of his robe.

"How unhappy you look," Arabella said when he returned to the breakfast room.

"Do I?"

"Anything to do with your wire?"

William spread marmalade on his buttered toast.

"Who was it from?"

William took a bite of the toast and a sip of coffee. "From the young woman on Long Island, whose property Lydia wants."

"You seem to be spending an awful lot of time on that." Arabella sounded petulant. She pushed her plate away.

"Only what the case demands. It's over now anyway." William brushed crumbs from the corner of his mouth.

"What does she look like?"

"Who?"

"Who do you think?"

"Your height—maybe a little shorter. Dark hair and eyes." William began to feel uneasy. "Quite ordinary, really," he added.

"If she's so ordinary, why is Bertie Penniman interested in her? Other than Vivian—and everyone knows he married her only because she was his cousin and he was expected to—I've never known Albert to be interested in any woman who wasn't quite stunning."

An icicle fell outside the breakfast room window, shattering on the stone sill below. "I don't know that Albert is interested in her." William glanced at the remaining icicles raining down droplets in the morning sun. "She might be a friend of the family, or a relative for all I know. It doesn't matter, in any case. She's not willing to sell her property or to negotiate further. Other than filing writs and issuing a check—a rather small one—it's over."

"You seem disappointed. And how thrilled you were to get her wire."

"What are you driving at?"

"Nothing." Arabella's tone was cool.

"And as far as Albert's concerned," he said, "if she is involved with him, I would wonder why she would be interested in him, not the other way around."

"Money." Arabella stood.

"Not this woman."

"Oh? Beautiful and virtuous." Arabella leaned down close to his ear. "Darling, they only exist in fairy tales," she whispered, then let her lips graze the lobe of his ear. She pulled her robe together and left.

William finished breakfast, then went to his room to change. He was just about to put on his shoes when there was a soft knock at the door.

"Come in," he said.

Arabella entered, still in her dressing gown. "Do you have to leave for the office just yet?"

Before he could reply, she raised a finger to his mouth and traced the outline of his lips.

"I've given the servants the morning off," she murmured, kissing William on the mouth and sliding down his suspenders. Something told him to pull back, but as she undid his tie, kissing him passionately, he could not resist reaching under her dressing gown and running his hands over her breasts. She pushed him back onto the bed and unbuttoned his shirt, then his trousers. When they were naked, curled around one another on the bed, she guided him inside her and thrust her hips forcefully against him. As he was about to climax, she pushed him away from her, rose quickly, and left without a word. William lay on the bed for some time, staring at the ceiling. Was there any hangover from drink or drugs that could make him feel as miserable and empty as he did at that moment? If there was such a thing as sin, he thought, they had both just committed one of the gravest kind. He took a deep breath, dressed, and went to work.

Chapter 14

For the following week, William spent long hours in his office trying to plow through the mounting piles of Consolidated briefs, but he was increasingly distracted by his deteriorating marriage and by Sybil's curt reply to his wire. He and Arabella argued less, but they talked less as well. For a day or two after their interlude in the bedroom, Arabella behaved in a more affectionate manner, as if a new intimacy had sprung up between them. But then she seemed to grow bored with the notion and withdrew into a cool civility. The iciness of his last moments with Sybil Curtis was a source of continuing regret for him, arousing both his anger and his guilt, and he resigned himself to simply letting matters take their own course. Even the return of the map of Bagatelle to Havering's office had not turned out as he had planned.

"I was looking for that map," Havering said sharply. "Why didn't you tell me you had taken it?"

"I had an idea for a compromise. I thought—"

"No, William. No more ideas. This case is closed as far as we're concerned. What has gotten into you?"

At his desk, William picked up his pen again and continued writing on the long white pad: "And as was made evident in the case of Standard Oil of New Jersey vs. North Atlantic Petroleum, the plaintiff had every reason to believe that North Atlantic Petroleum (hereinafter North Atlantic) would adhere to contractual obligations dating back to . . ." He thought for a moment. What *had* gotten into him? He shook his head and resumed writing: ". . . dating back to March of . . ." Was it March? He pushed aside the pile of notes on his calendar. He was about to look to the back of the calendar when he noticed the day's date. He stared at it. December fourteenth. The day Sybil Curtis was to be at the library, the day he had said he would meet her there. NO THANK YOU, he saw the smudged letters again in his head. He took out his pocket watch. Twenty after one. She had said her meeting was at two thirty. He thought a moment. "Miss Leary," he called to his secretary, "do I have any appointments this afternoon?"

William heard a page turn. "Only with the barber at three thirty, Mr. Dysart."

"I see." There was a long moment of silence. "Would you please cancel that for me. I have to go to the library." He could at least tell Miss Curtis that he was sorry for having brought up the subject—something personal—that was none of his business. He grabbed his coat and hat from the coatrack and ran into the hall.

"Will you be at the Christmas dinner, sir?" asked Miss Leary.

"Is that tonight?"

She nodded. "Fraunces Tavern."

"Oh, I'm afraid not, Miss Leary." Arabella would never deign to attend something so prosaic as his firm's Christmas dinner, and it was something William managed to avoid most years. "But have a wonderful time," he said, rushing for the elevator.

William arrived at the library on Fifth Avenue at two o'clock. He climbed the wide marble steps, two at a time, to the portico of the main entrance. The air was bitterly cold, but the sunlight penetrating it from the clear blue sky above imbued the afternoon with a kind of optimism.

As he waited, the sun moved slowly westward, casting the front of the library in shadow, making it an uncomfortable place to be. William danced from foot to foot, wrapping his arms around himself to ward off the cold. Finally he walked down the steps into the sunlight on a landing below. Just as he reached it, Sybil Curtis rushed past him, carrying a satchel. She was wearing a dark woolen coat with a white scarf wound loosely about her head. "Miss Curtis?"

She turned around. "Oh," she said coolly.

"I came today, as I said I would."

"I'd forgotten."

"If you'd rather I go, I will, but I'd first like to apologize for insinuating myself into your personal affairs."

She nodded.

"I hope your meeting goes well." William smiled politely. "Which I have no doubt it will." He turned to walk down the stairs.

"Mr. Dysart," she called to him. "I know it was only out of concern that you said what you did, but I can't have my life—"

"No, of course not." Her pale skin was flushed with the cold, and her dark eyes looked almost black. How strange, he wondered, that he had ever thought her anything but beautiful.

"There are things . . ." She looked at him uneasily.

"It was wrong of me to say anything."

She stared at him a moment. "If . . . if you would still like to accompany me, I would be most grateful. I am so nervous about this."

"I'd be happy to." William joined her and they began to walk up the steps together. He looked to the ornate beaux-arts facade of the recently completed library, trying to think of something inconsequential to say to alleviate the tension. "Impressive, isn't it?"

"Yes," she agreed.

"Can I carry your bag?"

"If you wouldn't mind, it's gotten so heavy."

In the library, Sybil asked for Mr. Fiske and was directed to the second floor. As they climbed the massive marble staircase, William reflected on her ease in this grand building, despite her nervousness. She had the simplicity and directness of a person from the country, but underlying it was an acquaintance with a much larger world.

They found Mr. Fiske's office at the end of the hall and went in. His secretary, sitting in an outer office, asked them to be seated and told them Mr. Fiske would be with them shortly. Sybil opened her satchel and took out her father's book. She held it on her lap, her hands pressing nervously into the soft leather binding.

"Mr. Fiske will see you now," his secretary called from the door to his office, and Sybil and William went in.

"William!" Arthur Fiske, a tall, urbane-looking man with sparse white hair, stood when they entered. "This is a surprise."

"I found out that my friend here, Miss Curtis, had an appointment with you, so I thought I'd stop in and say hello." Arthur Fiske and William spoke for a moment about mutual acquaintances before William managed to turn the conversation to more general topics so that Sybil might be included. She had a natural poise and an agreeable way of listening intently to others when they spoke, he noted. Soon she seemed to be completely at ease with Arthur Fiske, whom William could see was charmed. "Well, Arthur, I'm sure you would like to see what Miss Curtis has brought you today," said William, excusing himself, "so I'll leave you both to it."

William waited in the outer office for almost an hour. He was sure Fiske would want the books: the drawings were exceptional, the coloring superb. He recalled trying to draw the branch of an apple tree once, years ago, how difficult it had been to capture its exact color. He had been using the colored pencils given to him by their cook, Mary Conran, after she had seen drawings he had done in the margins of his schoolbook. He remembered his father coming upon him as he sketched the old apple tree behind the barn. His father demanded the pencils. William looked down at the beautiful wooden pencils in every color of the rainbow and refused to give them up. His father, enraged, tried to grab the pencils, but William ran away. That night William hid the pencils behind several books on the top shelf of a bookcase in his room. The next morning they were gone.

The door to Fiske's office opened. Arthur Fiske and Sybil emerged, shaking hands. "If you have any more friends like this young lady, please bring them around," Fiske told William.

After they left the office, William turned to her.

Her smile was radiant. "He loved them," she whispered. "He said my father is to flowers what Audubon is to birds. He wants all the books."

"I knew he would."

"He asked to see the others right away. Fortunately, I have them with me at the New Netherland Hotel, so I'm bringing them to him tomorrow. He said he might put them on permanent display. Can you imagine? Thank you so much, Mr. Dysart."

"I didn't do anything. It was you—your father's work." William thought for a moment. "I don't suppose you have a minute to hear my latest idea on how Lydia Billings can have her way, you can keep your cottage, and I can hold on to what's left of my integrity." There was a man reading intently at a nearby table, so he kept his voice low.

"Mr. Dysart, you have been so kind, but—"

"Just please hear me out. What if Mrs. Billings were to give you an equal amount of land at another site in exchange for your property, then were to pay to have your house moved to the new site?"

"Mr. Dysart—"

"It would cost her far less than what she was willing to pay you originally for your property alone."

She shook her head. "It's not possible."

"Please, Miss Curtis," William insisted, while trying to keep his voice low, "doesn't it matter to you that you could find yourself thrown out of your home without any recourse?"

"Of course it does."

"You have some power now. Use it. You won't have it in a few months' time."

"Power?"

"Mrs. Billings is afraid the press will pick up your story: 'Young woman of small means evicted from her property by the widow of Henry Billings.' "

"I know something about Mrs. Billings's power, Mr. Dysart. The press wouldn't dare go against her."

"Then what is she afraid of?"

She shook her head. "I know you want to do what's best for everyone," she said, "but it's an impossible situation."

"What if Mrs. Billings were to agree to my proposal?"

"She won't. This is not about my property." She reached for her satchel. "I am grateful for your concern, Mr. Dysart—touched by it, really—but nothing can be done." She hurried down the marble staircase. William watched her until she was out of sight, trying to make the pieces of information he knew about her fit together in a coherent way.

He glanced finally to the man reading at the table. What must he have made of their brief, intense conversation? But the man was gone.

William sat at the table. He had been so confident—certain—that he'd found a way to satisfy Lydia's demands without displacing Sybil. Now he felt foolish and frustrated by Sybil's stubborn, baffling refusal. What was she trying to hide? Whom was she protecting? He stood at last and wandered down the main staircase and out of the library.

As he walked home along Fifth Avenue, the sky began to darken, though it was just after four o'clock. And despite the fact the air was frigid, he made no attempt to close his coat against the chilling cold.

Chapter 15

That night William went to speak to Arabella in the library. He had hoped to say something to her earlier at dinner, but she seemed to have sensed his intention, as she communicated far more than was usual with the kitchen about the soup, the gravy, and the state of the silverware, always finding something to say to prevent a few moments of quiet. She was sitting at her desk in a far corner of the room writing a letter when he entered. The smell of evergreen from the Christmas tree that had been put up earlier that week and decorated by the servants filled the room. William sat in a chair by the fire and picked up his newspaper. Arabella's pen continued to scratch across the sheet of paper on the desk before her.

William put down his newspaper. He saw his wife glance away from her letter.

"Arabella."

"What is it?" she sighed.

"I think we need to talk."

"Talk?"

"About our marriage."

"How many times are you going to—"

"It won't work anymore, Belle," said William wearily. "There has got to be more to a marriage than what we have."

"I'm sorry if you're unhappy, but really, William, I think it's time you grew up."

"Grew up?"

"Expected a little bit less from life and a little bit more from yourself."

William went to her desk and leaned across it. "If I expected any less, Belle, I would expect nothing."

"This is about that girl, isn't it?"

"What girl?"

"That one on Long Island with the property."

"Don't be ridiculous."

"I'm not so sure."

"She's a perfectly nice young woman, who—"

"Perfectly nice young women do not run around with men like Albert Penniman." Arabella gathered up the papers from her desk. "You're thirty-one years old, William. I'm sorry your life hasn't turned out quite as you had hoped."

William thought of her coming to his bedroom the previous week and their perfunctory lovemaking.

"Everybody has regrets. Disappointments," she added. She opened the desk drawer and arranged her things neatly inside. "Everyone," she repeated, closing the drawer. "We all make compromises."

"For the life of me, Belle, I don't know what it is I've done to make you hate me."

"I don't hate you, William. But can you say you ever really loved me?"

"I have tried."

"Perhaps too hard."

"I think," William said, "we might both be happier under different circumstances."

"Actually, I'm quite content." She walked past him and slid back one of the heavy mahogany doors. "And if I were you, I wouldn't force your father to choose between us." She left the room.

William stood by the mantel for some time, then went finally and pulled the door closed. He returned to his chair by the fire, lowered his head, and covered his eyes. For six years he had stood before a dark mirror believing he gazed into the eyes of another human being. Now he realized he had always been utterly alone, with a bit of glass and tinseled silver reflecting back nothing but his own vanity.

Chapter 16

The next morning, instead of walking to work, William hailed a cab, though there was no reason he needed to go to work at all. It was the day after the firm's Christmas dinner, and when he arrived, the office was nearly empty, forsaken only to the ghostly scratching of his pen and the relentless clicking of the teetotaling Miss Leary's typewriter. He had already completed the preliminary work on the Consolidated Ironworks case, but he spent the morning organizing his files and making redundant notations to his research. By one o'clock, there was absolutely nothing further to detain him. He gathered some papers from his desk, put them in a folder, and got his coat.

"Miss Leary, I'm leaving," he said, handing her the folder. "Would you retype pages three and seven with the additions I've made?"

"Certainly." Miss Leary took the folder. "Will you be coming back, sir?"

"No. If anyone calls, please tell them I won't be in until Monday."

"Yes, sir."

He glanced down the empty hallway. "Must have been quite a party last night."

"When I left, Mr. Parrish was leading everyone

in a naughty rendition of 'The Night Before Christmas.' "

"Again? And did Mr. Havering do a tango with Miss Koop?"

"To 'Jingle Bells,' " Miss Leary replied with a pained expression.

"Well, let's hope the Vatican succeeds in its efforts to ban the tango by next Christmas." He was about to leave. "Miss Leary, why don't you take the rest of the day off? Those changes can wait until next week. You must have presents to buy or something to do."

"But, sir, what if someone calls?"

"They'll call back."

"What if it's important?"

"They'll find me."

Miss Leary smiled.

"Merry Christmas, Miss Leary."

Once outside, William walked up Broadway past City Hall. He thought about Arabella asking him if his frustration had anything to do with Miss Curtis. Anything, it seemed, would do to obfuscate their real problems. Miss Curtis. He imagined what her expression might have been had she heard Arabella. Probably the one she wore when she asked Walter Jameson if the Lozier was a *thrilling* car. Gravely earnest . . . almost comical. He smiled.

Waiting for a motorcar to pass on Thomas Street, he noticed a small saloon tucked into the basement of a nondescript building in the middle of the block. Without giving it a thought, he turned down the street toward the saloon and descended the several steps to its front door.

Walking in, he found the quiet darkness of the place, with its not unpleasant odor of beer and wood, soothing after the bustle of Broadway at midday. It reminded him of a place where he, Theodore, and their friends had passed many hours during their undergraduate days. The saloon was small and all but empty, except for three men who sat at the far end of the bar talking in a friendly way to the barmaid, a voluptuous, neatly dressed woman who appeared to be in her late forties. She and the men looked up at William when he entered.

He waited at the bar and could see by the dismissive smirk one of the men cast his way that his presence was resented in this working-class establishment. He began to regret having come in, but would not let himself be intimidated into leaving.

"Yes, sir?" asked the barmaid. She had a brogue.

"An ale, please," William said, loosening his tie.

The woman pulled a glass from beneath the bar and placed it under one of the taps as the three men, Irish laborers, fell back into talking among themselves. William relaxed a bit and sat down on a stool.

"There you are, sir, that will be ten cents."

William paid for the ale and tried to drink it slowly, though all he really wanted to do was to finish it quickly and leave. The barmaid began to wash glasses behind the bar, while the men, casting occasional glances at William, continued to talk about their foreman, whose ignorance was surpassed only by his greed, which was itself only exceeded by his cowardice. William had almost finished his ale when the men got up.

"We're back to work, Annie," one of them called to the barmaid.

"So soon?" she asked, drying her hands with a small towel as she accompanied them to the door.

"Sorry, Annie, got a lot to do today."

"Yeah, murder O'Callaghan," said another of the men.

"I'd like to send that bastard flying off a cross-beam from the fourteenth floor," said the third.

"Hey!" said the first, apparently Annie's admirer and defender of her virtue.

"Sorry, Tommy," said the transgressor a bit sheepishly. "Sorry, Annie."

"That's all right, Pat. After all"—she cupped a hand to the side of her face and feigned a whisper—"he is one, ain't he?"

They roared.

"Back again tonight, usual time, Annie," said Tommy.

"Don't be late."

Tommy paused at the open door directly behind

William. "Just be sure you don't run off with no gentlemen, even them what gives you the glad eye."

"Oh you!" Annie laughed and waved Tommy away with her towel as William heard the door close behind him. Turning to William, she said, "Mustn't mind him. He don't mean nothing by it." She spied William's nearly empty glass. "Would you like another?" Before he could say a word, she had his glass under the tap. "There you are." She placed the ale before him.

William reached into his pocket.

"No"—Annie waved her hand—"it's on the house on account of you being a good sport about my Tommy." She turned to clear away the empty glasses, then took a broom and began sweeping and cleaning up. She took a damp cloth and vigorously mopped the bar near William. "It's a woman, ain't it?"

"Pardon me?"

"That's why you're here in the middle of the day. Some woman's made you miserable."

He didn't know how to respond.

"An absolute wreck"—she thrust out her lower lip—"judging by the look o' things."

He laughed. "All right . . . yes, I suppose that's why I'm here."

"Do you love her?"

He took a long drink, then shook his head. "No." He drained the ale and got up to leave.

"Have one more with Annie before you go."

"I don't think so." He took out his pocket watch.

"Just one," she said. "Please," she cooed.

He couldn't help smiling. "All right." He sat down again. "Just one."

"I'll make it a Tiptons." She took his glass. *"It's the superior refresher,"* she said with a half curtsy. She placed the Tiptons on the bar in front of him. "So, you say you're not in love with her." She stared at him, as if considering several romantic scenarios in which to cast him.

"No, I'm afraid not."

"I've had this place for on to twenty-five years now. It's gotten so I can read men almost as soon as they walk in the door. I can tell whether they're happy or sad. And I can tell why, too. If not as soon as they come in, then after a glass or two."

"And here I'm on my third, Annie."

"I look at a man and I think: Oh, his wife left him last night for some bounder and he's wretched; I see another and can tell he's just lost a child and it's killing him; that man there's in love. You see?"

"Very scientific."

"Just so. Now as soon as I saw you today, I said to myself there's a man in love and it's making him miserable."

"Sorry, Annie." William glanced at his pocket watch again, then quickly drank the rest of his ale. He set the glass on the bar.

"Maybe it's because you're a gentleman; I don't get much chance to study them."

"I won't tell anyone you missed." He stood and put a dollar on the bar.

Annie saw the dollar. "You don't have to do that."

"But I want to, Annie."

"She must be crazy."

"Who?"

"The one who's breaking your heart."

"Annie . . ." William leaned toward her and whispered, "I don't have a heart."

"Sure you do, and it's breaking. First time, I'd say."

William laughed.

Leaving the bar, he walked along Thomas Street to Broadway, which seemed a far more pleasant place than it had earlier. He was just about to cross Canal Street when he looked up and saw Sybil Curtis walking half a block in front of him on Broadway.

"Miss Curtis," he called, running to catch her. "Miss Curtis," he called again, more loudly this time. "Miss Curtis," he said as he reached her.

"Pardon me?" The woman turned, and he was startled to see that she was not Sybil Curtis after all.

"Oh, I am sorry," William stuttered. "I thought you were someone else."

As the woman walked away, he stood on the pavement. Where had Sybil said she was staying when they met at the library yesterday? He stepped off the curb and hailed a cab.

Chapter 17

William got out of the cab in front of the New Netherland Hotel's arched brownstone and marble entrance and charged up the front steps, through the revolving door, straight to the hotel desk, where he asked for Miss Sybil Curtis. His voice sounded strange to him, and the clerk seemed to look at him peculiarly before turning around to check. William's face felt flushed. He remembered his tie was loosened and promptly slid the knot up to his throat. His heart beat rapidly. The man turned back to him. Miss Curtis was not in. Would he care to leave a message? He shook his head and went to find the men's washroom off the main lobby. He felt headachy and warm. Several minutes later he walked back into the lobby, which was crowded with people coming into town for the weekend. Porters moved about briskly, gathering up suitcases and putting them on trolleys. Sounds of happy reunions punctuated by bursts of muffled laughter filled the air. Bland, indifferent faces flashed quickly past him as he made his way toward the hotel's front door. Suddenly, there she was standing before him.

"I . . . I was in the neighborhood," said William, holding out his hand.

Sybil took it. "I was . . . just . . . out," she stammered, waving over her shoulder at the revolving door spinning behind her.

"I thought perhaps you might like to go for a walk in the park."

She looked toward the large brass clock at the center of the lobby. She was wearing a black velvet toque trimmed with a single egret plume. The hat covered her hair, emphasizing her lovely eyes and glowing complexion.

"Please," said William.

"All right." She smiled. "But you must promise we won't talk about Mrs. Billings or my property or any of that unpleasant business."

"I promise."

"I just need to go to my room for a moment."

William nodded and sat down in a leather wing chair near the entrance, breathing a sigh of relief. Glancing at the floor, he saw an envelope and picked it up. It was addressed to Arthur Fiske. She must have dropped it. He studied her handwriting—precise and intelligent, without any of the flourishes or curlicues some women favored. Leaning back in the chair, he admired the enormous painting behind the registry desk, *The Purchase of Manhattan Island from the Indians*, by Franklin Tuttle.

When she joined him a few minutes later, he rose and walked with her out of the hotel and across Fifth Avenue into Central Park. It was cold, but the sun warmed them as they made their way over the park's cobblestoned walks under a clear blue sky. "Do you plan to be in town long, Miss Curtis?" he asked.

"Only until tomorrow morning," she said as they paused to let a carriage pass on the East Drive of the park. "Mr. Dysart, are you married?"

"Miss Curtis," William replied, smiling, "you're far too plainspoken. Most women would ask three seemingly unrelated questions to get the answer to that one. I admire your directness. Yes, I am. My wife's name is Arabella and we have been married for six years."

"Arabella Dysart is your wife?"

"You know her?"

"I know of her. I would say most people have heard of Arabella Dysart."

"I suppose." William reached for the branch of a tree and pulled it down, then let it spring back toward the sky.

They continued on, passing through the mall at the center of the park until they came to Belvedere Terrace, where they descended the stairs and walked around the fountain.

She looked up at the angel peering down at them from atop the fountain. "Her head is out of proportion, don't you think? A bit too small."

He glanced up. "And she has that overly sentimental mid-nineteenth-century look to her."

"I like her all the same. I think she's sweet."

"I think she's an angel," he said.

She laughed and they walked over by the lagoon at the northern end of the terrace. Red rowboats were tied together on shore, awaiting the return of visitors to the park in the spring. They walked back up the stairs.

"Can I treat you to a cup of tea this time?" he asked, leading her along a gravel path toward the Casino restaurant inside the park off Seventy-second Street.

"Thank you."

Inside, they found a small table in the rustic main room. William pulled out a chair for her and she took off her coat. He was surprised to see her in a high-collared, dark maroon dress of some polished material that danced from deep red to blue-black as she moved. The dress was gathered at the waist with a black patent leather belt. How different from her usual simple white blouses, woolen skirts, and cardigans.

She read his mind. "You expected to see me in my cardy? I do like to dress up now and then, Mr. Dysart," she said, twisting the rope of jet beads hanging from her neck.

"So I see." William smiled. How beautiful she looked.

They ordered tea. William glanced out a nearby

window. "My nurse used to bring me to the lagoon when I was a boy." He laughed. "She took me out in one of those boats once, but I wouldn't behave. I kept trying to jump in the water."

"I can imagine you being quite willful, Mr. Dysart." She sipped her tea. "Were you happy as a child?"

"Early on, yes. Later, not especially. And you?"

She nodded. "I lived in a small village in England—Burford."

"Near Oxford?"

"You know it?" Her face brightened.

"Lovely place. I remember staying there with my father on a trip through the Cotswolds."

Her eyes drifted away. "Someday I'm going to go back."

In an alcove of the restaurant, a pianist and a violinist began to play "Alexander's Ragtime Band."

"Now there's one I haven't heard in a long time," said William dryly.

Sybil turned to watch the musicians, leaning her cheek against her hand. "I don't care if they do play it everywhere, I love it—so full of life." She hummed several bars of the tune, then began to sing along softly.

"That was lovely," said William.

She blushed. "I didn't realize."

"Won't you continue?"

"Now that I know you're listening?" She shook her head.

After he had paid the bill, they walked along the East Drive in the park. Suddenly a large yellow dog ran toward them on the walkway, pursued by three young boys. The dog leapt up against William's legs, muddying his pants and nearly knocking him over.

William reached down and rubbed the dog's neck. He took a ball from its mouth. "Is this what you're after?" he asked, tossing the ball to one of the boys. The boys apologized, then disappeared with the dog across the drive.

William took a handkerchief from his jacket and wiped the dog's saliva from his hand. "Well," he joked, "I guess you won't be holding my hand today."

There was an awkward silence. "Perhaps we should be getting back," Sybil murmured. "It will be dark soon."

"Of course."

They left the drive and followed a tree-lined path that wound its way south.

"I noticed your wife on Madison Avenue recently, Mr. Dysart—with an admiring crowd of friends around her. I think she must be the most beautiful woman I've ever seen."

"Do you?"

"And one hears so much about her work for

different charities. How lucky you are. Not only is she exceptionally beautiful, she—"

"Please don't."

They walked through the park the rest of the way in silence. Across the street from her hotel, Sybil held out her hand. "Thank you for the tea, Mr. Dysart."

William took her hand and held it. He didn't want the afternoon to end.

"Mr. Dysart," she said softly.

"Oh, yes, of course." He quickly withdrew his hand.

She darted across the street and up the polished marble steps of the hotel. As she disappeared through the revolving door, William wondered how she was able to afford the expense of such a hotel and her fine clothes, living as simply as she did in her cottage on Long Island. He wished that things could simply go on as they had, that he could see her from time to time and not have to think about all the troubling questions that gathered around her like dark clouds in the distance on a beautiful day.

Turning down Sixtieth Street, he began to walk home along Madison Avenue. At Sixty-eighth Street, he went to buy the evening paper from a newsboy. When he reached into his pocket for two cents, he felt something—the letter Sybil had written to Arthur Fiske. He turned back toward the hotel. He pictured her coming into the lobby to get the letter. There would probably be a moment of awkwardness. He had said too much on their walk in the park. That damn ale. He must think of the right words to say—clever, but not too clever, charming, but not glib—something to put her at her ease, that he might see that lovely smile of hers again.

He dashed across Sixtieth Street and rounded the corner onto Fifth Avenue, just in time to see Albert Penniman come out of the New Netherland Hotel. William watched him walk down Fifth Avenue. He took a breath, then entered the hotel. At the front desk, he handed the clerk the letter. "This belongs to Miss Curtis."

"Would you like me to ring her, sir?" the man asked.

"No, thank you," said William, turning to leave.

Chapter 18

After dropping off Sybil's letter, William arrived home and found a note from Arabella, apparently dictated over the telephone to one of the maids, pinned to his evening clothes. She had a late meeting with the planning committee for the Settlement House Ball, and would see him at the Belmonts' Christmas party at eight o'clock. "The Belmonts' Christmas party," William muttered. He tossed the rolled-up copy of his evening paper into a wastebasket, then changed to meet Arabella.

The next night they attended a dance given by Mrs. Osborn at her home on Madison Avenue for her debutante niece, Sarah Morgan. Two orchestras played until midnight, when supper was served, then there was more music and dancing, followed by breakfast at dawn. William and Arabella didn't arrive home until 5:30 a.m. The next afternoon William went for a walk in the park to clear his head. He had drunk too much wine the night before and had smoked a cigar after dinner, something he rarely did, and the combination left him with a powerful headache. Entering the park at Seventy-second Street, he saw the Casino restaurant directly ahead and turned north to avoid it. The park was wet, cold, and deserted, which fit his mood perfectly, and he walked almost to its limit at 110th Street before returning home to read his newspaper and go to bed early.

When he came downstairs the next morning, he was surprised to find Arabella sitting in the breakfast room. She glanced up from reading the *Society at Home and Abroad* column in the *Times*.

"An early appointment?" asked William.

"No. I heard someone at the door. Lydia Billings's chauffeur." She picked up a crisp white envelope by the side of her coffee cup and handed it to him. "He delivered this for you."

William quickly opened the envelope. It was a

154

note from Lydia, saying she wanted him to come by to see her later that morning. It was an odd note for someone of Lydia Billings's usual elegance to write, direct almost to the point of rudeness. William stared at the martial line of her script as he sat down.

"What is it?" Arabella passed him a cup of coffee.

"Lydia wants to see me this morning." He took a quick sip of his coffee.

"Anything important?"

"I don't know."

"I hope you're not getting on the wrong side of her with all this business. I've spent too much time getting that old hawk to like me to have you ruin it." She raised a silver lid and glanced at the eggs beneath.

"I have to leave," said William, bolting down a piece of toast and getting up from the table.

"Tonight is the Settlement House Ball," Arabella called as the breakfast-room door swung closed behind him.

William rushed down Madison Avenue toward Lydia's house on East Fifty-fourth Street. He couldn't imagine what had prompted her to write such a note, delivered by her chauffeur no less. He had just turned onto Fifty-fourth Street when he heard someone call him. It was Lydia. She was coming from a fitting at Madame Georges, her favorite dressmaker, she told him.

She took his arm. "How I love being on the arm of a handsome young man," she said, almost coquettishly.

When they arrived at her house, Lydia stopped to examine two holly trees on either side of her double front doors. "So festive, don't you think? Mr. Ker must have brought them while I was out." The dark green spheres of holly with their tiny red berries sparkled against the warm glow of her oak doors. "How right he was. I wanted ribbons, but he said that would detract from their natural beauty and that such effects were too *Belleclaire Hotel*." Lydia winced, referring to the baroque Upper West Side hotel favored by prairie debutantes.

"Such a marvelous day, Hammond," Lydia greeted her butler as she and William entered the house. "Isn't the holly lovely?"

"Yes, madam, it is."

"Hammond, we'll take coffee in the morning room. And tell Frau Flatscher no pastry for me." She thought for a moment, then reconsidered. "Perhaps one small piece. The linzer torte."

They entered her morning room just off the main hall. "Please have a seat, William." Lydia gestured to two small sofas facing one another. She walked toward one of the windows in the room. "How is Arabella? Beautiful as ever?" She adjusted the blinds at the window. "A bit too much sun, don't you think?" She walked over to a desk, opened a drawer, and took out a cigarette box. "Cigarette?"

"No, thank you."

She sat down across from him, lit her cigarette, and leaned back against the pillows of the sofa, exhaling a cloud of smoke. "William, why were you at the library the other day with that young woman?"

William was too shocked at first to respond. "Pardon me?" he asked.

Lydia stared at him.

"I was meeting with Miss Curtis," he finally explained. "I had an idea I wanted to discuss with her."

"At the library?"

"How do you know we met at the library?"

"It's not important." Lydia raised her cigarette to her lips and inhaled deeply.

"I'm afraid it is."

William's words hung in the air between them.

The door opened and Hammond entered carrying a tray, which he placed on the round marble-topped table near Lydia.

"Thank you, Hammond," said Lydia, "we'll serve ourselves." When he'd left, Lydia reached for the silver coffeepot. "Coffee, William?"

William ignored her. "I want to know how you know I met Miss Curtis at the library."

"How do you know she didn't tell me?"

"Why would she tell you?"

"Don't trust her, William." Lydia tamped out her cigarette.

"But you don't know her, Lydia."

"I have my reasons for saying what I did."

"Such as?"

She poured herself a cup of coffee, then surveyed the plate of small pastries, finally choosing one. "Ah, my linzer torte. You really must try these."

"Lydia, I asked you a question."

"Yes, I know." She paused and lit another cigarette. "But I don't know that I care to answer it."

"Then you can find yourself another lawyer."

"My, how grave you are." Lydia exhaled cigarette smoke in one long burst. "So much like your mother. You know I knew her, of course."

William stared at her silently.

"She had the same puritan earnestness. Quite irresistible. Combined as it was with all that beauty."

William sighed and got up to leave.

"Please don't leave me, William." Lydia's tone changed completely. "I'll tell you about Miss Curtis. Please sit down."

William sat again on the sofa.

"This is very difficult for me." Lydia's eyes shone. She blinked rapidly. For a moment, William thought she might cry. "I am so very proud," she said with a quick laugh. "As you may have guessed, this young woman, this—Miss Curtis—caused me no end of heartache when Mr. Billings was alive."

"How?"

"How do you think?" Lydia smiled ruefully. "He was obsessed with her. Utterly. To the point that I ceased to exist for him. Of course these things happen, even in the best families. Your mother with that writer or whatever from Boston."

"What writer from Boston?"

Lydia looked at William thoughtfully. "Oh, it was nothing," she said at last. "A little flirtation—*une amoureuse innocente*—but it upset your father." Lydia sighed. "Mr. Billings's *amoureuse* was, unfortunately, not so innocent. After he died, she came to me with her demands . . . threats."

"Miss Curtis?"

"Yes. Miss Curtis." Lydia gave a snide twist to the name. "She is very clever. Will say anything to get what she wants. Please, you must be careful."

"Why didn't you tell me all this before?"

"I was too ashamed."

"How has she threatened you?"

"She says things about Mr. Billings. Terrible things. Lies. I'm afraid she'll go to the newspapers with them one day. I have offered her a great deal of money to leave me alone, but it's never enough. Please, William, you must get her to leave that property somehow. I can't stand the thought of her being there."

"How did she meet Mr. Billings?"

"How?" The question seemed to rattle her. "I—I'm not sure. In a shop, I believe. Somewhere outside of London."

"Burford?"

"Yes. That might have been it. They're always shop girls, aren't they, William?" Lydia tried to smile.

"It would have been much better, Lydia, had I known all this from the start."

"I'm sorry. I just couldn't bring myself to tell you. But when I heard about your meeting with her at the library, I knew I had to do something."

"It was all very proper. Miss Curtis was in from the Island for some business at the library. I thought maybe I could still settle this without involving the State."

"Forgive me, William, but I was given to believe that your behavior toward her was rather ardent."

"Ardent?" asked William. The word stung him.

"Yes. Not the kind of behavior one would expect during a business encounter."

"And who told you this?"

"Albert Penniman."

"Albert?"

"You know, of course, that he's seeing her."

"I had some idea. But why, if she's so objectionable?"

"As you may have noticed, she is not without her charms. And although Albert might come from a good family, we both know . . . well, frankly, he might as well have been raised in a kennel. And water does, after all, seek its own level."

"I don't believe it. She is nothing like him."

"And I can't believe you can't see through her." She took a deep breath. "Though how can I blame you. Mr. Billings was so . . . And he was nobody's fool."

"Why would Albert tell you this?" William asked.

"He is the jealous type. Besides, Mr. Billings helped him with his investments and made him a very rich man. He is grateful."

"So grateful that he's willing to stand by and see Miss Curtis lose her property?"

"I could make it very expensive for Albert." Lydia's tone grew harsh. "He knows better than to mix business with pleasure."

William looked at Lydia thoughtfully.

"You will be careful, William. That girl could charm the devil."

"I appreciate your concern. But there is absolutely no reason for it."

Lydia went to him. "You will help me."

"I'll do what I can."

She looked into his eyes. "Thank you, William. Now, if you don't mind, Hammond will show you out. I have a frightful headache."

Chapter 19

William's father's sleek Delaunay-Belleville limousine glided down Fifth Avenue toward the Waldorf-Astoria Hotel on Thirty-fourth Street, carrying William and Arabella to the Settlement House Ball that night. Sitting in the backseat, they spoke hardly a word to one another. Arabella was wearing Cady's diamond and sapphire parure; the smooth oval sapphire at the center of the tiara shone softly like the night sky, and the necklace sent out blue and white sparks in the back of the limousine. Loosely draped over her shoulders was her peacock blue opera cape lined with Russian sables. William remembered the night she had come to his room wearing the cape. She had crept up behind him and kissed his neck. He turned and she opened the cape and gathered him in against her naked body. He remembered her exquisite breasts, the softness of her skin against the sable, and the night of lovemaking that followed. What had she wanted that night?

As their limousine passed Fortieth Street, William glanced out at Madame Lanier's, an exclusive millinery shop occupying the ground floor of a converted brownstone. *They're always shop girls, aren't they, William?*

Arabella reached into the slit-like pocket of her cape and took out a slim silver case with her initials on it. She looked for a moment at the elaborate scrollwork on the exquisite little case, then opened it and took out a cigarette. A Gitane, the brand she had sent to her from Paris. She tapped the cigarette lightly against the case, then put it to her lips. William reached over and lit it for her.

He looked ahead and saw the Waldorf-Astoria, a Second Empire masterpiece of towers, domes, and mansard roofs. It rose in the night sky above the surrounding converted mansions and office buildings of lower Fifth Avenue.

Their limousine swung onto Thirty-fourth Street and pulled up to the hotel's iron and glass canopy, which reached out over the sidewalk. Wilson, William's father's chauffeur, opened the car door for William and Arabella. They passed the Waldorf's doormen, dressed smartly in their blue and gold uniforms, and proceeded down Peacock Alley, the hotel's famed corridor where hotel guests and well-dressed tourists sat to watch the nightly procession of wealth and glamour passing beneath its high, deeply coffered ceiling. Pages moved about, quickly calling out the numbers of rooms, the names of guests, or the availability of tables in the exclusive Palm Room restaurant at the end of Peacock Alley. The conversation filling the corridor turned to a low excited hum when

Arabella entered. Her beauty alone might have accounted for it, but her fame had grown now beyond the world of New York society, so that many there would have read about her in their local newspapers or seen a picture of her in a national magazine. She held on to William's arm, her face flawless and serene, seemingly oblivious to the sensation she was creating. Her dress of fluttering blue silk broke perfectly over her satin shoes and wound its way elegantly over the graceful contours of her slim body, its long train rippling over the hall's thick Turkish carpets and bright mosaic floor.

"William, where have you been hiding?" William's friend George Meade called to him as they entered the ballroom on the second floor. George and his wife, Marian, walked quickly across the floor to greet them.

George was short and wiry with a large forehead, a man of seemingly boundless energy. His wife was taller than he and had, as most women said, "a fine figure," but her broad shoulders gave an almost masculine impression of strength and she had a hawk-like nose, which on a man might have been called distinguished but on Marian was simply called unfortunate.

"It's been an age since we've seen you." George looked from William to Arabella. "And look, dear." He turned to his wife. "Arabella is as stunning as ever."

"Yes," Marian agreed with genuine admiration. "What a magnificent dress."

"Thank you," said Arabella, glancing at Marian's Paris gown of ten seasons back, with its drooping flounce in want of a needle and its tiny velvet bows, creased this way and that from a too intimate acquaintance with its neighbors in Marian's wardrobe. "Yours is lovely, too. Have Sunny and Gladys arrived?" she asked.

"The Duke of Marlborough?" asked Marian. "Yes, I saw them five minutes ago over by the orchestra."

"Will you pardon me?" Arabella turned toward the orchestra. "I promised Kitty Livingston I would help keep them entertained. She must be furious with me. Did we miss the grand march?"

"I'm afraid so," said Marian.

Arabella walked gracefully across the room into the welcoming arms of a crowd of bright young things. William saw her carefully position herself next to Gladys Deacon, the Duke of Marlborough's mistress, confident, he thought, that any comparison between her and the famously beautiful Miss Deacon would be in her favor.

At one end of the ballroom was an enormous evergreen swathed in red ribbon and hung with silver ornaments; garlands framed all the doors and windows. "The room looks beautiful," William told Marian, who had been in charge of decorating.

A waiter carrying flutes of champagne stopped in front of them. "Polly," said George, using his pet name for Marian, as he handed her a glass of champagne.

George and Marian Meade, thought William, were perhaps the least romantic couple he could imagine in terms of physical beauty or personal magnetism, yet their marriage was one of the most passionate he knew.

George clinked his champagne glass with William's. "How are things on Wall Street?"

"Quiet." William took a sip of champagne and recalled that one of George's uncles had been involved with Henry Billings in his first business venture, a glassworks company that had been wildly successful in the construction boom following the Civil War. "I am working on something right now for Lydia Billings involving her place on Long Island."

"Wilbur de Forest told me about it," said George. "He's chief landscape designer."

"Is he? I'd be interested in talking to him about a problem I'm having."

"I'm afraid he's in England—studying Capability Brown's landscapes, in fact, for the project. What is the problem?"

As George already knew about Lydia's plans, William felt he could discuss the case with him, at least in a general way.

"I'm trying to buy a small piece of property

Lydia feels she needs to carry out her plans." William glanced at Marian to include her in their conversation, but she seemed interested only in the ball. "She is determined to have it no matter the cost, and the young woman who owns the land is equally determined not to sell for any price."

"A young woman?" Marian turned to William. She had been listening after all.

"Yes," said William.

"Can you tell me her name?"

"A Miss Curtis. Sybil Curtis."

Marian nodded without inquiring further.

"Do you know her?" asked William.

"I may." Marian blushed. "That is, I know someone who might. It's nothing, really."

Marian's obvious reticence to say anything further made it impossible for William to pursue the matter.

"Probably Lydia is trying to pull another of her fast ones," said George. "She's not about to let anyone get in the way of her remaking the reputation of that scoundrel husband of hers."

The orchestra could be heard tuning their instruments.

"My Uncle Charlie was nearly destroyed by Billings," George continued, "because he was foolish enough to deal with him in an open, honest fashion."

A waltz began.

"But enough of Henry Billings." George's tone

changed. "I've come here tonight to drink too much champagne and to dance with the most glorious woman in the room, if not all New York." George held out his arm to his wife and he and Marian glided out onto the dance floor.

After William had finished his champagne, he stood for a time watching the many couples spinning past him. He saw the Parrishes whirl by and smile. A waiter stopped and offered him another glass of champagne. He drank it, but found no pleasure at the bottom of the glass. People came and spoke to him.

Across the dance floor he saw Arabella surrounded by admirers and thought of the first time he had seen her, at a ball given by the Bradley-Martins. Arabella—all grace and staggering beauty—a woman who asked nothing of him but to be indulged and admired.

"William, you have been hiding here in this corner all night." Theodore Parrish walked up to him. "People are beginning to wonder if you're not some socialist spy."

"Tell them I am," said William, "and I'm bored to death."

"I suppose these gatherings do have a certain predictability to them." Theodore took a glass of champagne from a passing waiter and looked out at the crowded dance floor. "Have you seen Bertie Penniman tonight?"

William shook his head. He watched the crowd

before them dip, swell, and turn in time to the music.

"Well, here's a bit of excitement for your socialist friends. Bertie's come here tonight"—Theodore lowered his voice—"with a woman he's been introducing as his cousin from Boston. No one believes him. She's far too beautiful to be anyone's cousin."

"His cousin?"

"Dark. Quite the little stunner. Everyone's being very worldly about it, of course, but some of the old bats like Eugenia Beckwith want to show them the door. Of course, it's all right that the Duke of Marlborough shows up with his mistress. They'll accept anything from the English aristocracy—makes you wonder why we didn't just skip the Revolution." Theodore looked out past William onto the dance floor. "There they are now."

William turned and saw Sybil Curtis dancing with Albert. She wore a simple ivory-colored dress with a tunic that made everyone around her look overdressed.

"Beautiful, isn't she?"

"Yes." William caught his breath.

"Looks interesting, too."

William nodded. "So why aren't you out there, Theo?" he asked, attempting to sound blasé. "I've never known you to sit out a dance, if there's so much as a harmonica wheezing away somewhere."

"You're not even going to speculate about Penniman and this woman?"

"These little intrigues bore me," William replied, his mind spinning. The music ended.

"I suppose." Theodore nodded. "She probably is his cousin, after all. Why else would she be with that dolt? Of course, we could start a rumor that she's Teddy Roosevelt's love child."

"Or blew up the *Maine*," said William. On the dance floor, all the couples stood waiting for the music to begin again. He could not help staring at Sybil Curtis. The orchestra burst into a spirited waltz. He watched her dance, her feet moving lightly over the floor, executing a half turn, then a dip into a graceful spin. How he wished it were he and not Albert dancing with her.

"She's quite a dancer," said Theodore, "and look at Albert, two left feet—doesn't realize she's carrying him."

"Like so many we know—people carrying them all their lives."

"You are a socialist spy," said Theodore. "Looks like his *cousin* got tired of the heavy lifting."

William saw Sybil walk out a set of doors at the far end of the room. "Pardon me." William turned and walked away.

"What the devil?" He heard Theodore over his shoulder.

Sybil Curtis was adjusting her cape as she walked rapidly down the long hall outside the ballroom. She moved swiftly over the thick carpeting toward the staircase at the end of the hall. William rushed to catch up with her, but she had already descended past the first landing on the staircase and had almost reached the second when he called to her from the top of the stairs. She stopped and reached for the brass handrail at her side. "Yes, Mr. Dysart," she said without turning around.

He walked down to where she stood. "Why are you leaving?"

She glanced at him, then looked away.

"Are you Albert Penniman's cousin?"

She shook her head.

"Who are you?"

She turned and looked into his face. "I can't tell you." How different she looked with her hair swept up, a fringe of curls grazing her forehead.

"Why?"

"Because I don't think you would understand. Because I think I would lose the respect I sometimes flatter myself you have for me."

"You flatter neither of us. Me for my understanding, nor yourself for the depth of my respect."

She looked away. "How kind your words are, Mr. Dysart." She hesitated. "How kind you are."

William moved closer. His hand grazed hers.

Turning, she met his eyes. Without thinking, he leaned down and kissed her softly on the lips, then backed away. They stared at one another.

Her eyes searched his face. She looked as if she might cry.

Suddenly there was the sound of someone clearing his throat. William looked up and saw the Duke of Marlborough and Gladys Deacon at the top of the stairs, Gladys with a conspiratorial gleam in her eye. "Really now, Mr. Dysart," she murmured.

Sybil turned and hurried down the remaining stairs.

"Wait." William ran to catch her.

Sybil reached Peacock Alley and proceeded toward the Palm Room. William followed her. She stopped abruptly when she realized there was no exit in that direction. People lounging in Peacock Alley looked up expectantly.

Mrs. Schuyler Oelrichs, a society matron in a glittering black dress with a plume of feathers in her hair, was leaving the Palm Room with a large party. She fixed her eyes on William, then on Sybil.

Sybil turned in confusion. William approached her.

"Please call me the week after Christmas," he said in a low voice. He thought quickly. "Thursday. I want to see you again. I'll work out something with Mrs. Billings. I don't care about anything that's happened between . . . you . . . her . . . none of it's important. Please call me."

"I can't."

"Please," he implored.

She looked at him with an anguished expression.

"Please."

She nodded, then hurried past him down the corridor and out of the hotel.

William turned then to see Mrs. Schuyler Oelrichs glaring at him. She walked by him in stony silence, followed by her party.

Chapter 20

Moonlight fell through the partially opened shutters in William Dysart's bedroom, forming odd geometric patterns on the floor. He lay in bed unable to sleep. He kept spinning out in his mind all that he knew about Sybil Curtis. Finally he threw aside the covers and went to the window to close the shutters. Instead he pushed up the window sash, and frigid night air slipped in. He looked up at the moon in the starless December sky and raised his fingers over his lips. What had she thought of his kissing her? The expression on her face afterward gave him no clue. Then he remembered the gentle pressure of her hand on his forearm as he pressed his lips to hers. That would have meant she was as engaged in the moment as he. Or would it? He took a deep breath, then reached up and pushed the window sash down and locked the shutters.

The next afternoon he called Lydia Billings, but was told she was in Maine and not expected to return to town until sometime after the New Year. He replaced the phone on the hook and went to one of the drawing room windows. It was a gray day. A woman passed by directly below, one gloved hand pressed against the scarf at her throat, the other holding tightly to a little boy at her side. They moved quickly up the street toward the park. The woman, pretty and dark, said something to the boy and smiled at him. William watched them until they were out of sight. He recalled Lydia Billings's remark about his mother's puritan earnestness, and remembered a time when he was a small boy and didn't want to make his bed. It was the servants' job, he had told his mother, but she insisted, promising if he made it every day, she would buy him something. What was it? He remembered facing his unmade bed every morning as if it were a mountain to be climbed and getting it done one way or another, but he never got his prize.

Arabella entered the room putting on her gloves.

"Going out?" William asked.

"Yes, and so are you. The Houghtons' Christmas reception is in half an hour."

William groaned. "I completely forgot." He went upstairs to change.

Mattias and Ardith Houghton were an elderly couple who gave a Christmas reception every year to which only certain New York families were invited; generally, those whose grandparents had known Ardith Houghton's grandparents. It wasn't that she was a snob. As far as she was concerned, she was simply inviting old friends to share Christmas, but an invitation to the Houghtons' had become over the years a significant measure of one's social standing. Mrs. Houghton would have been astonished to learn the number of people who vacated their Fifth Avenue mansions for Long Island or Tuxedo Park the weekend of her reception to avoid having to admit they had not been invited. Ironically, it was a deadly dull affair, precisely the same year after year. There was the enormous Christmas tree in the drawing room of the Houghtons' town house on Fifth Avenue at Seventy-ninth Street, beneath which the Grace Church choir would sing Christmas carols. Women and children were expected to take part in the caroling. The men were allowed to retreat to the library, the music room, or wherever they could find a quiet corner to be served by a small army of attentive waiters hired by Mattias Houghton, who could not abide Christmas music and wanted his male guests to enjoy the reception as he did, with talk, brandy, and cigars.

William and Arabella arrived just as the drawing room was exploding into a rousing rendition of

"Deck the Halls." Arabella took a deep breath, and as the drawing room door was opened for her, a booming concatenation of *fa la la la la, la la la la*'s escaped, sending William flying to the conservatory at the back of the house.

Happy to find it empty, he sat in a comfortable wicker chair and took out his pocket watch. Six o'clock. Perhaps by eight they could politely leave. A waiter appeared. William asked for a whiskey and the *New York Tribune*. The whiskey and paper arrived in short order and William settled in to what he hoped would be a quiet hour or two alone. He was reading only a short while when he heard footsteps outside the conservatory. He sighed and prepared to engage in small talk. The door opened and William looked up from his paper. It was Albert Penniman.

"Hello, Will," said Albert. "They said I might find you here. Mind if I join you?"

"Not at all." William closed his newspaper.

A waiter appeared with whiskeys for Albert and William. "I ordered one for you, too. Hope you don't mind." The waiter set the whiskey down next to William's drink already on the table. Albert took a case from his jacket. "Cigar?"

William shook his head.

Albert lit his cigar and sat down in a wicker chair across from William. "So, I hear you're trying to buy Sybil Curtis's place for Lydia Billings."

William stared at Albert a moment. "Yes. Something like that."

"She'll sell . . . eventually."

"Do you think so?"

Albert nodded. "She's just waiting for Lydia to make it interesting for her."

"Interesting?"

"Fifty thousand dollars." Albert drank some brandy.

"That's not going to happen."

"It will."

"Albert, the place is going to be condemned by the State. Miss Curtis will be lucky to get three thousand dollars for it—unless she comes to some kind of an agreement with Lydia beforehand."

"Miss Curtis." Albert leaned back in his chair. "You have to understand, Will, it's like a chess game with those two. Lydia may have the money and the power, but believe me, Sybil . . . *Miss Curtis* . . . will come out on top."

"I'm not so sure."

"She will. She always does. Henry Billings could have had any woman in the world, and he chose her. Have you asked yourself why? Oh, she's pretty enough. But the real reason, Will, is that she has a genius for knowing just what kind of woman a man wants her to be, and for being that woman." Albert picked up his whiskey and drank the remainder in one swallow. "Hello.

Hello," he called toward the door. A waiter entered. "Another glass, Will?" he asked.

William shook his head. "And why are you telling me this?"

"I saw the way you ran after her last night." Albert handed his empty glass to the waiter. "You know she was Billings's mistress."

"Lydia alluded to it," said William. "I thought she might be lying."

"Why would she lie about something like that?"

"It just didn't seem to fit."

"It fits all right."

William took a deep breath. "I suppose with her parents dead, she—"

"Dead? Her mother manages the Hotel New Point on Long Island—Amityville. Goes by the name of Burns—Mrs. Burns. Ask *her* about Sybil."

"It can't be true."

"Believe what you like."

"Well, whatever the truth about her parents, it doesn't explain why Lydia is obsessed with her. Men have had mistresses before. Lydia is no innocent. It might have been difficult for her at the time, but to go to such lengths now . . ."

"Sybil doesn't fit in with how Lydia would like the old man remembered. Or herself, for that matter. She's afraid people will visit her park in a hundred years and see that little house and whisper, 'That's where he kept his mistress.'"

Albert laughed. "It's killing her. And when I think of all the women Billings had."

The waiter delivered Albert's drink. "Cheers." Albert raised his glass and took a long swallow. "Be careful, Will."

"Careful?"

"There's nothing Sybil would like better than to draw you into all this."

"Have you been drawn in?"

"She wouldn't have a chance and she knows it."

William turned to look out the glass wall of the conservatory. The bare branches of the trees across the street in Central Park swayed and turned heedlessly, buffeted about by winds against the dark December sky.

"No one knew better than old Billings how to find someone's greatest weakness or fear, then to strike at it until he had you." Albert leaned toward William and began to speak in an eager whisper. "When he found out he was dying, he bought that property. Put Sybil there, then had his lawyer, that old lizard Barclay Philbin, set up a trust—a regular Chinese puzzle—so that there was no way Lydia could take the place away from her after he was gone."

"Any trust would have done that," said William.

Albert shook his head. "There was a technicality, which only Lydia knew about. She could easily have challenged the trust, but then the whole thing would have come tumbling down."

"What whole thing?"

"The extent of Billings's philandering. But the minute Lydia heard old Barc Philbin was dead"— Albert laughed and leaned back again in his chair—"she was on it, ready to drive Sybil out. I don't think Billings or Philbin ever thought Lydia would go so far as to have the place condemned by the State."

"If Henry Billings tormented Lydia as you say," said William, "why is she working so hard to make sure he's remembered—respected?"

"She loved him. Completely. Insanely."

"Did he love her?"

"He never loved anyone."

"Sybil?"

"She interested him for a while, then he found others."

"Lydia said Henry was obsessed with Sybil."

"He was, until he had her. That's the way it was with him."

"He introduced you to her?"

"He knew I would appreciate her. I guess it's no secret I like pretty women. That's one thing the old man and I had in common. Someday I'll tell you about the time I spent with him in Paris. Truly outstanding! I've never seen so many incredible women.

"He was a rough character all right, but he knew how to have a good time. I'll tell you something else." Albert's hushed voice contrasted sharply with his bright eyes. "When I met Henry Billings, I didn't have much, but thanks to him, I'm a rich man today."

William stared at Albert. It could not have been difficult for Henry Billings to find Albert's weakness. Had Sybil, he wondered, been part of Billings's design for Albert's soul? He thought back to that moment on the staircase with her the night before.

"I'm getting tired of Sybil," Albert said, swirling his brandy around in its glass. "Besides"—he fixed William with a smile—"I think she's seeing someone behind my back."

"I have to leave." William stood.

"Will, wait," Albert slurred. "Sit down." He slapped the arm of William's chair. "I want to tell you more about her."

"I've heard enough."

"Never have you seen such a body."

"What?"

"Or have you?"

William felt his hands tighten. "Good-bye, Albert," he managed to say evenly at last and he went to the door.

"You're no better than I am, Will Dysart," Albert called. "I know all about you, and your little meeting in Central Park. How you hovered over her like a lovesick schoolboy."

William walked out.

Chapter 21

The following evening, William sat in his library reading a book. Arabella was in the drawing room on the telephone going over every detail of the Settlement House Ball with Mrs. Beckwith.

William's mind kept wandering to his conversation the night before with Albert Penniman. Sybil's mother still alive? But she had said her mother was dead for years—said it the moment they had first met. Why would she have had reason to lie? Could she have meant dead to her? William set aside his book.

On his way down to the drawing room, he saw Fanny, who told him Mrs. Dysart had gone to bed. William closed the drawing room doors and picked up the telephone. He was connected by an operator to a woman at a main switchboard in Amityville. She put him through to the Hotel New Point. Mrs. Burns was not in, he was told, but would be in the next day. William left a message that he would like to meet with her the following afternoon.

The next morning, he hailed a cab to Pennsylvania Station. It was snowing as the cab pulled in front of the arcade entrance to the new station, which covered a city block in pink granite colonnades. He strode along a corridor, then down a broad marble staircase into an immense waiting room with grand arches, columns a hundred and fifty feet high and a coffered ceiling inspired by the Roman Baths of Caracalla. The room, built on a scale to take one's breath away, was hardly noticed by William, who immediately descended another set of stairs to a platform to catch his train.

By the time the train pulled into the station at Amityville an hour later, there was more than an inch of snow on the ground. A number of commercial carriages with W. POWELL'S STAGE SERVICE written on the side in gold and black letters were waiting in the station. A young man doffed his cap to William and to an older man, who had gotten off the train with him. The man asked to be taken to the Brunswick Home, apparently a sanitarium nearby. William saw tears in the man's eyes when he gave his destination. The young man with the cap called to one of his partners to take the man to the sanitarium, then walked with William to another carriage and they climbed in.

"Would you like a blanket?" the driver asked as they pulled away from the station.

William shook his head. "No, thank you," he said.

They drove down Broadway, the main street in Amityville, past several small shops and two country churches, toward the water. "Robbie Ketcham's the name," said the boy cheerily.

"Nice to meet you, Mr. Ketcham."

"Come to the hotel often?" asked Robbie Ketcham.

"No, I've never been. I'm here to see a Mrs. Burns, the manager."

"They get a lot of people from the city out at the hotel. But this time of year, so close to Christmas, it's pretty desolate. Sorry about the carriage, a little cramped, but I just don't trust the motorcar if there's snow. Besides"—Robbie nodded toward the horse—"Sally's faster than any motorcar. Right, Sally?" he called affectionately to her, making a clicking sound with his tongue, and Sally, who looked to William as close to death as a very long life could bring her, managed to pick up a little speed.

They turned onto a street called Grand Central Avenue, and as they drove the length of it, majestic maple trees and the snow-covered lawns of gracious summer homes gave way gradually to reed-filled wetlands and scrub pine. William looked out over the wetlands.

A fishing rod, he thought. His mother had said she would buy him a fishing rod if he made his bed and that she would take him fishing. But it never happened.

They came finally to the end of the road. The Hotel New Point stood on a spit of land jutting out into the Great South Bay. It was a handsome shingled building, four stories high with gables, dormers, and an octagonal tower with a peaked roof at its center. A porch facing the bay wrapped itself around the first floor.

The carriage pulled beneath the porte cochere at the front of the hotel, and William stepped down. The brisk salt air whipped through the porte cochere, stinging his cheeks. "Mr. Ketcham, would you mind stopping back in about an hour?"

"Heck no. Next train's not due in 'til three thirty. I'll wait here—be in the kitchen visiting." Robbie Ketcham gave a tug to the reins. "Just tell the front desk to get me when you're ready," he said as the carriage moved slowly away.

William entered the hotel and asked for Mrs. Burns. The front desk clerk, an elderly man, knocked at a door behind the desk. A moment later, Mrs. Burns appeared. She was a tall woman, neatly dressed, her gray and black hair swept up carefully on her head. The moment he saw her, William realized he had come expecting to find either a saint or a monster. Mrs. Burns, whoever she was, was neither, and seeing her in all her ordinariness made him realize that a boundary had been crossed between his professional and personal interest in Sybil Curtis to the point where he was risking either behaving unethically or making an utter fool of himself.

"Good afternoon, Mr. Dysart," said Mrs. Burns, walking over to him.

"Thank you for agreeing to see me, Mrs.

Burns," said William as he tried to think of a legitimate reason for his call.

"How can I help you?"

"Is there somewhere we can talk?"

"Of course." She turned to the man at the front desk. "Herbert, I'll be in the dining room." She walked with William toward double oak doors across a hall from the lobby. William glanced at her as they approached the doors, but could not see any resemblance between her and Sybil Curtis.

They entered the dining room, which included an enclosed section of the front porch. Most of the dark wooden tables were bare, but two or three had tablecloths. The paned windows enclosing the porch looked out over snow-covered wetlands to the Great South Bay.

"Beautiful view," said William, still trying to think of how to justify discussing Sybil's case with this woman.

"We don't use this dining room much in the winter. We have only a few guests—hearty souls. We use the small back dining room mostly."

By the time they sat down at a table, William had managed to concoct an acceptable reason for his wanting to see her. "Mrs. Burns, I am a lawyer, and I'm trying to purchase some property from your daughter, Miss Curtis, on behalf of a client."

"Property?" She sounded annoyed. "Sybil owns property?"

William nodded. "And before I proceed further, I need to make sure it's not entailed in any way. I was unaware, until recently, that either of Miss Curtis's parents was living."

"Did she tell you that?"

"I . . ." he fumbled. "She said something. I obviously misunderstood."

She sighed in irritation. "What do you mean by property?"

"A small cottage, several acres of land on the North Shore. You've never been there?"

"No." Mrs. Burns shrugged. "Probably some gentleman's," she said pointedly. William was surprised she would make such a comment about her daughter. "She was here two summers back with a man, who I didn't believe for a minute was her husband. When she saw me, they left. How she'd changed. I knew it would happen. Pretty girl, people always making much of her. And Mr. Curtis constantly letting her have her own way."

"Mr. Curtis is dead?"

Mrs. Burns nodded.

"And you have remarried."

"Yes."

"Pardon my asking, but Miss Curtis *is* your daughter?"

Mrs. Burns stared at him for a long moment, then nodded.

"Do you know a man named Albert Penniman?"

She shook her head.

"Odd. He told me about you."

"Really? Penniman," she repeated the name. She thought for a moment. "Will you excuse me?" She got up. A moment later she returned with a card. "'Albert Penniman,'" she read from the card. "'841 Fifth Avenue, New York.' That's the man she was with. I copied the address from the hotel register and wrote to her there—several times— but she never answered. Will you be seeing her?"

"Yes."

"You tell her I want those books."

"Books?"

"My husband was a botanist. There are books filled with drawings of plants, flowers, that sort of thing. Three of them. They're quite valuable. They're mine and I want them. And if she continues to ignore my letters, I will get my own lawyer."

William concluded his meeting with Mrs. Burns as quickly as he could and left the hotel. He was surprised to find the carriage waiting for him. Robbie Ketcham's smiling, open face was a relief from the bitterness of Mrs. Burns's, as the cold sea air was from that of the musty dining room. William jumped into the carriage.

"Nice, isn't she?" said Robbie Ketcham.

"You're joking." William reacted, surprised at his own candor.

Robbie Ketcham nodded, a sly smile playing at the corners of his mouth.

Robbie let him off at the station and he boarded his train. As it made its way back to New York, he peered out at the darkening landscape. How could Sybil possibly be the daughter of someone like Mrs. Burns? He didn't know what to believe anymore. Albert was a liar; that was obvious. But Lydia Billings? There was no denying the fear in her eyes when she talked about Sybil. A woman like Lydia Billings was genuinely afraid of her. Why?

The train picked up speed as it entered the tunnel that took it under the East River into Pennsylvania Station, the sounds of its wheels screeching and growing louder in the enclosed space, the train's interior in the darkness of the tunnel reflected sharply in its windows. William saw his face in the window, and looked away. The woman he thought Sybil was, like the woman he had married, never existed except in his own head. Still, despite his awareness of this fact, his feelings for her were not going to go away easily.

I can't tell you. Because I think I would lose the respect I sometimes flatter myself you have for me, he heard her whisper over the clattering of the rapidly moving train.

Chapter 22

William and Arabella's Christmas three days later was a perfunctory affair; they exchanged presents, neither extravagant nor personal, then called their five servants into the library and gave them their gifts from beneath the Christmas tree. In the afternoon they went to their friends the Chanlers' for Christmas dinner as they did every year.

The next day, William worked in his library. After several hours, he went down to the breakfast room to eat the lunch that Agnes, their cook, had left out for him. He had just passed through the front hall toward the back of the house when the telephone rang in the drawing room. He went in and picked it up. There was no sound at first, then a voice speaking in such a low whisper that he could not be sure if it was a man or a woman:

"Ask Lydia Billings about Dr. Keating on Orchard Street."

William stood with the phone pressed to his ear. He heard a click, then the phone went dead. He put it down, then pressed rapidly on the hook a number of times for an operator. "Operator, this is Lenox 831. I just received a call on this line. Can you tell me where it came from?" He heard the young woman speaking to someone. She got back on the line. "The call was made locally, sir. Other than that, we can't say."

William placed the receiver back on the hook. He stared at the maroon and blue pattern in the drawing room carpet, the name "Dr. Keating" vibrating in his ear, the desperate, whispered tone giving the words a ghastly spin.

He took a deep breath. Who could have made the call? Sybil? Albert? Lydia even? Perhaps Lydia wasn't in Maine at all. How could he believe a word any of them said?

He opened the door to the cabinet beneath the telephone and looked through the directories there. There was no listing for a Dr. Keating on Orchard Street. He looked at the hall clock. It was quarter-to-three, Tuesday afternoon. Dr. Keating—if there were such a person—would probably have office hours now. He went to the hall closet and reached for his coat and hat.

He found a cab on Park Avenue. "Orchard Street," he told the driver.

The cabman looked surprised. "Any cross street?"

"How long is Orchard Street?"

"About six blocks."

"Drop me off somewhere in the middle."

The cabman left William at the intersection of Delancey and Orchard Streets, and William headed north on Orchard. The Lower East Side streets and sidewalks were crowded with noise and people. He asked a man selling hot sweet potatoes if he knew a Dr. Keating. The man shook his head. William walked until he came to Houston Street, where Orchard ended. He asked passersby along the way about Dr. Keating, but no one seemed to have heard of him. He looked at door signs up and down the street, still nothing.

He walked back down Orchard. After crossing Delancey, he finally found an old man who knew Dr. Keating. The man directed William to an address just south of Grand Street. Narrow tenements reached out to one another over the grimy streets with their sooty fire escapes. William kept his head down as he walked, to avoid the stares of all the poorly dressed people crowding past. At last he came to a two-story federal brick house collapsing into its twin next door, two survivors from the eighteenth century and the last of their kind on the block. A sign in peeling black and white paint announced, HENRY R. KEATING, M.D. William walked up the broken cement stoop with its rusted cast iron railing and knocked at the door.

"Why didn't you just walk in?" asked the short, heavy woman in a nurse's uniform who came to the door. "As if I have time to be answering doors." She cast an appraising eye at William's dark chesterfield coat and derby hat. "Are you sure it's Dr. Keating you're wanting to see?"

"Yes, I was wondering if I might have a word with him?"

"Is he expecting you?"

"No, but it's important that I see him."

The woman opened the door and William stepped inside the shabby house. "Well, he's seeing patients right now." William saw people sitting on chairs in the hall. A young girl rocking her sick baby in her arms. The child cried weakly. "If you like, you can wait in the parlor until he's done." The woman opened a door directly off the hallway. "He'll be with you as soon as he can."

"Thank you," said William. He sat in a chair near a coal-burning stove, whose flue ran through the bricked-up mantel of an old fireplace. On the murky gray walls, faded sentimental prints hung askew. A half hour passed. The room grew darker and more depressing. Finally Dr. Keating entered.

"I'm sorry to have kept you waiting," said the doctor, a tall man with red hair and a face covered with freckles. He wore a white coat and seemed not to notice William's fine clothes. "I had far more patients than usual this afternoon. What can I do for you?"

"I'm a lawyer, Dr. Keating. This afternoon I received a phone call from someone—I don't know who—telling me that you might have some information about a client of mine."

"Is your client one of my patients?"

"I don't think so."

"No." Dr. Keating gave a quick laugh. "You don't look like someone who'd be representing one of my patients."

"My client's name is Lydia Billings." William purposely sprang the name on Dr. Keating.

Dr. Keating stared at William.

"Do you know her?"

Dr. Keating shook his head. "No."

"Are you sure?"

"Yes. Is there anything else I can help you with?"

"No, that's all I needed to know. Thank you, Dr. Keating."

Once again outside, knowing it would be useless to try to find a cab in that neighborhood, William retraced his steps north on Orchard Street. Dr. Keating had lied to him, he was certain of it. William guessed it was difficult for a man like Dr. Keating to lie.

Once he reached Houston Street, he turned west toward Greenwich Village and walked until he came to a small restaurant on University Place. He sat at an obscure table in the back and ordered dinner and a glass of wine. But when his food arrived, he hardly touched it. In the darkness of the restaurant he drank the wine, pondering what to do. He decided he would see Havering the next day and resign from the Billings case.

He had had enough.

Chapter 23

Havering said he was disappointed when William told him he had to resign from the Billings case, citing the pressing demands of Consolidated Ironworks about to go to trial, but William could see that Havering was actually quite pleased and probably looked forward to handling the case as a way of ingratiating himself with Lydia Billings. Havering was also, William knew, quite lazy. He probably assumed the case would require little of his time. How different Havering would feel, thought William, once he tried to untangle a skein that started with Henry Billings and ended—if only for the moment—at Dr. Keating's door on Orchard Street. The difficulty for William lay not in resigning from the case, but in trying to determine what he would say to Sybil Curtis when she called him the next day, as he had asked her to do the night of the Settlement House Ball. His uneasiness was sharpened by an item that had appeared in *Town Topics* under the Saunterer's byline:

What handsome young lawyer from one of New York's best families was seen racing through Peacock Alley on the night of the

Settlement House Ball in reckless pursuit of one of the loveliest creatures ever seen to grace that aviary, and where can his wife—a true bird of paradise, if ever there was one—have been?

If Arabella saw it—and William did not know how she could have missed it—she said nothing.

The winds howled through the canyons of lower Manhattan, rattling the windows in William's office the next day. He glanced out at the snow flurries blowing scattershot through the air and rubbed his hands together. Miss Leary walked past his door. "Miss Leary, is there a problem with the radiators?"

"I don't think so." She went to the radiator in his office and held her hand over it. "No, sir, it's working properly."

"I'm sure it is. Thank you, Miss Leary." William looked down at his desk as if to read something there. "Miss Leary," he said suddenly, "I'm expecting a call today from a Miss Curtis. When she calls, I'd like you to tell her I'm no longer working on her case and that if she has any questions, they should be directed to Mr. Havering."

"Of course, sir," Miss Leary said and left.

William worked the rest of the morning, waiting for the high-pitched ring of the telephone, which seemed so unusually silent that he lifted the receiver and pressed down on the hook to make sure it was still in working order.

"Number please?"

"I'm sorry, operator, I've changed my mind." He put the receiver back on the hook.

At twelve thirty he got his coat and left the office.

The sun had burned away some of the chill and darkness from the morning sky, leaving it a dreary quilt of gray and white. William walked up Wall Street, then down Broadway, feeling more relaxed now that he was out of the office. He was right not to speak to Sybil. He continued down Broadway until he reached the Battery. There he wandered by the water until the strong winds blowing across New York Bay made it unbearably cold, driving him back to Broadway. Why take her call? What could he say to her?

There is the matter of your friendship with Mr. Billings . . .

People walked hurriedly past without expression. Some seemed to glance at William, then to quickly look away. Everyone, it seemed, was struggling after an illusion, some fevered dream.

I was given to believe that your behavior toward her was rather ardent.

As he approached Wall Street, it started to snow, but he resisted the idea of going back to his office.

He crossed Broadway to Trinity Church. After

passing through the gate at its front, he pulled open a heavy bronze door and slipped inside. What little daylight there was filtered its way through the church's stained glass windows. William stood for a moment, waiting for his eyes to adjust to the darkness. Gradually the pews and other objects in the church took form from the deep shadows. He went to a side aisle and sat in the far corner of a pew there. The church seemed unusually damp and cold. He put his hands in his pockets and hunched his shoulders. He looked at the altar, the pulpit, and all the ornate tracery, and thought of the many cathedrals, temples, and mosques he had seen in his travels. They all seemed to share something, a vocabulary of some sort, expressed in stone, wood, and glass, the deep quiet and mysterious light, the scent of old incense.

He looked up at the great ceiling high overhead, the fluted Gothic columns and stained glass windows, and recalled the last time he had been there. It was over a year ago, late summer, for the wedding of a friend. How different it looked then, on a bright summer morning with flowers banking the altar, and all the radiant young women in gauzy summer dresses. An impressive stage, he thought, on which to act out yet another of life's foolish pageants sanctified by tradition and contrived to give meaning to the meaningless.

Finally he rose and crept out a side door of the church. Through the cast iron fence in the churchyard, he could see people crowding past on Broadway. He made his way out the front gate, then dodged across Broadway to Wall Street, and returned to his office.

"Good afternoon," Miss Leary greeted him. She and another young woman, wearing striped cotton aprons to protect their blouses and skirts, were unpacking boxes of office supplies outside William's door.

"Good afternoon." William went into his office and hung up his coat and hat. He hesitated, then stepped back into the hall. "Miss Leary, are there any messages for me?"

"Yes." Miss Leary looked up from a box filled with sheaves of paper. "Mr. Parrish was here. He wanted to speak to you about the Wheeler bequest. But said it wasn't important. Then there was a call from downstairs. They said there was a man here to see you. I went right down, but when I got there, he was gone. They said an older man. He didn't give his name."

William shrugged. "Anything else?"

"No, sir." Miss Leary returned to her work.

William sat at his desk. She had not called, which surprised him. Perhaps she never intended to.

"I'm sorry, Mr. Dysart." Miss Leary walked in, somewhat flustered. "The Miss Curtis you mentioned this morning called, but left no message."

"I see." William reached for a stack of papers. "And you told her I was no longer working on the case?" William bounced the papers against the top of his desk.

"Yes, sir."

William nodded. "Thank you, Miss Leary."

She turned to leave.

"Miss Leary." William hesitated. "Did Miss Curtis say anything after you gave her my message?"

"No. Only that she understood."

"She understood?"

"Yes, she said, 'I understand,' then hung up."

"Thank you, Miss Leary."

William's eyes moved fitfully over the different objects on his desk. *I understand.* The words lingered like a soft whisper in his ear, and in them he heard a betrayal acknowledged and forgiven in a single breath.

Chapter 24

William had hoped that in resigning from the Billings case, he would be free as well from the hold Sybil Curtis had on his imagination. But the memory of her clung to him, and there were times when the desire to drive out to Long

Island to see her would almost overwhelm him. Once, he had even called to have his motorcar brought around, only to have it sent back at the last minute.

With Sybil gone, William felt more lost than ever in the desert of his marriage—yet, unable to see any life for himself beyond its endless scorching horizon, he determined, almost with a kind of desperation, to make something take root there and grow.

Two weeks after Sybil's call, he and Arabella were in the middle of dinner. He suddenly put down his fork and took a deep breath.

Arabella looked up. "Is everything all right?"

William nodded. "I have been doing quite a bit of thinking." He pushed his plate away.

"Have you?" Arabella sat back in her chair uneasily.

"Yes. I think it's time we built that house."

"Build the house?" Arabella whispered. "Do you mean it?"

"Yes." He smiled briefly.

Arabella got up and threw her arms around him. "Oh, darling. It will be wonderful. You'll see." She looked into his face. "What made you change your mind?"

"I think . . ." He paused for a moment. "I think I need to take hold of my life."

"Oh, William." She embraced him again.

"I think I've been holding on for too long to a

foolish notion of what life . . . can . . . should be."

"Yes," Arabella said, taking his hand, "and it's that that has made you so unhappy." Kissing his hand, she held it against her cheek. "Let's call your father and Cady right now!"

"Yes." William kissed the top of her head.

It took almost an hour for the call to go through to the Villa Corsini outside Florence, where William's father and stepmother were staying, but they said they were thrilled for Arabella and William.

"Damn the expense," Charles shouted through the phone. "You have them get that place up in a year—six months. And make sure you build something that'll make the Vanderbilt houses look like shacks. Now, you'll need the deeds to those lots. Howland Bayard has them," his father said, referring to his attorney. "No," he immediately corrected himself, "they're in the safe out on Long Island."

After they hung up, William and Arabella drank champagne in the library, then locked the door and made love on the floor before the fire. There was something awkward about the sex, thought William—a performance—well intentioned on both sides, but a performance nevertheless, that left him feeling emptier than before. He'd hoped, childishly he now realized, that in making the difficult decision to commit himself once more to his marriage, that all the pieces would somehow fall into place, that every jagged edge would be smoothed. He looked at Arabella stretched out languorously on the carpet before him. She reached up and brushed his cheek. He smiled. Perhaps he wanted too much too quickly. They had, after all, just shared the kind of intimacy that had been absent from their marriage for so long; if it had been less than he had hoped for, it might still deepen over time.

The next morning, Arabella set off for the architectural firm of Osgood & Platt, and William drove out to Long Island for the deeds, almost welcoming the test of his resolve to never see Sybil again. He and Arabella were starting over again—a fresh slate—and the house they would build together was to mark that new beginning. Still, when he arrived at his father's Long Island estate, the smell of the sea air oppressed him.

Henry helped William look through files in the walk-in safe in his father's dressing room. Neither man was familiar with the layout of the safe, however, and they spent the first half hour looking through drawers of jewelry and ancient family silverware before coming upon a small safe within the safe. In it they found three drawers filled with deeds and certificates. William pulled one out of its dusty envelope.

"Look, Henry," he said, "the original deed of sale for Mulberry Farm from 1753. Why, it's even older than you."

"Let me have a look." Henry peered at the deed over his glasses. "I want to see who it was your people swindled."

Laughing, William continued checking through files. At last he found the deeds he needed. "Here they are," he said, handing them to Henry.

As they were returning files to the safe, William saw a dusty folder with WILLIAM written on its side. Curious, he opened it and found a letter from a law firm in Boston dated 1890. Attached to the letter was a deed and an envelope with two rusted keys. Someone had died, and left William a cabin in the Adirondacks, but everywhere in the letter and on the attached deed, the name of that person had been obliterated. "This is odd," he said aloud, as much to himself as to Henry. "A letter from a law firm in Boston. Someone left some property to me years ago, and I know nothing about it."

Henry was uncharacteristically silent.

William searched the letter. At the bottom-left-hand corner was written AG90. Most likely a file number, he thought, similar to the type of file numbers they used at his firm, and 1890 must have been the year he . . . or she . . . died. But AG? Henry had still not said a word. William examined the blacked-out portions in the letter and deed. There seemed something almost violent about the impression made by the pen stylus as it had gone back and forth over the name. William remembered Lydia's mentioning his mother's flirtation with someone from New England. Was it Boston? Yes. A writer from Boston.

"Henry," he said at last, "my mother had a friend from Boston. I think his initials were A.G. Do you know anything about him?"

"Oh," said Henry, "I don't think I would . . . I mean, that was such a long time ago."

"Henry, it's important," William urged.

Henry shuffled some papers together. "I think," he said at last, "I do remember someone, name of Arthur or Andrew from Boston. But I don't know the last name."

"Did my father like him?"

"That I don't know, Mr. William," said Henry, in a way that made William believe that he did.

William hesitated. "Was he a writer?"

"No," said Henry, "an artist."

William looked at Henry a moment, then placed the letter, deed, and keys into the folder, put the folder back, and shut the door of the safe.

Chapter 25

It was a raw, rainy Saturday afternoon in mid-January. William was reviewing the preliminary sketches for the new house on a long table set against a window in the library. The architects had prepared a surprisingly simple design: a four-story limestone house with deeply recessed double doors to one side. The three first-floor windows were a bit florid, with the faces of Greek gods in high relief peering down from the center of each, but overall William was happy with the clean lines of the place. Reaching for the floor plans, he happened to glance out the window to see Marian Meade, whom he had not seen since the night of the Settlement House Ball, walking determinedly on the opposite side of the street. What could she possibly be doing out on such a day, he wondered. And without an umbrella. For all her kindness, there was something hopeless and clumsy about Marian. Perhaps, William thought, watching her disappear up the street, that was what drew people to her, as to some shabby doll that hears painful secrets whispered late at night, while bisque and glass-eyed beauties sit untouched and revered on a shelf far away.

William turned back to the sketches before him and began looking through the plans for the first and second floors. He heard a motorcar stop in front of the house. He looked out the window again and saw a chauffeur dash up the front steps with an umbrella. A moment later, the man descended, accompanying Arabella into the motorcar, which then sped silently off into the rain. William stared thoughtfully for a moment at where the motorcar had been, then returned to the floor plans. At that point, he heard a knock at the front door.

Who could that be? He heard Rose open the front door, then came the muffled sound of a woman's voice. The stairs creaked softly as Rose ascended them.

"Mr. Dysart," said Rose, appearing at the library door. "Mrs. Meade is downstairs. She asks if you're in."

"Mrs. Meade?" asked William. "Did you tell her Mrs. Dysart was out?"

"I did, sir, but she said it was you she wished to see."

Why on earth had Marian Meade come out on such a day to see him?

"Shall I tell her you're not at home, sir?" asked Rose.

"No." William began putting the floor plans back into their cardboard jacket. "Please show her into the drawing room. I'll be down in a moment."

When William entered the drawing room, Marian was sitting by the fire, smoothing back her wet hair and arranging her rain-soaked dress in what seemed a futile attempt to make it appear she had merely stopped in on an impulse. She did not see him enter and was startled when he greeted her.

"Oh, William!" She took his hand. "Good afternoon. I—I was so happy to find you at home."

"Yes. Would you like some tea, Marian, coffee or something?"

"No, thank you."

"You're looking a little damp there." William sat down. "Maybe you'd like to sit closer to the fire."

"I'm fine." She flashed the mantelpiece a winning smile. "Did you enjoy the Settlement House Ball this year?"

"Yes, I did." And as he spoke, it occurred to him that Marian must have waited for Arabella to leave before calling.

Marian smiled at him nervously.

"Very much," he added in an attempt to keep alive a conversation that seemed ready to be extinguished at any moment.

Marian's lips moved promisingly, but she remained mute.

"Everyone was so beautifully dressed," William threw out, cringing at the fatuousness of his words.

"Weren't they just!" Marian seized on the remark. "Especially Arabella! I have never seen such an exquisite gown," she prattled on. "What was it, silk? And such a shade of red."

"I believe"—William hesitated—"it was blue, Marian."

"Blue? Oh, but of course it was."

"I don't wonder you've never seen such a shade of red," William quipped, desperate to ease the nervousness Marian was obviously feeling.

"Yes." She nodded, although she seemed hardly to have heard him. "My, and how everyone enjoyed themselves." The tips of her intertwined fingers danced over the backs of her hands. "In fact, Mrs. . . . said . . ." Marian stopped and looked at William mutely.

"Marian, what is it?" William leaned toward her. "What's wrong? Is something the matter with George?"

"No." She shook her head. "It has nothing to do with George. I need to ask you if you will do something for me."

William noticed her glance toward the open drawing room doors. He went and pulled them together.

"William," she began as he sat again across from her, "I know that at one time, you and your family were quite friendly with the Holborns."

"Thomas Holborn?"

She nodded. "He told me that when you were a child, you stayed with him and Charlotte."

"Yes. I spent a summer with them years ago."

"William, do you know what has become of him?"

William began to feel uneasy. "I know that since Mrs. Holborn's death he's been quite miserable. And"—William hesitated—"that he drinks."

Marian nodded.

"In fact, I saw him recently and hardly recognized him."

"What I tell you will go no further?"

"No."

Marian paused. "Charlotte Holborn was my mother's friend, and when she died, I went to see Thomas. He refused to see me, as he did everyone else at the time, but I persisted. His man, Laurence—hoping, I suppose, I might help in some way—finally let me in. When I saw Thomas, he was drunk and there was an ugly scene."

Marian took a deep breath. "Weeks later, I received a letter from him, which I could hardly decipher, asking me to come see him. I went, but he denied ever having written the letter and told me to leave. The next day, Laurence came to my door and begged me to come with him. When I got to the house, Thomas was sitting in a corner of his drawing room shivering like a wretched animal."

Marian's voice trembled as she recalled the scene. "He said he was going to kill himself. He had killed Charlotte and he was going to kill himself. I tried to reason with him." Marian's eyes filled with tears. "I told him it wasn't his fault, but he wouldn't listen. Finally he broke down and told me something of his torment." Marian took a handkerchief from her pocket.

"What can I do to help, Marian? Of course I'll do whatever I can."

"Do you remember at the ball? You told me that you were trying to buy some young woman's property—a Miss Curtis?"

"Yes."

"Would you take Thomas to see Miss Curtis?"

"Why?"

"He wants to see her before he dies."

"Why?"

She took William's arm. "Please, William, try not to judge him."

"Of course not, Marian." William tugged his arm away. "Everyone should take his happiness, wherever he can find it."

"I don't know that I would call Thomas Holborn happy."

"Damn it, Marian, you know very well what I'm talking about. No, I will not take him to see her. Now, if you'll excuse me, I have —"

"Not until you agree to take him."

"What?" William stared at her. "Marian, I am not going to take Thomas Holborn to see Miss Curtis under any circumstances."

"You must."

"No."

"I'm sorry, William, I'm afraid then I am going to have to insist."

"Marian, have you lost your mind?"

"I promised myself I wouldn't leave until you agreed."

"Have you always been such a bulldozer?"

"Yes. Ask poor George."

William looked at Marian's homely face with its kind, compassionate eyes, at her ungainly figure and the way she had one foot crossed over the other at the ankle with ineffable femininity. "He has known only dread and suffering these last years," he heard her say. "You might help him find some peace before he dies."

"Perhaps he doesn't deserve peace."

"Who are you to say?"

William heaved a frustrated sigh.

"This isn't like you, William. Why is this making you so angry?"

"Perhaps I know more about this situation than you do, Marian."

"And perhaps you don't." Marian watched the fire die to sparks and embers. "I've offered to take him myself, but he's refused. Then, the night of the ball, you mentioned her name and I told Thomas you knew her. I told him, if he agreed, I would ask if you would take him. He was terrified at first. Afraid you might find out about . . . about everything. He thinks a great deal of you, William."

"Does he?"

"Yes. Then last week—suddenly—he said he would go if you would take him. Will you, William? Please. He hasn't long to live."

"You won't give up."

"Oh, no."

William looked at Marian, astonished at the onslaught coming from so unexpected a quarter. So, Thomas Holborn wanted to atone for his sins now that eternal darkness waited to engulf him, and he would do so through the ministrations of an artless woman with her highly sentimental views of the world. William recalled Arabella saying that Thomas Holborn had taken a mistress, and that when his wife, Charlotte, found out, she just couldn't accept it. Where, William wondered, did Charlotte Holborn's suffering fit in with Marian's scheme of redemption?

Marian waited.

William lowered his eyes, determined to tell Marian again that he would not do what she asked. He raised his eyes and saw the desperate look on her face. He leaned back in his chair. "Marian, I—"

"Please, William."

He sighed.

"I beg you."

"Damn it, Marian!"

Her gaze didn't waver.

"I—" he began again.

"Please, William, for me? Will you do it for me?"

"An absolute bulldozer!" He threw his hands up in surrender. "All right."

"Thank you." She took his hand. "You do more good than you know."

"Yes, yes," said William, pulling his hand away.

"He'll go whenever you like."

"I'm very busy at work right now," William said abruptly. He thought for a moment. "Next

Thursday would be the earliest. In the morning—around eleven o'clock."

"I'll tell Thomas. Next Thursday. Eleven o'clock." Marian went to him. "William, I can't tell you how much—"

William gave a peremptory shake of his head. "Thanks are not necessary, Marian."

"No," said Marian, kissing him, shaking his steely composure. Turning, she bolted toward the drawing room doors.

"Marian," William called, "let me send for the motorcar, or get you a cab. You can't go out in this rain."

"Thank you, William," she said as she sent one of the drawing room doors flying, "but I'm only going two blocks to see the Warburgs."

William followed her into the hallway, where Rose was getting her wrap for her. "Have you a good deed for them to do as well?" He smiled, trying to dispel any lingering unpleasantness from their meeting. "Here," he said, grabbing an umbrella from the stand by the door, "take this at least."

Marian took the umbrella and kissed William again before turning to run out into the pouring rain.

After she'd left, he returned to the drawing room and slid the door closed behind him. He looked around the room, at the high front windows whose foggy panes were being pelted with rain, and at the two chairs he and Marian had just occupied. He went to the far end of the room, opened one of the double doors, and entered the dining room. As he pulled the door closed after him, he felt a sense of relief. The heat had not been turned up in the room and he found the chill and the deep, somber blue of its walls reassuring.

He went to a mahogany sideboard that sat between two windows overlooking the garden at the back of the house and took out a decanter of whiskey and a glass. After pouring himself some whiskey, he pulled a chair from the dining table and turned it so that it faced one of the windows. He sat in the chair and watched the rain through the clear panes of glass. The leafless branches of the trees vibrated in the downpour. Skittish puddles of brown water collected around the dead remains of the flowers of summer and overflowed onto the brick walkways traversing the yard. He looked at the long, sodden wall formed by the backs of all the houses facing the next street. He thought of Thomas and Charlotte Holborn in their garden so long ago, when he had stayed with them as a boy. Thomas Holborn with his arm around his wife's waist, the soft sound of Charlotte's laughter. He recalled Arabella's account of Charlotte Holborn's drunken behavior at the Newington's house party.

That was the last anybody saw her. She died not long after—drank herself to death.

William raised the glass of whiskey to his lips. A small brown bird landed on the branch of a tree, perched there, then flew away.

How kind your words are, Mr. Dysart. How kind you are. William bit his lower lip.

There's nothing Sybil would like better than to draw you into all this. William raised the glass again to his lips.

I know all about your meeting in Central Park. And how you hovered over her like a lovesick schoolboy. He took a deep breath. How Sybil Curtis and Albert Penniman must have laughed. He remembered the moment on the staircase at the Settlement House Ball, his body trembling after barely grazing her lips in a modest kiss. What a fool she must have thought him, what a fool he was. He drank the remainder of the whiskey in one swallow, then slammed the glass onto the dining room table. "Rose," he called, opening the dining room doors. "Rose," he repeated as he made his way across the drawing room.

"Yes, Mr. Dysart," answered Rose, pulling at the closed drawing room doors.

"Rose, ring the garage and tell them to bring the motorcar around."

Chapter 26

The heavy rain made it a slow drive out to Long Island, taking almost three hours, but to William it seemed only moments had passed before he reached the rutted, muddy road leading to Sybil Curtis's cottage. He pulled his motorcar by her front steps, got out, and knocked at the door. Darkness had descended early with the rain, but light shone from the two windows by the porch. He knocked again. Rain thumped on the roof overhead and gurgled down a nearby drainpipe. He heard the sound of the latch being lifted and a creaking from the door. She stood before him. Light fell from behind her onto the cold, dark porch. Her lips parted, but she said nothing.

"I'd like to speak to you," he said.

She moved away from the door and he entered.

He turned to her. "Do you know a Dr. Keating?" he asked. He noticed how she remained by the door.

She shook her head.

"You didn't call me about Dr. Keating?"

"No," she said at last. She walked into the room and began lighting kerosene sconces on either side of the fireplace.

"I suppose I have no alternative but to believe you."

"Is there a reason you're being so insulting?"

"I had a talk with a Mrs. Burns."

There was a momentary look of dread in her eyes, but she spoke evenly. "Did you?" The wick in her hand began to flare up. She quickly shook it out.

"She wants those books," said William, pushing back wet strands of hair from his forehead.

"She's not going to get them."

"She said she's your mother."

"She's a liar."

"Are Mrs. Billings and Albert Penniman liars? Would you like to know what they told me?"

She stared at him.

"Aren't you going to say anything?"

"What do you want me to say?"

"That you didn't tell Albert about our meeting at the library."

"I don't know what you're talking about."

"Our walk in the park?"

She sat down on the sofa and was quiet a moment. "He saw us from my hotel room," she said, quietly fingering a button on her blouse. "I told him I didn't want to see him anymore, but somehow he found out where I was staying. He was waiting for me when I got back."

"How did he get into your room?"

She looked up at him. "The way all of you get whatever it is you want. He paid someone."

"But you were at the ball with him."

"Yes."

"Why?"

She was silent.

"Why did you tell him you didn't want to see him anymore?"

"That is no concern of yours." She stood. "I want you to get out."

"Was it because you found someone you thought might be more useful to you? Someone you might not have to pay the kind of attentions a woman like you has to pay to men like Henry Billings and Albert Penniman."

She stared at him in disbelief.

William felt a pang of remorse. "I suppose it didn't matter, so long as you got what you wanted."

"You have a bottomless fund of pity for yourself, haven't you?"

Her accusation hit its mark. "I suppose it also didn't matter," he shot back, "that Mrs. Holborn should suffer the way she did?"

"I didn't want her to know. She saw me with him one day. It was not my fault . . . ." Her voice faltered. "She—"

"Not your fault? That she drank herself to death? I suppose Henry Billings wasn't your fault either."

She shook her head.

"Lydia Billings seems to think he was. In fact she told me—"

"I don't care what she told you!" She raised her hands to her ears. "I want you to get out!"

"She said you'll say anything—do anything—to get what you want—"

Sybil flew at him, grabbing the lapel of his coat. He felt a stinging where her fingernail grazed his chin. She twisted the lapel tightly. "You're right, we have been horribly mistaken about one another." She paused to catch her breath. "You thought I was a woman worthy of your admiration. No small distinction, I'm sure. But then I thought you were a kind and decent man. Of the two, I believe I have been the more bitterly deceived. Now"—she released his lapel—"I want you to get out of my house at once."

William raised his hand to his chin. He saw blood on his fingers. He looked at her a last time and left.

Chapter 27

William hardly slept at all after his confrontation with Sybil Curtis. He awoke the next morning with a horrible headache, the kind he had so often suffered from as a child. All Sunday he tried to distract himself from the haunting emptiness he felt. He went to bed early, hoping to escape his misery in sleep, but had another awful night. When he awoke on Monday, his headache was a little less severe, but his mood was, if anything, blacker. He went into his office, still in a foul temper.

"Miss Leary," he called from his desk when he heard her speaking to someone in the hallway outside his door.

"All right, Kitty, this afternoon then." Miss Leary smiled and waved good-bye to a coworker as she entered William's office. "Yes, Mr. Dysart?"

"Miss Leary," he asked, continuing to write furiously at his desk, "where are the pleadings in the Consolidated case?"

"The pleadings, sir?"

William sighed audibly. "The pleadings, Miss Leary, in the Consolidated case, which I asked you to have on my desk this morning."

"No, sir." Miss Leary's face reddened, and her voice faltered. "You didn't."

"Didn't I?" William asked in a manner that made Miss Leary seem no less culpable. "Well, I need them." William glanced up from his writing. "That will be all, Miss Leary."

Theodore Parrish entered the office as Miss Leary rushed past him.

"What's the matter with Leary?" Theodore asked, sitting down.

William continued writing.

"Or should I say what's the matter with you?"

William stopped writing long enough to glance at Theodore. "I'm busy."

"Are you?"

William returned to his writing, his pen moving quickly across his notepad. "Did you come in here for some reason?"

"No," Theodore answered, "no reason, Will. I just like to see you at your stuffed shirt best."

"Do you?" William said. "Well, it's unfortunate we can't all be radicals like you and Lucie." He sat back in his chair. "Smug—rather self-satisfied."

"You've got a lot of nerve."

"If you'll excuse me . . ." William turned back to the notepad on his desk.

"I'll excuse you. You horse's ass." Theodore got up and walked out.

"Idiot," said William under his breath. "All a bunch of idiots."

William continued to write, filling three notepads in his clipped, precise script. At seven o'clock in the evening, he paused to go to the firm's small, two-room library on the floor below. There, he pulled out book after book, throwing aside those he didn't need and placing paper markers in those he did, with notes to Miss Leary indicating which passages and legal precedents he needed typed.

The next morning the three notepads were on Miss Leary's desk, barricaded behind a wall of legal books, papers sprouting from them like so much lichen. On top of the notepads was a message from William for Miss Leary saying that two lady typewriters would need to be hired for the next two days, as his brief had to be finished by Wednesday afternoon. William, who had worked through the night, heard Miss Leary sigh when she saw her desk.

Later that day, as she was typing, William dumped more books on her desk. "This should be the last of it, Miss Leary," he said, then went into his office to get his coat. "Did you get the lady typewriters?" he asked, pulling on his coat.

"Yes, sir, the agency sent them over an hour ago. They're working downstairs."

"Good. There are two more notepads on my desk. I'm going home for a few hours. Please put all the typed pages on my desk as soon as they're done."

"Yes, sir."

In less than two hours, he returned in a change of clothes.

"Miss Leary, please have a pot of coffee sent up." He walked into his office and shut the door behind him.

On his desk, William found a neat pile of typed pages awaiting him. He took his pen and began to mark them. Sometime later, Miss Leary entered to deliver more newly typed pages and to take away those William had annotated. He never looked up from his work. Night came. Miss

Leary left. William worked on into the morning.

At five o'clock he stretched his arms toward the ceiling and glanced out the window. A reddish light was just beginning to appear over the buildings. Dawn or dusk? he wondered as he looked at the sky through burning eyes. He leaned his elbows on his desk and recalled as a boy watching from his room as the last light of day, a burst of red flame, sank into the Sound. The lamps by the front gate of Tekahoka flared up brightly as they were lit by a servant using a long pole with a wicker. William remembered lying down finally on the window seat in his room, light slipping in beneath the door from the hallway, a thin yellow ribbon that grew brighter in the darkening room.

A shadow blocking the light under the door came vividly back to him. Someone stood outside the door. The door began to rattle. A voice, very softly at first, then with a kind of desperation. *Master William!* Who was it? His mother's maid Anna. *Master William,* she whispered, *open the door!*

William turned from the window in his office. Why would his door have been locked? And why would Anna, of all people, have been so desperate to have him open it? He must be misremembering the scene. Still, perhaps he heard Anna call to him once in that desperate way—he could hear too clearly the sound of terror in her voice. He shook his head. He would never know what in his early childhood was real and what was imagined.

He left his office and walked down a long hallway of closed doors, the frosted glass of their transoms lighting up icy white with the dawn. He came to the watercooler at the end of the hall and took a drink. He leaned against the wall and stared out a window at the sunlight of a new day falling across the rooftops of lower Manhattan in bright squares and dark shadows. He took a deep breath and closed his eyes. His sleepless eyes stung and his mouth had the bitter taste of too much coffee. He slowly opened his eyes, but the rising sun, a small red circle of fire in the sky, forced them closed again. He wanted to sleep. How he wanted to sleep. There was just a bit of water left in his cup. He threw it in his face and cleared away the excess with his hand. Only a few hours more and he would be done. He had done an excellent job, he knew that. But what would he do tomorrow, and next week, and all the rest of his life?

Chapter 28

William waited in his motorcar in front of Thomas Holborn's town house on East Eighty-third Street the next day. He took out his pocket watch. He had told Marian he would be by to pick up Holborn at eleven o'clock; it was now almost quarter past the hour and still there was no sign of him.

William, who had not fully recovered from his formidable effort on behalf of Consolidated Ironworks during the previous three days, was greatly provoked to find himself in such a position on a day when he might have been resting, and as he waited, his anger grew at having allowed himself to be dragged back into the whole sordid affair.

"Come on," he said impatiently. He looked again to the silent front door of Thomas Holborn's town house. Holborn's man, Laurence, had told him Holborn would be out momentarily. William reached over and opened the window on the opposite side of the motorcar. After several days of severe cold, the weather had turned unseasonably warm. "Damn it," he muttered, then got out of the car and walked toward Holborn's town house. The glass of the wrought iron door shivered as it was opened. Thomas Holborn appeared, taking his hat from an anonymous hand. He seemed unaware of William's presence. He mumbled something to the person behind the door, then stepped out into the morning sun as the door closed behind him.

"Hello, Mr. Holborn," said William, brusquely holding out his hand.

"I'm sorry I kept you waiting." Holborn took William's hand, but kept his face turned away.

"Quite all right," said William, trying to get the better of his impatience. He quickly disengaged the bony hand in his grasp and turned toward his car. William began to unbutton his coat. "You might want to take your coat off," he called to Holborn, "it's supposed to be quite warm today."

Holborn got in the car without answering.

"It shouldn't take more than an hour or so to get there." William tossed his own coat into the back of the car, then climbed in next to his passenger. "I don't imagine there will be much traffic."

Holborn only nodded and stared through the windshield.

He was so much thinner than William had remembered, looking even more gaunt than he had at the Hamiltons' reception. He sat hunched forward, with his pale hands pressed tightly together between his knees. His features offered only the dimmest outline of the handsome man he had once been. William's one or two halfhearted attempts to engage him in conversation were unsuccessful, and an eerie silence prevailed during the rest of their drive out to Long Island. It was only after they had turned off the main road and were within a mile or two of Sybil Curtis's cottage that Thomas Holborn spoke.

"Does she," he asked, "does she know I'm coming?"

"No." William glanced at Holborn. "I thought it best not to say anything."

"Oh," Holborn replied distractedly. "I suppose,"

he added, looking down and rubbing his hands together.

They turned up the road to Sybil's. William steered the car to the side. "Her house is up the way a bit on the left," he said as he put the car into gear. "You'll see it as soon as you get over the rise of that hill."

"But I thought you were going to come with me." Holborn turned to him with a fearful expression.

"I'm sorry," said William. "I can't possibly go with you, I . . ." he demurred. "I have reasons for not wanting to see Miss Curtis. When I told Marian that I would accompany you, I didn't mean—"

"But," Holborn pleaded, "couldn't you make an introduction of some kind, and then leave?"

"An introduction?" William asked coldly, and the meaning of his words was not lost on Holborn, who stared at him helplessly before slowly looking away. William turned to gaze out the window. A moment later, he heard a low, painful sigh, then the sound of the car door opening as Holborn got out.

William watched him walk slowly up the road toward Sybil's cottage, with his head down and the hem of his coat swaying slightly as it hung away from his wasted body. *An introduction?* William heard his words again with the same snide twist he had given them, and a momentary sense of shame touched him like a hot iron applied carelessly to his skin. "Damn them all," he whispered, striking the steering wheel of the motorcar. He sat back in his seat and closed his eyes. There was a painful tightening in the back of his throat.

A short while later, he was surprised to see Thomas Holborn walking back down the road toward the motorcar.

"Did you see her?" he asked as Holborn got into the car.

"No one was there." Holborn shook his head. "I knocked at the door a number of times."

"I wonder where she can be?" William murmured to himself. "Perhaps I should have let her know you were coming, but . . ." He reached into a compartment at the front of the car and took out a piece of paper and a pen. "I'll leave a note for her with my father's telephone exchange," he said as he began to write. "She can telephone us there." William finished the note and began to fold it. "If she wishes," he added pragmatically, doubting very much they would hear from her. Thomas Holborn nodded, but William wondered if he had heard any of what he had said. "If for some reason she doesn't call, perhaps a meeting in town can be arranged." There was a note of genuine kindness in William's voice for the first time that day. He got out of the car to deliver the note.

When Sybil's house came into view, William experienced an unsettling feeling of remorse, which came upon him unexpectedly. He walked up her front steps and wedged the note into the doorjamb. He was about to return to his car when he turned back around and knocked at her door. He was sorry the moment he did it, but he waited. He knocked again, louder this time. Still no answer. He walked to the far end of her porch and looked out over the stretch of land reaching to the water. Where could she be, he wondered with a vague sense of foreboding. He was just about to try the door to see if it were locked when he saw a flash of white out near the water by the old maple tree. He stepped down from the porch and began to walk toward the tree. As he drew closer, he moved very quietly until he could see around the side of it.

There she was, sitting on the small bench with her arms crossed, leaning over a book lying open in her lap, one hand absentmindedly stroking the back of her arm. William watched as her hand moved gracefully over her arm. He looked at her hair, plaited in a thick braid that hung down her back, over her white sweater. He could just see her cheek, and the desire to speak to her almost overwhelmed him. The sudden surge of feeling for her infuriated him, and he turned quietly away to make his way back to his motorcar.

He had almost reached the car when he

remembered the note left at her door. He ran back and retrieved it. He would at least have the satisfaction of her never knowing he had been there. He returned once again to the car, none of his anger abated. "She's there," he said rudely to Thomas Holborn as he got into the car. "Sitting under a tree, directly out from the house, by the Sound."

"Under a tree?" Holborn asked nervously.

"Yes. A large maple—standing by itself near the water," William explained with audible impatience. "You'll see it as soon as you turn in by her house."

"Oh," Thomas Holborn whispered. "I see."

"One more thing," said William, putting his hand on Holborn's arm. "I don't want Miss Curtis to know I brought you here today. Do you understand?"

"Yes," Holborn answered. He moved to get out of the car, but stopped.

"What is it?"

Holborn looked down.

"Well?"

"I can't. I'm sorry"—his voice shook—"I can't."

William threw him a look of contempt. "Very well, if that's what you want."

"I don't know what I want." Holborn wrapped his arms around himself and rocked in his seat. "But I can't . . . I can't face her."

"Why? Why can't you face her?"

Holborn shook his head.

"Very well," said William, getting out of the car. He turned the crank, but the car wouldn't start. He grabbed it again and turned it violently once, twice, and a third time. Finally the motor turned over. He got back into the car and threw it into gear and was about to drive off.

"Wait, no. Please." Holborn took hold of his arm. "I'll go. I promised Lottie I would."

William looked at Thomas Holborn shivering in the warm sunlight filtering through the windshield. "Mrs. Holborn?" he asked.

Thomas Holborn read the expression on William's face. He leaned back in his seat and closed his eyes, tears collecting at the corners. "No, I'm not mad," he whispered, "though I wish I were."

William took the car out of gear and turned away. The two men sat together in the front seat as the motor hummed quietly on.

"You're different than you were as a boy, Willy."

"Am I?" William asked curtly.

"Yes. You're smug . . . proud."

"We've all changed," said William cruelly.

"Yes," agreed Thomas Holborn.

William felt ashamed, but his anger was greater than his shame.

"You don't know anything," Holborn struck back.

"I know more than I care to."

"Do you?"

William sighed. "I think it's time we left."

"How old do you think she is?"

"How old?" William repeated, certain he had misunderstood. "Miss Curtis?"

"Yes."

William considered the question. "I don't know, I suppose she's . . ." He stopped. Incidents and dates began to crowd against one another in a way that made his head pound. "She must be"—he turned to face Thomas Holborn—"twenty-seven. Twenty-eight."

"She's not more than twenty-one, if she's that."

"It's not possible."

"I'm afraid it is."

"No . . . It can't be."

Holborn nodded. "Do you want to know the truth?" he asked. "I've never told anyone, not even Marian, though I think she's guessed it."

William stared at him silently.

Thomas Holborn looked away. "She . . . she was the daughter of my gardener." Holborn's voice was flat. "His name was Charles Curtis. We met him while visiting England one spring. Friends recommended him to us. We brought Curtis and his children to America." Holborn nodded as if to confirm what he said. "She was about ten or eleven. Her mother had died years before—a schoolteacher, I think. There was a boy, several

233

years older." Holborn paused and pressed his lips together. "One afternoon after they had been here only two or three years, the father and the boy went sailing. There was a terrible storm. They found the father's body the next day. Two days later, the boy's." Thomas Holborn fell silent again.

"Mrs. Holborn took the girl in. She loved her. Lottie had always wanted a child. Weeks later, Henry Billings called me to his office." Holborn sat up nervously. "He said he had heard about the accident and wanted to help the girl." Holborn turned to William, his eyes those of a cornered animal. "You see, she had sung at a Christmas party Lottie had given. Billings saw her there. She had a lovely, sweet voice. I remember his commenting on it at the time." Holborn's voice began to shake. "Billings said he would take her back to England. He told me he had one of his people in London locate her relatives, and they were anxious to have her back. It was all very simple. He was crossing the Atlantic on some business, and would make sure she was delivered safely to them. Of course he was lying. For years I'd heard stories about Billings, but I was afraid of him. He had made me a very rich man, and he could as easily have made me a poor one. I pretended to myself that I believed him and told Lottie it was only right the girl should be with her own people. Lottie didn't want to give her up, but

I insisted, and finally she relented. I took the girl down to Billings's yacht, but she sensed something was wrong. She begged me not to leave her. I couldn't calm her down. I told her to wait. I would speak to Billings and tell him she had changed her mind. I did speak to him, but he told me not to worry—told me more lies about relatives in England. Still, I wasn't sure. I didn't know what to do.

"Then all at once the boat was to leave and I . . . I ran. But"—tears welled in Thomas Holborn's eyes—"I turned back. Turned back and saw those eyes of hers looking out over the railing at me. And still I ran. Still . . ." Thomas Holborn raised his hand to his mouth. "I tried to forget—to pretend that she was living in England with her people. Then, when I thought the whole thing was buried away and forgotten, Charlotte came to me. She had seen the girl with Billings in his motorcar somewhere. 'We must do something,' she said, 'we must find Sybil.' I tried to put her off, but she wouldn't have it. Finally, I told her there was nothing we could do, it was too late. She looked at me as if I were a stranger. It wasn't long before she realized everything. Of course, I denied it. She begged me to consider what I had done, to show some remorse, but I turned from her instead. Finally, she said she would go to Billings herself and demand he tell her where he kept the girl.

"I didn't think she would go through with it,

Lottie was such a timid woman. But she did go. Someone had tipped off Billings that she was coming and he had the girl taken to Europe. He told Lottie she was mad—imagining things. She thought I had warned him. I hadn't. But she wouldn't believe me, she never believed me again. I, who had been everything to her. She fell to pieces. Drank—just couldn't bear it."

Thomas Holborn bit savagely at his lips. "Then she died, and it was all before me. That poor girl." Thomas Holborn dropped his head and covered his eyes. "My Lottie," he cried, weeping "I did not protect the girl."

William turned away.

Holborn took several deep breaths. He pulled out a handkerchief and wiped his eyes. "I'm sorry," he said at last.

William said nothing.

Holborn took another breath and got out of the car.

Chapter 29

William Dysart sat in his motorcar and watched Thomas Holborn drift silently up the quiet country road for the second time that day. He stared at the empty road when Holborn was no longer in sight, and waited for him as the time passed in ghostly silence. And still his head throbbed.

There was a technicality, which only Lydia knew about.

A technicality, thought William. That she was little more than a child. He reached for the car door and got out. He paused by the car, thinking of what she must have endured, and it made him dizzy with revulsion. He walked along the side of the road, remembering all the cruel words he had spoken to her. He could not bear what he had said, or accept what she had suffered, and for it all, he blamed Thomas Holborn. The throbbing in his head continued, pounding against his temples and pushing against the sides of his skull, until it exploded in a burst of fury that sent him running in a blind rage after Thomas Holborn.

He shot down the road. After a short distance, he jumped a fence and ran through a field of tall grass in a desperate attempt to get to Holborn before he reached Sybil. He came to another fence at the far end of the field and was over it in an instant. He stood for a moment in a shallow valley and searched until he saw the top of the old maple tree in the distance. He ran as fast as he could, but the tree was too far off. Thomas Holborn was moving slowly toward the tree, and Sybil Curtis was reading at its foot, unaware of his approach. William realized that he would never be able to get to Holborn in time to prevent Sybil's seeing him. He stopped and watched as Holborn approached Sybil.

Gulls flew by overhead. A breeze swept in off the water. William heard the sound of young trees swaying nearby and the rhythmic sound of his own exhausted breathing. Holborn took off his hat as he stood before Sybil. He had come upon her so quietly that she was unaware of his presence. She slowly moved her eyes from the page of her book and saw him. Her mouth opened with a small cry and she drew back in surprise. Holborn started to speak, fidgeting with the hat in his hand.

All at once Sybil stood. She lost her balance for an instant and leaned against the tree to steady herself. She dropped her book and ran past Holborn in the direction of the cottage.

William bent over, braced his hands against his knees, and took a deep breath. It was over. He would wait until Sybil was out of sight, then drag Holborn back to his car. There would be no further damage done.

Holborn stood beneath the tree staring at the ground. William looked away from him with contempt, then glanced toward Sybil. She had stopped running, had stopped so abruptly that her cardigan had fallen from her shoulders. She lurched forward as if she were going to be ill.

William felt a sharp stab of pity and was about to go to her when he saw her turn and begin walking back to Thomas Holborn.

Holborn looked up with a start when he saw her moving toward him, then stiffened as if he expected her to strike him. She shrank back, then said something, and began to cry. Holborn bowed his head, and she turned to leave. Holborn said something quickly. She looked back and nodded, then turned once again to leave. Suddenly Holborn leaned forward and spoke in a desperate way. She turned back to him. Neither of them moved for some time. Then William saw Sybil hold out her hand to Holborn; he looked at it and shook his head uncertainly. She moved toward him, and as Holborn reached for her hand, he began to stagger and fall as if under a crushing weight, and she reached up and caught him in her arms.

William didn't know how long it was before Thomas Holborn returned to the car, but as they drove over the narrow isthmus of land connecting the broad peninsula of Lydia Billings's property to the rest of Long Island, the late afternoon sun was moving quickly to the west, draining the eastern sky of its brilliant unseasonable blue and turning it deep gray.

Holborn said nothing when he got into the car, and the two men drove the distance back into town without a word. Night had fallen by the time William pulled in front of Holborn's house on East Eighty-third Street.

"Thank you," said Holborn.

William looked at him. Death seemed so close

that the shadow of its approach could be seen clearly in the pallor of his skin, but William could see he was at peace—Thomas Holborn again, the man he had known as a child. "It was you, wasn't it?" asked William.

Holborn looked at him.

"The call about Dr. Keating."

Holborn looked down. "Yes."

"Why?"

"Marian Meade told me you were working with Lydia trying to get the Curtis girl's property. I could only imagine the lies Lydia was telling you. I wanted you to know the truth."

"But who is Dr. Keating?" asked William. "He denied even knowing Lydia."

Holborn took a deep breath. "Billings took advantage of others before Sybil and others after, none older than fifteen or sixteen. Some had no homes, and some he simply paid their parents for letting him use them. Mostly girls. But boys, too. He had someone in his employ who would . . ." Holborn paused. "Who would drug them, if necessary.

"Something happened to one of the girls. She was never the same. Lydia pays for her to be taken care of somewhere upstate and handles everything through Dr. Keating."

"Dr. Keating was involved in this?"

Holborn shook his head. "No, never."

"How did you find all this out?"

Holborn continued, his voice now resolute. "I became obsessed with Henry Billings. His sins were my sins. After Lottie died, I bought a gun. I was going to kill him at a ball in Newport, but I got drunk. I woke up the next afternoon in a strange bed. The gun was gone.

"After Billings returned from Europe," Holborn continued, "he kept Sybil at the Union Square Hotel for a short while, then I heard he'd passed her along to Albert Penniman, as you might a pair of cufflinks. That was the last I knew of her until about two years ago, when I learned she was living near Bagatelle. I wanted to go to see her, but the thought of it terrified me."

"Do you know a Mrs. Burns?" William asked.

"She was our housekeeper," Holborn spoke ruefully. "She married Charles Curtis shortly after they arrived here. He was very lonely after his wife died, and wanted a mother for his children. She was hard on Sybil's brother, Percy. He was a good boy, didn't deserve it. Smart. Handsome. You could tell he was going to make something of himself. She seemed all right, but . . ." Holborn shook his head. "She left Curtis—ran off with a Mr. Burns, who had a bit of money."

Her brother was named Percy, William thought. She had told him he reminded her of Percy.

"Did you come to see me at my office?" William asked after a moment.

"As far as the desk downstairs. How did you know?"

"Just a guess." William shrugged.

"Thank you for taking me to see her." Holborn reached for William's hand and pressed it. "You're the same, the boy I knew. I'm glad." He stared into William's eyes for a moment, then got out of the car and walked slowly toward his front door.

When William returned home, he parked right in front of the door. Rose approached to take his coat and told him Mrs. Dysart was in the library.

Arabella was sitting on the sofa when William entered. "Where have you been?" she asked. "We're expected at the Goelets' in an hour."

"I'm sorry. I won't be able to go. I had some business on Long Island and I'm exhausted."

"Your little friend?"

"Her name is Miss Curtis." William sat down. "I took Thomas Holborn out to see her."

"Why on earth would Thomas Holborn want to see her? Don't tell me she was the one he was involved with."

William said nothing.

"Oh, I know, attorney-client privilege. I don't really care."

"I'm sorry, Arabella, I really have to go to bed."

"Well. If you must. I'll make your excuses with the Goelets. They're beginning to think you don't like them."

William stood. "I don't."

He left the library and climbed the stairs to his room. Once inside, he leaned against the door. He thought back to the man he had been when he picked up Thomas Holborn that morning; it seemed as if that man no longer existed. Arabella thought she was talking to him, but he was gone.

He took off his clothes and slipped into bed, hoping to escape into the oblivion of sleep. He turned fitfully, imagining himself running once more trying to catch Thomas Holborn, Holborn getting farther and farther from him and closer and closer to Sybil. Holborn was going to harm her somehow. William ran faster, but there was nothing he could do to stop Holborn and he realized he would not be able to save Sybil, either.

Either? William sat up in his bed, his thoughts spinning, some distinct, some half-remembered, all disturbing. He looked around the room for a moment, then lay down again.

Sleep came to him fitfully. Sybil Curtis kept appearing and disappearing. They were sitting together by a river in England. Did he ever think there might be a reason horrible things happen? she was asking him. A tall man with blond hair suddenly came from the shadows and stabbed Sybil, then ran away. William held her as she died. He was in a church with his father as a mahogany casket with silver handles floated down the aisle. William began to cry. His father reached down and squeezed his shoulder tightly, a look of rage on his face.

William awoke and rolled over on his back, as words ricocheted through his head. *She's a liar, William . . . she is a liar . . . she . . .*

He remembered clearly now how as a child he would lie alone in his bed at night, trying desperately not to think of the newly turned earth over his mother's grave. How terror would lunge at him in the dark. He would walk down the back stairs to the kitchen, finding some small solace in the pots and pans hanging from the ceiling in the shadows, their everyday ordinariness seeming to offer a quiet challenge to the shrieking terror pursuing him. There he would press his body against the cool tile surface of the floor and utter a low suffocating sound. How many mornings did Mary Conran, their cook, find him on the kitchen floor, never guessing at the torment that drove him there?

At last he fell into a deep sleep and dreamed.

He was in a beautiful field of high green grass, so high he could barely see over it. His mother took his hand and pointed to the sunny endless stretch of blue sky overhead. They began to run. His mother laughed as William ran ahead.

He ran in circles, making figure eights, flattening all the tall grass before him, imagining his mother's delight at his inventiveness. He stood breathless and perspiring amid all the flattened and broken grass. He turned to where his mother was waiting for him. But she was gone.

He ran to the spot and saw her lying in the deep grass. She was dead. The air was too thick and she had succumbed to it. She was suffocating, when all the while he thought she was only trying to catch her breath amid all their laughter. He looked again to where her lifeless body lay in the grass. It had vanished! He ran into the grass to find her. As he ran, the grass began to disappear, until he was running along a city street.

He came to a mansion. The windows were broken and grimy curtains fluttered through the broken glass. When he entered the mansion, he found Arabella and his father sitting in the dining room.

"William wants to do the figure eights," Arabella said, pouring his father coffee.

"He does, does he?"

Pigeons flew in through the broken windows and perched on the windowsills and furniture. There was pigeon excrement everywhere. He walked out a door and found himself on a long road in the cemetery, monstrous headstones looming everywhere.

He ran but couldn't find his way out of the cemetery. Suddenly he was in a field whose tall grass lay flattened against the ground. The sky overhead was a bright, clear blue. He walked for some time by himself, then saw a woman with long dark hair running in front of him. He raced to catch her, but she disappeared. He found himself at the edge of a cliff. The woman was far below, standing amid the rocks on a white sandy beach looking up at him. He had no fear of the great height and moved to the edge of the cliff, knowing he would glide down to where she waited for him. He stepped off. It was only then that he realized his mind had tricked him, and he began to hurtle through the air, the jagged rocks coming at him faster and faster . . .

William sat up in his bed and looked around his room, his heart beating rapidly. Night had just begun to lift. The cold light of another winter's dawn shrouded the room in drab shadow. He caught his breath. The image of Sybil Curtis being stabbed by a tall man with blond hair returned to him. He knew that man, had seen him one day when he was a child. He had been hiding from his governess in the old fir tree by his father's front gate when he heard voices on the driveway far below. He looked through the branches of the tree and saw that very man—tall, fair-haired —walking with his father. They were yelling at each other in a frightening way. William had never before seen adults behave with such naked emotion, and the sight terrified him. His father's face was contorted with rage. He was screaming at the other man. What was he screaming?

William lay on his back and stared at the ceiling. He was screaming that the man with the fair hair had killed William's mother.

William threw back the covers and went to his wardrobe. He found a pair of pajamas and put them on, then opened another door and reached for a robe and a pair of slippers. He stepped into the slippers, tied the robe closed, and walked out into the dark hall. In the bathroom he splashed cold water against his face, then ran his damp fingers through his hair, pushing it back away from his forehead. He walked out into the hall and down the stairs to the library. Closing the doors behind him, he went to the small writing desk at the back of the room, sat down, and turned on a light. He took out several sheets of plain white stationery, thought for a moment, then picked up a pen and wrote:

January 17, 1912

Dear Miss Curtis,

I owe you a profound apology for my conduct toward you at our last meeting. Unfortunately, there is nothing I can do (or, believe me, nothing I would not do, if it were only possible) to change my reprehensible words and behavior toward you on that occasion. To say that I misjudged you offers only the flimsiest excuse for my actions. I can now only tell you how deeply sorry I am.

Since it is unlikely we will meet again, I would like to take this opportunity to tell you that my respect and regard for you are without limit, measure, or end.

I remain yours, most sincerely,
  William B. Dysart

He read the letter, then lay it on the desk. He looked around the room. All was quiet but for the ticking of the gilt clock on the mantel. A faint gray light still lingered outside. He heard Rose and the two newly hired Irish girls on the stairs outside, descending from their rooms on the fourth floor to the kitchen in the basement. He read the letter again. It was all very nicely done—neat and clean. He would send it and the matter would be at an end. He would retreat back into the quiet security of his comfortable, unhappy life.

William pushed his chair away from the desk and walked over to the fireplace. He looked into the mirror above the mantel.

William wants to do the figure eights.

He does, does he?

He went back to the desk, picked up the letter, and tore it up.

Chapter 30

William sat on the low railing of Sybil Curtis's porch that afternoon. He had been waiting there for more than an hour, and as the time passed, he had, with rhythmic regularity, gotten up to pace the length of the porch or stepped from it to stand in the warmth of the early afternoon sun. He was about to begin his pacing again when he heard the thrum of a motor and turned to see Sybil's friend Caroline Jameson's car swing into the circular drive in front of the cottage and pull to a stop. Sybil, sitting in the front passenger seat, glanced at him, then turned away. Two young children in the back piled against the window to stare at William.

"Hello," said Caroline Jameson, getting out and smiling pleasantly across the roof of the car to William. "Mr. Dysart, is it?"

"Yes, hello." William smiled back at her.

"Excuse me." She ducked down and spoke into the backseat. "If you girls don't behave yourselves, this will be the last time I take you when we go shopping. Do you understand me?"

Sybil got out of the car and reached down to get two canvas bags filled with groceries.

"Can I help you with those?" asked William, bending down next to her to take the larger bag.

"Please," he pleaded in a hushed voice, "I have to speak to you."

"I tell you, Veronica," Caroline Jameson was still attempting to restore order in the backseat, "I mean it, you will stay with Mrs. Moreau next time."

"But I just wanted to look out the window," the young girl began to wail, "and Helen pushed me."

"All right, stop crying. We'll discuss it later." Caroline Jameson closed the car door. "Sybil, I'm sorry, I'm going to have to run. They haven't had their naps today and they're going to drive me completely mad." She held out her hand to William. "So nice to see you again, Mr. Dysart."

"Oh, Caroline," said Sybil, taking a small package from her handbag, "I almost forgot."

"Mr. Dysart," said Caroline Jameson, "perhaps you'd like to help?" She opened the package and held up a beautifully hand-tinted program for William to see:

THE COMMITTEE FOR THE EMERGENCY
HOSPITAL OF HUNTINGTON, L.I.
PRESENTS
THE COBURN PLAYERS
IN
As You Like It.

"It's to raise money to build a hospital. I am chair. Sybil has spent months hand coloring these programs. We're all contributing in whatever way we can. Now, can we count on you to buy a ticket or two?"

"Certainly. I'll take twenty."

"Well," said Caroline Jameson, smiling. "Then you may keep this." She handed him the program.

There was a sudden commotion from the backseat of the car. "Pardon me." Caroline Jameson tapped at the back window vigorously. "All right, you're both going to bed early tonight." She turned to Sybil and William. "I'm sorry." She hurried to the other side of the car. "Sybil, I'll be by tomorrow at three. Childless!" she whispered across the roof of the car. "Mr. Dysart, a check will do very nicely, the address is on the back of the program." She drove off.

Sybil waited in the driveway with William. When the car was out of sight, Sybil carried her bag of groceries onto the porch. William followed with the other bag. She stopped at the front door to take the bag from him. "I don't want you to come in," she said.

"Please, I have to speak to you," said William in a preoccupied way as he handed the bag to her.

"I'm sorry." She took the bag and turned toward the door.

"Won't you at least let me explain?"

"Mr. Dysart, please go."

"I don't blame you for feeling the way you do after what I said and how I behaved. I'm not surprised you despise me."

"I don't despise you."

"Then won't you please let me speak to you."

Sybil opened the door finally and walked in, leaving it open behind her. William entered. She went to the kitchen as he waited in the front room. He could hear the rustling of thick brown paper as she untied her parcels from the market. He went finally and stood in the doorway to the kitchen. She was reaching up to get a tin from a cabinet by the sink.

"Let me get that for you." William took the tin down for her.

She took the tin without comment and began to pour sugar into it.

"I had no right to speak to you the way I did," he said. "All I know is that I was angry and wanted to hurt you."

"Why should you want to hurt me?" She looked at him for the first time.

"Because . . ." William struggled to find an answer.

"Mr. Dysart . . ." She picked up the top of the tin and began turning it over in her hands. "I accept your apology. There is no need for you to say anything further."

"Sybil," he spoke suddenly, "I would do anything for you."

She glanced at him uneasily, then went and stood by the sideboard. She held on to it as she stared out the window.

William went to her. "I'm sorry."

"I want you to leave."

"Oh," said William quietly. "I see." He took a breath. "Of course."

She went with him to the front door and opened it.

"May I come again?" he asked.

"No."

William took a deep breath, then turned to walk out the door. Without warning, he felt a blow to the side of his head, which sent a flash of light shooting across his eye and almost caused him to lose his balance. He looked at her. What had happened? She stared at him without expression. Everything seemed suddenly unreal. He saw her lift her hand to hit him again. He could hardly make sense of it. It was terrifying to see her like this. He grabbed her arm. She tried to pull it free, then raised her other hand to strike him. He held up his arm to deflect the blow. He felt fear and pity at once and tried desperately to think what to do as she continued to spin out of control in front of him. She stared at him with the same expressionless face, her breathing swift and shallow. She went to bite his hand that held her arm. He let go and she ran out the door toward the Sound. William raced after her. "Stop!" he called. She ran faster. William ran until he was right behind her. He caught her around the waist and held her. She struggled to get away, pummeling him with her fists, her breathing becoming more labored until she began to gasp for air, at last letting out a hideous wail. Her legs gave way beneath her and William fell to his knees, struggling to hold on to her as she sank to the ground. She clung to his neck, her head falling against his chest, and she began to cry as if she would never stop.

The afternoon sun slanted through a nearby window, suffusing Sybil Curtis's bedroom with a light that seemed to wrap itself around the stillness. And although Sybil slept quietly in her bed, there seemed something tragic about her, like a body from some ferocious night's shipwreck lying peacefully on a sunny beach. William sat in a nearby chair watching her with concern. A tapping at the window in the front room roused him.

"Sybil," he heard a woman's voice call. "Sybil, are you there?"

He went into the front room and saw Caroline Jameson on the porch. He opened the front door. Caroline Jameson drew back at the sight of him, and it occurred to him how he must look to her, unshaven, in his shirtsleeves, with his suspenders down.

"I'm sorry," he said, quickly pulling up his suspenders. "I know this must look very odd, but Sybil is ill and I had to stay."

Caroline Jameson stared at him uneasily.

"She's in the bedroom." William reached inside the door for his coat. "I'll wait out here." William pulled on his coat and stepped off the porch. Caroline Jameson entered the cottage. A short while later she came out. "What happened?" she asked.

William related the facts of the previous afternoon. "She has been in this state ever since. She thrashed about all night, calling out names and saying unintelligible things. When I would go to her, she didn't seem to recognize me."

Caroline Jameson looked very concerned. "We'll take her to my house. My husband is a doctor. She'll stay with me."

"Can I talk with you for a moment?" asked William. They walked a short distance from the cottage. "How long have you known her?"

She read the look on his face. "Long enough to know something terrible must have happened to her. I know that her father and her brother drowned. But something else besides. Quite horrible, I'm afraid. I don't know exactly what, but I have an idea."

"It's not my place to tell you, or I would," said William.

They turned back toward the cottage. "Don't worry." Caroline Jameson pressed his arm.

They went to Sybil's bedroom. Caroline leaned across the bed. "Sybil," she said softly. She took

Sybil's face in her hands and looked directly into her eyes. "Sybil, dear, it's me, Caroline."

Sybil's eyes drifted slowly over Caroline's face.

"You're not feeling well. Mr. Dysart and I are going to take you to my house so you can get better. Do you understand what I'm saying?"

Sybil stared at Caroline. She nodded.

"Good." Caroline smiled. "Good," she repeated and kissed Sybil's forehead. She tucked the blankets around Sybil and turned to William.

William took Sybil in his arms and carried her out to Caroline's car. He placed her in the backseat as Caroline put an extra blanket over her. He turned the hand crank on the car and, when it started, went to his own car and started it. He followed Caroline Jameson the mile to her house.

Her housekeeper, a dark, heavyset woman who spoke with a French accent, met them at Caroline's door.

"Mrs. Moreau," said Caroline, "Miss Curtis is ill and will be staying with us for a time. Is the back bedroom made up?"

While Caroline and her housekeeper were settling Sybil in the bedroom, William paced about the parlor, not trusting himself even to sit down, until Caroline appeared.

"She's sleeping comfortably," she said. "Mrs. Moreau is with her."

William took a deep breath.

"Would you like a drink, Mr. Dysart?"

"Yes." William fell into a chair. "Yes, I think I would. Thank you."

"I'm sorry I took so long, but I also had to see to the children." She poured him a whiskey, then sat across from him.

"You mustn't worry. She'll be all right."

"Do you think so?"

"She's strong. She has a wonderful spirit. A father and a brother she was mad about. Good men. Some women—girls—who have been through what she has been through don't have that."

"You know, then."

She breathed a deep sigh. "Not the details or the extent, but yes. It must have been horrific."

"Yes, horrific." William was quiet for a moment. "I would hate to do anything to upset her further, or . . ."

She looked at him expectantly.

"I'm a married man, Mrs. Jameson."

"Yes, I know," she said at last. She got up. "I think I'll have a drink, too." She poured herself a sherry, then sat down again across from William. "I know your wife. Or perhaps I should say I knew her." She took a sip of her drink. "We went to school together in Pittsburgh. The Unqua Corinthian Academy for Young Ladies. It was where mothers and fathers in Pittsburgh with notions sent their daughters to get more—learn bad French, that sort of thing." She smiled and took another sip of sherry. "Arabella Harrison was the most beautiful girl in our school. Probably the most beautiful girl in Pittsburgh. So many of the girls were jealous of her."

"Did you like her?"

"She was a few years younger than I."

"But did you like her," William persisted.

"We had different interests."

He nodded.

"Since you have made your confession, Mr. Dysart, I'll make mine. I was married before."

"Your first husband died?"

She shook her head. "Only the marriage." She sipped her drink. "I lived in Paris and was married to an aristocrat of sorts, a Monsieur de Roussillon. My parents couldn't have been happier; I was never more miserable. I wish I could tell you that Monsieur beat me, but he was just a pompous ass with money.

"I am Catholic," she went on. "My church told me if I left my husband, it would be a sin. I thought the far bigger sin would be to live half a life, so I left him *and* the church. Though I do sneak into Saint Patrick's in town occasionally. Once a Catholic, you know . . . I hope you'll keep my secret. Around here I am simply Dr. Jameson's wife. I drive my Model T, which we can scarcely afford, and take care of my children, and am happier than I ever thought possible. My dreams led me to the rue D'Anjou, but my heart led me to this old farmhouse. Dreams can be wonderful things, they can also be . . . well, nightmares." She put down her drink. "I hope you won't mind my saying that you remind me of myself in Paris—toward the end."

"Do I?"

"Yes. You drive a lovely car, Mr. Dysart—in fact, my guess is that my son Walter is out there right now crawling all over it. I don't know that I can picture you driving a Model T."

"A Packard?"

"Perhaps." She smiled.

William finished his drink. "Thank you, Mrs. Jameson." He stood. "I am so glad that Sybil has you for a friend."

Caroline Jameson walked him to the door.

"Would you mind if I called to see how she is?" asked William.

"Of course not."

William was about to leave. He turned back. "Is it so obvious?" he asked.

She hesitated. "That you're in love with her?" She thought for a moment. "Yes. Very."

Chapter 31

William arrived home just after nine o'clock and went directly to his room. He was surprised to find Arabella reading in a chair there.

"Hello," said William. He stood at the threshold for a moment before closing the door.

"Where have you been since yesterday afternoon?" She closed her book.

"Out on Long Island."

"With your little friend?"

William loosened his tie and sat on the edge of his bed. "As I've said before, my little friend's name is Miss Curtis."

"I know. I know a lot about Miss Curtis. I know, for instance, that you spent last night with her."

"You're jumping to conclusions."

"No, I know it for a fact. I also know that you have been seeing her in New York. The library. Central Park. A cozy little rendezvous at the Casino."

"How do you know?"

"I called Albert Penniman today. We met and had a long chat. He's been having your Miss Curtis followed."

"Followed?"

"Since November."

"Why?"

"She told him she didn't want to see him

anymore. He thought there must be a reason. Apparently there was."

William went for the door.

"Where are you going?"

"To see that snake Albert Penniman."

"It won't do any good—especially not in the mood you're in."

William opened the door.

Arabella grabbed his arm. "He's called off his detectives."

William stared at his wife. "I don't believe you."

"He has. He's realized he's never going to get her back. I told him I was furious. Do you think I want him knowing more about our affairs than I do?"

William looked unconvinced.

"He promised me he would."

"A promise from Albert Penniman."

"He'll do anything I ask. Especially now that he thinks you're otherwise engaged."

"I see."

"Do you seriously think I would ever have anything to do with him?" Arabella asked.

"I don't know anymore."

"Please. Give me some credit."

William sat again on the bed.

"And honestly," said Arabella, closing the door, "I don't know what all the fuss is about. When I saw her at the ball, I thought: *her*. I knew Albert had no taste, but I expected more of you."

"Why did she go to the ball with him, if she didn't want to see him anymore?"

"He threatened to tell me everything, if she didn't."

"There was nothing to tell."

"She seemed to think there was. Albert thought if you saw them together, it might dampen your ardor—having no idea, of course, of the extent of your pigheadedness. Now, I want you to tell me everything."

"As I said, there's nothing to tell."

"Don't play me for a fool, William."

"Nothing."

"The Saunterer thought there was—with your *reckless* pursuit of her down Peacock Alley? Mrs. Oelrichs also gave a rather persuasive report. She came by the next day. Of course she was very sorry and there was probably nothing to it, but how she warmed to describing the look on your face as you *cornered* Miss Curtis. I almost laughed. She'd make a wonderful—if long-winded—witness." Arabella returned to her chair. "I think we need to talk."

"You want a divorce."

"On the contrary. I want us to continue on as we have. You may see your Miss Curtis as much as you like. Provided, of course, you are more discreet than you have been recently, which, frankly, I don't think is too much to ask. I will come and go as I please, see whomever I please—

also discreetly—without any questions from you."

"It's time we divorced."

Arabella shook her head. "I like being Mrs. William Dysart. Besides, if I divorce you, even if I got all your money, how much would that be?"

"You're counting on my father's money?"

"Since you ask. Yes. He has shown me his will."

"How very cozy. Pity you couldn't marry him."

"Don't think I couldn't, but betraying the sainted Cady—*quel scandale*—I might just as well move back to Pittsburgh."

William stared at his wife. "You must hate me a great deal."

Arabella shrugged. "I hate your sanctimony."

"I see."

"Don't take it too personally."

William looked at her thoughtfully. "I am afraid," he said at last, "I'm going to have to insist on a divorce."

"Then I'm afraid I'm going to have to drag your Miss Curtis into court for sleeping with my husband."

"She has done no such thing."

"I have a private investigator who will swear you spent the night with her in her house."

"She was sick."

"I'm sure. Well, the poor dear can tell it all to the judge and the reporters. And I'm sure Mrs.

Oelrichs will enjoy her spell on the witness stand. But tell your Miss Curtis not to worry, Albert has promised to provide her a sterling character reference."

"Albert should be in jail for what he's done. She was little more than a child when he forced himself on her."

"He said she can't prove a thing."

William got up from the bed and looked out the window. He took a deep breath. "I will divorce you."

"If you like. But don't think I won't have your Miss Curtis's name and picture in every newspaper in New York and London. Albert tells me she is not the most stable creature—moody, cries for no reason."

"She has reason, I assure you," William said.

"Then she doesn't need another." Arabella walked over to him. "What are you so upset about? You can see her as much as you like. You can even bring her to parties at our new house. She is Albert's cousin after all. Or your cousin now." Arabella suddenly noticed something. She reached up and ran her finger across the scab on William's chin, where Sybil had scratched him. "What *have* the two of you been up to?"

Then she turned and picked up her book. "I think I'm being more than fair," she said as she walked out of the room.

William slowly closed the shutters and got ready

for bed. He would call the office in the morning and tell them he would be out one more day. He could no longer battle his wife and his father with the demons from his childhood still clawing at him.

Chapter 32

The sun was in William's eyes the next morning as he walked past the small brownstone church on Park Avenue and turned onto East Twenty-first Street. He had imagined walking this way so many times that now as he made his way across Twenty-first Street to the east side of Gramercy Park, and stood within sight of his destination, there seemed something almost dreamlike in the long line of red brick town houses stretching down the block before him.

He came to a cast iron enclosure and paused at the door to Edith Bradford's house. He took a deep breath, gripped the gate, and entered. The door was answered by a short, trim woman in a black uniform with starched white collar and cap. "Yes?" she asked in a way that made William feel he had called her away from some important task.

"I wonder if I might speak to Miss—"

"Who is it, Catherine?" a voice called from the drawing room.

"A young man, madam."

"Do I know him?"

"No, madam."

"Do you know him?"

"No, madam."

"Then close the door. This is hardly a suitable hour for anyone to call." There was a pause. "Is he good-looking?"

Catherine looked William up and down. "I would say so. Yes."

"Then tell him to come by for tea. Four o'clock sharp."

"If you will return this afternoon, sir, we will be—"

"Wait, please." William placed his hand on the door. "I'm Miss Bradford's—"

"As I'm sure." Catherine began to close the door firmly.

"What is all this fuss?" His Aunt Edith stepped into the hallway and saw him. "William Dysart." Her voice quavered.

"Yes—Aunt—I thought it's time we got to know one another."

"Oh?" She studied his face.

"Long overdue, in fact."

"Yes," she whispered. "Come in. Please come in."

Catherine took William's coat and hat, and his aunt clasped his arm and led him into the drawing room. She was taller than he had thought, and though he knew she must be over eighty, she moved with the vitality of a much younger woman.

"Sit down, please," she directed, sitting opposite him by her front windows looking out over the park. Her clothes were trim and gave the impression that their wearer, while not at all fashionable, knew all she needed of style. "Catherine," she called, "please bring us some coffee." She took William's hand. "You look so much like your mother." Her hair, now almost all white and gray, was gathered in a simple way at the top of her head.

"You were close?"

"After Gracie died—your grandmother Grace Bradford—your mother was like a daughter to me. I can't tell you how much I still miss her."

"What was she like?"

"Enchanting."

"You sound like a proud aunt."

"It's true all the same. I remember when we went to Europe. By the time our boat docked in Southampton, everyone from the cabin boy to the captain was in love with her.

"She had such a passion for everything. There might have been women more beautiful, and better dressed, God knows. Your mother never gave a damn about clothes—or jewelry. I remember I had to force her into a decent dress when she had her portrait painted." She glanced at William. "I can still see her, those lovely dark eyes interested in everything and everyone."

Edith Bradford paused when Catherine came into the room and placed a tray on a low marble-topped table between William and his aunt. After Edith poured coffee for them both from a silver coffeepot, she settled back into her chair. "I can't believe you're here," she said, sipping her coffee. "What made you come?"

"When I saw you on the night of Mrs. Huffam's speech, I knew you couldn't be the woman my father said you were."

She smiled. "Lucrezia Borgia would, I imagine, have trouble living up to what you must have been told. Does he speak much about your mother?"

William shook his head. "I thought you might be able to tell me something. I've always been rather haunted by her memory. When I was younger, if I asked Father about her at all, he would either stop the conversation, or get up and leave."

"Oh, dear." His aunt sighed.

"Why is he so bitter?"

She thought for a moment. "He loved her a great deal, but he did everything, I'm afraid, to make it impossible for her to love him. I suppose it's easier for him to be bitter than to accept that."

William felt suddenly very anxious. "Bitterness doesn't make a person disappear—doesn't kill them."

"Kill?"

"When she died, something terrible happened."

"No, dear. Nothing terrible happened. She died of pneumonia."

"Pneumonia?"

"Yes, that's all."

"Are you sure?"

"Of course," she said softly.

"But there was a tall man. Fair-haired. I remember seeing him soon after she died, arguing with my father. My father accused him of killing her."

"I'm so sorry, William." His aunt leaned over and took his hand. "I know the man you're talking about. He had nothing to do with your mother's death."

"Someone left me property. Someone with the initials 'A.G.' Was that him?"

"Yes." His aunt's lip trembled and she began to cry. "William, I know a great many things you probably don't. And I will tell you, I promise you. But can you give me a little time—just a little? This is all quite a shock, your coming here today. I need time to think things through. Do you mind?"

William shook his head. "I know this can't be easy for you."

"Or you. What do you know?"

"Only that my parents' marriage was not a happy one."

"No." Edith dried her eyes and took another sip of coffee. "Your mother had been engaged to a wonderful young man, who died of diphtheria shortly before they were to be married. It devastated her. Soon after—too soon, I'm afraid—your father came calling. Your mother didn't know her own mind. I think she just accepted his proposal to escape the memory of the boy who had died. Your father truly loved her, but it was a disastrous match." She pushed her cup away. "Sometime after you were born, he turned against your mother. He became cold, distant—he would berate her, even in front of the servants. I didn't realize at the time"—her voice faltered—"just how bad things had become. Your mother tried to hide it all from me. But I should have known. I saw a vital young woman fade away little by little before my eyes.

"After she died, her Uncle Henry and I spoke to your father. We asked him if we could raise you. I thought he might hit Henry—he said he would see that we never had any contact with you; he called us the *crackpot Bradfords*." Edith smiled. "I rather liked that." She glanced out a nearby window. "The crackpot Bradfords," she repeated.

William watched his aunt, whose eyes seemed to be looking far beyond the trees in the park across the street. "Aunt Edith," he said finally, "I was told recently you have a portrait of my mother."

"Yes." His aunt sprang to life. "I do indeed. By Sargent. Painted when your mother was barely twenty. Would you like to see it?"

"Very much."

"You moved your head just now exactly as your mother used to! Pardon me." She searched the pocket of her dress for a handkerchief. "Now," she began again, "let me show you the painting." She placed her hands on the arms of her chair and attempted to get up. "Damn it all," she said as she fell back into the chair. "William"—she held out her hands—"will you give your old aunt some nephew-style assistance?"

"With pleasure." William stood and helped his aunt from her chair.

"Either I'm getting old, or that chair is getting deeper. I must have the springs checked." She smiled. "You certainly have grown into a fine young man," she said, holding on to his arm as they walked from the room. "Your mother would be very proud of you."

"Do you think so?"

"Indeed. You must have the world at your feet."

"I'm afraid I've made more than a few mistakes along the way."

"Well, then, unmake them. That's what life's about—making and unmaking mistakes, getting back on the track and moving on. The problem with mistakes is that they have the habit of growing into such big, fat, lovely excuses." She paused. "Rather preachy, aren't I? You're going to leave today thinking your aunt is just an old bore, and that coming here was the biggest mistake you ever made."

"That's already grown into something big and fat and lovely."

"Oh, you little charmer." She smiled at him. "A Bradford through and through, I see."

William laughed.

"Now," she said as they entered the hallway, "your mother's portrait is hanging over the mantel in my bedroom. It's probably a bit different from the photographs you've seen of her."

"I've never seen any."

"Oh, but you must have."

"My father said they were all lost in a fire."

"A fire!" she exclaimed. "Your father. Of all the nasty . . ." She shook her head. "Oh, it's not worth my breath. Do you remember her, William?" she asked as they paused at the bottom of the stairs. "I mean remember what she looked like?"

"No."

"Would you rather see it by yourself?"

"If you wouldn't mind."

"Not at all. My bedroom is the first door to the left at the top of the stairs. I'll wait for you down here. Take as much time as you like." She patted his arm and walked back toward the parlor.

William climbed the narrow staircase to his aunt's bedroom. He hesitated before placing his hand on the knob and slowly turning it.

He stood before the portrait—of a beautiful young woman in a white dress—for some time, then backed away to better observe the artist's genius in the delicate sheen of the flawless skin, the sparkle in the eyes forever young and hopeful, and the bright, flirtatious curl at the corner of the mouth that age and time would never darken.

He could not remember the face, but the sight of it evoked strong feelings in him, profound but inexpressible. Staring now at her vivid features, he began to recall more distinctly the shadowy figure who read to him as a child and put him to bed. He remembered standing with her once. The summer before she disappeared. She was wearing a white dress then, too; he remembered the clean smell of it. They were in front of his father's house. A carriage waited. Someone was with them. Tommy Ackroyd, his friend, the hostler's little boy. His mother was going to take them into Oyster Bay to buy something. Fishing rods. His father came from the house. The carriage was sent away. If she were determined to take him fishing by the dock with the Irish trash and colored boys, he said, then she would have to walk to town to buy the rods. His father pointed to William and said something about how she had him doing the servants' work and told Tommy to go home. His father said something else, then went back into the house.

William recalled his mother starting down the long driveway. She told him to stay, that his father would be angry. He sat on the lawn and watched her, a sad, lonely figure, growing smaller, moving farther and farther away.

William looked at the painting. He remembered now. Remembered getting up and running after his mother as fast as he could. Remembered a hand suddenly grabbing him by the collar, jerking him back violently. Remembered looking up and seeing his father with an almost murderous look on his face, slapping him again and again until his mother took hold of his arm to stop him. He remembered the taste of blood in his mouth and wondering what it was he had done to make his father hate him so.

When William descended the stairs and entered his aunt's parlor a short while later, she was reading a newspaper. "Is everything all right?" she asked, taking off her glasses.

William gave a quick nod.

"Can you stay for lunch?"

"Any other time I would, but . . ."

"No explanation necessary, I understand completely." She stood and took his arm, "But I'm going to make you promise to come and see me again very soon."

"Of course." William put his hand over his aunt's.

"William, what did your father tell you about me?" she asked as they walked toward her front door.

William hesitated. "He said you were responsible for my mother's death."

"Oh, dear. Well, if it makes it any easier for him to believe that. Anything else?"

William hesitated.

"What?"

"He said that you were unnatural."

"Oh, really." She smiled. "I wouldn't say so, though I suppose the world would." She thought for a moment. "What do you think he meant?"

"I'm not sure. It could mean many things."

"Exactly," said his aunt, stopping in her hallway, "and all the more damning for it, so I may as well tell you the truth." She took a deep breath. "I was engaged once to a man who was injured horribly in the Civil War. He lingered on for a year in a hospital near Washington. After he died, I thought I'd go mad. I started to correspond with the nurse who took care of him—it seems she fell in love with him, too. The letters helped lighten the load for us both. Eventually, she came to New York and . . . well . . . one thing led to another. Miss Ada Bryant. How I miss her. Unnatural? It seemed like the most natural thing in the world to me."

"I see," said William.

"What do you think of your old aunt now?"

He smiled at her. "She's unique."

"Maybe just a little more honest than most. I'll walk you outside," Edith offered as William opened her front door. "It's such a beautiful day, and I am enough of an aunt to want all my neighbors to see me with my handsome nephew."

They came to the cast iron gate at the bottom of her front steps. William opened it and stepped out onto the sidewalk. She closed the gate behind him. "Thank you, Aunt Edith." William leaned down and kissed her cheek.

"You!" She took his face in her hands. "You've made a crabby old woman very happy today." She kissed his forehead.

William smiled. As he was about to leave, he paused. "Aunt Edith, you said it was sometime after my birth that my father began to change toward my mother." He hesitated. "How long after?"

Edith stared into William's eyes. "Soon," she said at last, and William, seeing the tears collecting in her eyes, nodded. He bent down and kissed her a last time and left.

Chapter 33

William and Sybil Curtis strolled along a winding country road that ran by the shore of the Sound. It was early April; two months after Caroline Jameson had taken Sybil into her house. Sybil had stayed there for two weeks, during which time William had visited her several times. She had not remembered striking him, or running from him toward the Sound that afternoon. Her last memory, she told him, was his getting down the tin from the kitchen shelf for her and her filling it with sugar. William continued to see her after she returned to her cottage, stopping in once or twice a week. He wasn't sure how she felt about him, but every time he asked if he could come again to see her, she agreed. She knew his marriage was unhappy and that he and Arabella were living separate lives, but beyond that he had never discussed his personal life, or his feelings for her.

Winter still hid in the shadows cast by the old trees where they walked, but the warmth of the coming spring lay in the wide patches of sunlight in between.

"Look, a robin," said Sybil.

William turned to see the bird perching in a nearby tree. "Should we start keeping an eye out for the elusive Hibernian Warbler?"

"Blackburnian," she laughed.

"Pardon me," he said, casting her a sideways glance. Except for his visits to Sybil, William was living a mostly solitary life. He saw Arabella rarely, even at breakfast, as she had taken to sleeping in late in the mornings. They did manage for the sake of appearances to attend one or two events together a week. William was surprised by how little people seemed to notice the change. Theodore and Lucie would have known something was amiss, but Lucie had inherited a large piece of property in Cornwall from one of her uncles, and she and Theodore were in England. He had not, in fact, seen Theodore since he had been so insulting to him that morning. His

Aunt Edith had likewise left the city for Washington to stay with a sick friend, so he had not seen her either after their initial encounter.

William and Sybil turned off the road onto a small stretch of beach. He took off his woolen jacket and laid it out on the sand so they could sit down. A mild breeze cut across the water, rippling their clothes. He reached into the pocket of his jacket. "I have something for you," he said. He took out a small cardboard casing and handed it to her.

Sybil untied the brown ribbon holding the casing together. Inside was a pen and ink drawing of a tree.

"Do you like it?"

"It's beautiful."

"I did it," said William, his face flushing. "Do you recognize it?"

She studied the drawing. "It's my tree."

William nodded. "It's autumn, and you're reading beneath it."

"Where?"

"There." He pointed to a shadowy figure by the side of the tree. "How else could I have stumbled upon you? It's the day we met. Do you remember?"

"Of course," she said. "I thought you were lost."

"I was. Utterly."

"It's lovely," she whispered. "Thank you, Mr. Dysart."

"I don't suppose you'll ever call me William."

"William," she said.

"Thank you, Miss Curtis," he said dryly.

She laughed.

William gazed out over the water. "Do you find it strange my coming to see you like this? A married man," he added uneasily.

She did not respond.

"I would hate it if you thought I were someone like Albert."

"Of course I don't," she said, "though I . . ."

"Yes?" he asked.

She shook her head.

William picked up a handful of sand and let it slide through his fingers.

"I . . ." she began again, "I would be lying if I didn't tell you I'm terrified every time I see your motorcar pull into the driveway."

"Are you?"

She nodded. "But then, I don't think I could stand it if you stopped coming to see me." She shook her head. "I'm rather a disaster, you see." She tried to smile.

"No, you're not."

"But I am." She took the cardboard casing and turned it over and over in her hands. "Perhaps, if . . . if I had been older," she said, "when it happened . . . I might . . ."

William could hear the anguish in her voice and felt a wave of sympathy and anger wash over him.

"I remember," she said, her breath catching in her throat, "standing at an open window in Paris, a small wrought iron balcony all that stood between me and the street far below . . . I cannot tell you how the street called to me." She closed her eyes and trembled.

William put his arm around her.

"I wanted to die . . . I wanted to die." She hid her face in his shoulder and cried. William took the handkerchief from his jacket pocket, and gave it to her.

"When . . . I was a child," she began after a moment or two, "I asked my father why people killed themselves in such horrible ways. He said it was because their pain was so great that a violent death seemed as nothing if it would end it all quickly." She brushed the corners of her eyes. "That day at the window I understood."

She took a deep breath. "I went to the police in Paris, but the gendarme took me back to Mr. Billings. I gave up all hope then, but after that, Mr. Billings became wary of me and we returned to New York. He took me here, then brought Albert by, and I never saw Mr. Billings again. Albert said it was because he had told Mr. Billings to leave me alone, but the truth, I later found out, was that Mr. Billings was dying.

"I believed Albert, believed he had saved me, and I tried to make myself believe I was in love with him. It made it endurable. Albert knew the cottage was mine, but told me it was his." She rolled the handkerchief into a ball. "The only money I had was what he gave me. I was alone and Albert did everything to keep me that way. Not that I wanted to see anyone. I felt so ashamed, and thought no one would want to have anything to do with me if they knew the truth.

"Then I met Caroline Jameson. She saw me from time to time in Huntington Village and wondered who I was and why I was always alone. Caroline invited me to her home, and though I was terrified, I went. Meeting her was the beginning of the end of the nightmare—like breaking through to the surface of the water for brief moments at a time."

Sybil was careful, she told William, that Caroline should never meet Albert, and Caroline seemed to know not to intrude and never to press her for answers. Caroline noticed how little money Sybil had, and acting on the belief that Mr. Curtis, her father, must have left her something when he died, had her banker, a Mr. Glasco in Huntington, look into the matter. Mr. Glasco found a savings account at the Bank of New York in Charles Curtis's name, with over seven thousand dollars in it. Sybil finally had money of her own.

"When Albert was no longer my only means of survival, I was able to see things more clearly; to see Albert not as my savior or protector, but as someone who preyed upon me as Mr. Billings had, and I grew to loathe him."

At around this same time, she told William, Lydia Billings began her campaign to try to wrest the cottage from her. It was then Sybil realized that she, not Albert, was its owner. By then she was strong enough to fight back. When William appeared on the scene, she had been battling Lydia Billings and Albert Penniman for almost a year. The evening William saw her in Greenwich Village, she was meeting with Albert at his insistence. She agreed to the meeting only so that she could tell Albert emphatically, and for the last time, that she was never going to see him again, and that if he continued to come to the cottage or to threaten her, she had bought a gun and would not hesitate to use it.

William watched a wave roll in from the Sound and reach up almost to where they sat. He took a deep breath and picked up a stone and pitched it into the water.

"Did you?"

She looked at him.

"Did you really buy a gun?" he asked.

"No." She looked back out at the water. "I can't bear the sight of them. But I prayed Albert would believe it. Which he did, for a short while at least."

"Not many could survive what you have."

"Have I survived?" She pressed her fingers into the sand.

William looked at her, wanting to say so much, but knowing that whatever he might say could only sound facile.

She laid her head against her knees. "Tell me," she said, looking at him, "do you think I was mad not to sell my cottage to Mrs. Billings when she was willing to pay me so much for it?"

William sat up and looked out at the water. "No." He shook his head.

"I couldn't do it. Let her take it, without so much as an apology. Take it, as she—they—had taken everything."

"Of course not," said William.

They watched a boat hung with nets and tackle heading for the harbor of Huntington Bay, the fishermen raising and lowering their oars in unison, the oars splashing softly as they broke the water.

They got up at last and she brushed the sand from her skirt. "I hope you know," she said, "I will always be so grateful that you came into my life."

"Thank you . . . Sybil."

Her eyes softened and she smiled. The wind had ruffled William's hair so that it fell across his forehead. She reached up to smooth it back, then stopped. There was a moment of awkwardness. William offered her his arm. She took it and they began the long walk to her cottage.

"After stopping in at my father's house," he

said, "I would like to come to see you again for an hour or so if you wouldn't mind."

"I would like that," she replied as a postal motor wagon pulled up next to them.

"Hello, Mr. Ellis," said Sybil to the elderly driver, who was reaching into his mailbag. "How is Grace?"

"Fine." Mr. Ellis squinted at her through his glasses, revealing his discolored front teeth.

William saw Sybil push stray strands of hair from her face as she listened attentively to Mr. Ellis. "She stopped in yesterday with our new granddaughter." Mr. Ellis handed Sybil her mail.

"Really? What's her name?" Sybil asked.

"Grace." Mr. Ellis put his truck in gear.

"Well, that makes it easy." Sybil smiled. "Tell Mrs. Ellis I said hello."

"I will, missy," called Mr. Ellis, his truck rolling down the road, raising a fine cloud of brown dust.

William observed Sybil silently as she looked through her mail, his heart filled with admiration for her and her spirit that not all the sickness in Henry Billings's soul could crush.

Chapter 34

That evening, William sat reading a newspaper in Sybil's front room. When he had returned from his father's, she had asked if he could stay the night on her sofa. She didn't want to be alone, was all she had told him, and he didn't inquire further, knowing that she suffered from bouts of anxiety and fear. Still, he thought, something had changed between the time he had left for his father's and his return some three hours later. There was a tentativeness to her behavior that had not been there earlier.

Sybil put down her book. "Are you sure I can't help you make up the sofa?"

"I'll be fine." William looked up from his newspaper. "Making a bed is probably the only thing I know how to do properly."

"If you need another blanket, there's one in the cupboard."

William nodded and returned to his paper.

Sybil went into the bathroom. William heard the sound of her bathwater running. A short while later, he heard a click as the latch of the bathroom door was lifted. She walked into the front room. William was surprised to see her wearing only a simple cotton wrapper; her hair, damp from her bath, was gathered at the top of her head with a tortoiseshell comb. He could feel the blood rush to his face. "Good night," she said at last, then went into her room and shut the door.

William read awhile longer, glancing up from time to time at her closed door. Finally, he put down his paper and made up the sofa with the linens and blanket she had given him. He went into the bathroom and turned the two taps by the tub so that the water flew from them furiously. He took off his clothes, and as he waited for the tub to fill, he noticed the few items on the glass shelf above the sink. Several cakes of soap, a toothbrush in a glass, a tin of tooth powder, a small covered ceramic dish filled with dusting powder, and a little dark green wooden box painted with tiny yellow flowers. William opened the box. It was filled with hairpins. He reached in and scooped up a number of them and held them tightly in his hand. He opened his palm and examined them closely, then put them back in the box. He lifted the ceramic lid from the dusting powder and breathed deeply, expecting something floral, but instead, there was the sharp, clean aroma of citrus. He smiled and put the lid back and got in the tub.

When he was done bathing, he put on his shirt to use as a nightshirt and picked up the rest of his clothes. He turned down the kerosene lamp, and went out into the front room and lay down on the sofa. He turned on his side and was surprised to see the door to Sybil's room open. The thought of her sleeping so close, just beyond the open door, made it difficult for him to fall asleep. He turned restlessly. Time passed—hours, it seemed—and still sleep eluded him through the distraction of her open door. At last he fell into a fitful sleep.

He awoke with a start when he heard the sound of breaking glass. He sat up on the sofa still half asleep and looked around. Through the window behind him, far across the open fields, he saw a red slash of dawn appearing just over the tree-tops. The sound had come from the kitchen.

"Sybil?" he called expectantly.

There was no answer.

"Sybil?" he called again. Still no answer. He was about to get up when suddenly she came running from the kitchen, moving so quickly that she seemed to be hurtling toward him. For an instant, he wondered if he were dreaming. She untied her wrapper, letting it slip from her shoulders to the floor as she moved. Before he could fully comprehend what was happening, she was kneeling naked before him on the floor. He looked at her amazed. She paused breathlessly, then reached up and took his face in her hands and kissed him, lightly at first, then passionately.

Dazed, he broke away. "What is—" he started to ask.

She shook her head. "Please." She took his hand and pressed it against her breasts.

"But . . ."

"Please," she whispered.

He looked into her eyes.

"Please," she begged.

William looked at the beautiful face before him, felt her skin next to his, warm and alive. He could feel his heart beating rapidly as feelings of desire stirred throughout his body. He brought her face close to his and kissed her, then took the comb from her hair, and it tumbled down her back. She unbuttoned his shirt and pushed it away from his shoulders. She put her hand on his chest, and he felt the intense beating of his heart against it. He kissed her again, and as she lay back against the pillows of the sofa, his hand moved gently over her thighs. She ran her fingers through his hair and stroked the side of his face. He looked at her. Her face was expressionless. She kissed him quickly. He pulled away.

"What's wrong?" he asked.

"Nothing," she whispered.

"You're sure?"

She nodded emphatically, then kissed him intensely, running her fingers over his ears.

"I love you, Sybil," he whispered, softly kissing her cheek.

She broke away and stared at him.

"What's the matter?"

She shook her head with a tentative smile.

"I love you so much," he said, stroking her

face. He cradled her head in his hands and kissed the corners of her mouth, gently tugging at her lips with his own. He raised his thumbs to her eyebrows and temples, tracing them in small circles. He kissed her cheeks and her eyelids, then ran his lips down over her neck to her breasts. He ran his hand lightly over her abdomen and her thighs, caressing her gently.

She caught her breath.

He looked into her eyes and smoothed away the hair at the side of her face. He whispered her name softly to her. She closed her eyes and he could feel her respond to the vibration of his words in her ear. She arched her back and her breath came in short, quick gasps as she laid her cheek against his shoulder. She kissed his shoulder and his neck.

Then something happened. Her body went rigid. He looked into her eyes. They were filled with terror.

"What is it?"

Her lips trembled, but no words came, then she began to cry. "Please don't," she said at last. "Please."

William pushed himself away from her and took her in his arms. "It's all right," he whispered. "It's all right." He continued to hold her, reaching for her wrapper to cover her, as he rocked her in his arms until she fell asleep.

By the time he carried her into her bedroom, the early morning sun was already beginning to fill the room. He laid her down on the bed and reached for the covers. As he was placing them around her, she opened her eyes.

"Are you all right?" he asked.

She nodded.

"I'll stay."

"No, please. Caroline is coming over with the children this morning."

William nodded, then bent down and kissed her forehead. She closed her eyes and was soon asleep again.

William returned to the front room, put on his clothes, and went into the kitchen. On the table he was surprised to find an unopened bottle of whiskey and a can of toothpowder. On the floor he saw a broken glass coated in a white powdery film. He thought back to her open bedroom door the night before. Had she wanted him to enter her bedroom? He remembered the sound of glass breaking. Was the tooth powder to hide the smell of alcohol on her breath? But why the need to drink? He recalled the blank expression on her face—a seduction that was not about pleasure or feeling, but something else—not feeling. Then that moment of terror. William sighed and began to pick up the larger pieces of glass and put them on the table.

He left the cottage. A mist still hung just above the ground, but the sun was slowly beginning to burn it away. Crocuses were in bloom, purple and gold, by the porch. He began picking them until he had a small bunch. He pulled the shoelace from one of his shoes, tied the crocuses together, and walked back into the cottage. Sybil was sleeping soundly. He left the small bouquet on the table at the side of her bed.

He went into the kitchen and put the whiskey bottle away, then took a broom and swept the broken glass into a dustpan. He found a small trash can. He lifted the top and was about to empty the bits of glass into the can when he saw two half-smoked Gitanes at the bottom. He stared at the two crushed cigarettes with their blackened ends. Arabella. He recalled how differently Sybil had behaved upon his return —asking him to stay the night. In the few hours he had been to his father's, Arabella had come and gone. What must she have said to Sybil? Sybil's behavior from the night before no longer seemed so inexplicable. He quietly poured the broken glass on top of the Gitane cigarettes, pressed the cover down, and left.

Chapter 35

The next morning William sat at his desk mulling over something he had been considering for some time: resigning from his firm. He had no intention of standing by and watching Havering and Lydia Billings, or the State for that matter, take Sybil's cottage without helping her fight them. He opened a drawer, took out an envelope he had prepared a week earlier, then pushed his chair away from his desk.

He went first to find Theodore Parrish, who was to have returned from England that day. He wanted to apologize to Theo for his rudeness back in January and to ask if he might be interested in joining him in opening their own practice. William thought he would also invite David Isaacson, their mutual friend at the firm, to join them. As he was about to enter Theodore's office, his secretary told him that Mr. Parrish had to change plans at the last minute and was not expected back for at least another three weeks.

When William entered Havering's office, Havering was reading the "Town and Country" column in *The New York Times*.

"I'm sorry, William, I'm busy," Havering said. "I can see you in an hour or so."

"This will only take a moment, Phil." William handed him the envelope.

Havering gave him an annoyed look. Still, he took the envelope and read the letter inside.

"Is this some kind of joke?"

William shook his head. "No, I'm leaving. And you may as well know, I plan to help Miss Curtis in whatever way I can."

"Are you out of your mind?" Havering glared

across his desk at William. He moved forward, ready for blood, then stopped. "Oh, I know what this is about—you're involved with the young woman. That's it."

William did not respond.

"Don't do it, William." Havering threw his newspaper aside. "You will be throwing away your career—your reputation as well."

"Lydia has no right to Miss Curtis's property."

"She needs it for the public good."

"The public good has nothing to do with this, Phil, and you know it."

"You'll accomplish nothing by resigning. At best, you'll only slow her down. Lydia Billings, William! And she has the State behind her. She could have the goddamn Statue of Liberty condemned!"

William shrugged.

Havering leaned back in his chair. "Let's forget we ever had this conversation. Take a few weeks off. When your father returns from Europe, we can discuss it."

"Phil, I am thirty-one years old. I have no intention of waiting to discuss any decision I've made with my father."

"Your father is a very dear friend of mine, William," Havering said with feeling.

His father, thought William, wouldn't know Havering if he passed him on the street.

"And I want him to know that when you came

to me and told me you wanted to throw your life away, I did everything I could to stop you."

"Tell him whatever you like."

"Of course, you know that when Lydia finds out about this, she'll bring charges against you at the Bar. She was your client and you, as her counsel, had a duty, a sworn duty to protect—" Havering pounded his desk, warming to his subject.

"Phil," William commanded.

Havering stopped and looked up, astonished. William had never spoken to him that way.

"This case was presented to me, from the beginning, in an entirely fraudulent manner. Important information was withheld and my client lied to me repeatedly. I'm not bound to it legally or ethically, and you know it." William stood.

"Is that right?"

"I'm afraid it is."

"Well, I'm going to fight you on this." Havering shot up from his chair. "The reputation of our firm is at stake, and I will use every means available to me to blacken your professional reputation and to see that you never work again!"

"Have at it, Phil."

Havering shook his head. "I think you should be locked up."

"No, you don't. Because you know the truth about what went on with Henry Billings."

"I don't know what you're talking about."

"Don't you?" William turned to leave.

"It was despicable," Havering said suddenly. "What he did." The air seemed to go out of him all at once. He waved for William to close the door. "I think you're mad, and what you are attempting is impossible. And I'm still going to fight you every step of the way." There was an odd, unreadable expression on his face. "But—and if you ever tell anyone I said this, I'll deny it—I hope you succeed."

Chapter 36

William never said a word to Arabella about her having visited Sybil Curtis. He knew she would not tell him the truth and he was not interested in hearing her lies. From the way Sybil behaved, he imagined Arabella had told her she was ruining not only a beautiful marriage, but also William's career. He wondered which approach she had used in confronting Sybil, cold and imperious or tearful and wretched. He waited a few days, then wrote to Sybil, telling her how he had found the two Gitane cigarettes and asking to see her again. When almost a week passed without a reply, he sent another letter.

Finally she answered his second letter. Her reply was in the breast pocket of his jacket as he sat on the Third Avenue El while it rattled its way downtown. "Fourteenth Street," he heard someone call out as the train pulled to a stop. He got up from the train's grimy rattan seat and walked from the platform down into the street. He stopped first in Gramercy Park, intending to see his Aunt Edith, who had recently returned from Washington. But her maid, Catherine, told him that Miss Bradford had been called away, and gave him a note his aunt had written asking if he could come by for dinner the following evening.

William walked a few blocks to the Union Square Hotel, where Henry Billings had kept Sybil. The entrance to the hotel was at the corner of Union Square and Fifteenth Street. William entered the lobby, whose faded carpet was badly worn. Brown water stains marked the wallpaper near the corners of several of the windows. A number of cheap alterations had been made to the lobby, marring its once elegant lines with work of inferior quality and craftsmanship. Permeating everything was the dank smell of a room that had not been properly cleaned or aired in many years.

"Pardon me," William said to the clerk at the front desk, "perhaps you can help me?"

The elderly man, who wore long old-fashioned whiskers, eyed him suspiciously.

"A young girl lived here some years back—about seven or eight years, I would say."

"Is that right?" the clerk replied brusquely.

"I wonder if you might remember her? Very pretty. Dark hair. Probably thirteen or fourteen."

The man shrugged.

William took out his wallet.

"You can put that away," said the man. "Who do you think you are?"

"I suppose I deserved that," William said, returning his wallet to the pocket of his spring jacket.

"Well, I've nothing to tell you."

William nodded. "I'm sorry."

"I'm sure."

William glanced at the elderly clerk. "No. I am, truly. I didn't mean to insult you."

The man twisted up his mouth and stared at William. "Maybe I do know the girl you're talking about. Was her name Cecilia or . . ."

"Sybil," said William.

"Yes, that's it. Sweet girl, rather sad. I suppose because her parents died."

"How did you know?"

"Her uncle told me. He put her up here after they died, checked on her from time to time. He had different women who would look after her. She was here for a while, then her uncle said he found a place for her. I always wondered if it was with her aunt—thought the girl meant more to her."

"Her aunt?"

"She came around a lot. Would bring her things—books, chocolates, that kind of thing." He thought for a minute. "Mrs. Spencer."

"What did she look like?"

"Tall, thin. Posh. Very posh."

"Can you tell me how old she was?"

"Sixty-some-odd I'd say. She never wanted the uncle to know she came. You know how families are. And she never saw the girl. Would just leave things for her. Odd."

"Yes," William agreed.

"Working in a hotel all these years"—the man grinned—"you see a lot of things!"

"I'm sure." William smiled politely. "Would you happen to remember anything else?"

The clerk thought for a moment. "No, that's about it."

"Well . . ." William took a deep breath. "Thank you."

He emerged from the hotel, where streetcars, motorcars, and horse-drawn wagons kicked up dust as they rumbled by the crowded noontime sidewalk. People out on their lunch hours pushed past him as he made his way across to Union Square Park and sat on a bench.

He looked back at the hotel with its row after row of sooty striped awnings, drawn down like so many drooping eyelids over its many windows. A streetcar tooted its horn loudly at a stalled motorcar nearby. William tried to fend off feelings of confusion and anger.

On the roof of a bank across the street from the park, a huge American flag fluttered in the mild spring breeze. The wide Corinthian columns of the bank's portico dwarfed the many people rushing past them. All around, the life of the city clanged and churned. He looked again at the Union Square Hotel and thought of Sybil—a mere whisper in the deafening roar—supervised, watched, and kept by Henry Billings's hired women. The woman who had brought her books and chocolates was Lydia Billings, he had no doubt. He reached into the pocket of his jacket and took out the folded piece of white paper edged in deep blue. The letter unfolded easily in his hands. His eyes traveled down to the bottom of the page:

. . . and so I have decided in the end to settle with Mr. Havering. I know you will be furious with me, and I can't in any way blame you for feeling as you must, but please know it is for the best.

I'll be leaving for England soon, and I don't know when or if I shall ever return. In any event, I think it best we not see one another again. I will never forget you, nor will I ever forget your great kindness and generosity toward me.

Please try not to think too harshly of me,
Sybil

William stared at the signature for some time, then folded the letter and returned it to his pocket.

He crossed his arms over his chest and stretched out his legs before him as the minutes ticked away. People passed, sometimes alone, sometimes in small groups, some glancing William's way before moving on. The changing light finally caused William to take out his watch. Quarter past four. He rose from the bench. His father would have just returned from Europe. William was going to see him at dinner that night and he did not want to be late. Just outside the park, he passed a post box and dropped in a letter that he had been carrying for two days, addressed to Sybil Curtis.

Chapter 37

"It's too enchanting!" Arabella exclaimed at dinner that evening. William's father had given them a painting for their new house—a full-length portrait by Joshua Reynolds of Lady Arabella Leighton, Viscountess Alanbroke, a beautiful young aristocrat in furs and silks. The painting was leaning against the dining room wall. "Wherever did you find her?" asked Arabella, studying the painting.

"An auction at Bonhams," Charles Dysart said proudly. "Cady and I fell in love with it. And when we learned her name, we knew we had to have it for you. The two of you," he added.

"It's too generous. Really! Darling"—Arabella looked to William—"shall we put it over the mantel in the ballroom?"

"The ballroom?" asked William.

"The large drawing room, I mean." Arabella turned to her mother-in law. "Thank you."

Cady Dysart smiled.

"I think I'll tell everyone she's my great-great-grandmamma. And you're not any of you to contradict me." Arabella held up a reproving finger. "And if people assume the *L* in my name stands for Leighton rather than Louise—why, we'll just let them!"

Cady Dysart took a sip of wine.

William looked at the three of them, remembering the last time they had been together in that same room.

"William," his father began casually, "I spoke to Philipse Havering this afternoon."

Cady gave William a sympathetic glance.

"He told me what a fine job you did for Consolidated. I said, of course he did, Phil, his dear old *pater* has a lot of money invested there. He's just minding his inheritance."

"William," Cady said, "how is work progressing on the house?"

He looked at her, grateful to have the conversation turn to something other than his work. "I've been so busy, Cady, I haven't had a chance to think about it."

"Well, you're going to have to start giving it a bit more of your attention," his father said. "I stopped by this afternoon. The fountain for the courtyard arrived today."

"The courtyard?" William asked.

"A later change I authorized while in Europe," his father explained. "I didn't want you bothered. I knew how busy you were."

"Did you?"

"Don't let's get into a temper," Charles Dysart goaded his son good-naturedly. "You're going to love it."

"Seems I'm bound to."

"Do you know this Warren Olness?" asked Charles, cutting into the glazed duck on his plate.

"The managing architect?" William replied. "Yes, I spoke to him a few times early on. I liked him."

Charles Dysart looked askance at his son. "Do you know he authorized the purchase of a four-hundred-year-old fountain from an Italian monastery for the courtyard—at twenty times the cost of the marble reproduction I had approved?"

"I can't believe he'd do that on his own," said William.

"Well, he did. I told Ossie Platt I wanted him removed from the project at once. Of course, Ossie tried to defend him, but then I could have told Ossie a thing or two about this Olness's lying and double-dealing."

"How extraordinary," said Arabella.

"Yes, isn't it," said Cady, her eyes fixedly on Arabella.

William's father continued on about the house and its appointments and their time in Europe as Arabella listened avidly. Cady ate in silence and William bided his time, awaiting the moment of his inevitable confrontation with his father. Charles's high spirits were so stimulated by Arabella's seemingly inexhaustible sense of delight at whatever he had to say that it was some time before the two men adjourned finally to the library.

"All right, William." His father settled down opposite him on one of the twin brown leather sofas. "I didn't say anything before, because I didn't want to embarrass Arabella, but what *exactly* has been going on here since I left?"

William looked at his father. He had changed. He was still a vigorous-looking man, but there was something different about his eyes. Where they had once been all steely blue determination, there was now a shade of doubt in them, an uncertainty in the way they darted away from William's face.

"Embarrass Arabella?" asked William. "How is that possible, Father? As I'm fairly certain that whatever it is you have to say to me, you've already discussed with her."

"Is that right!" Charles exploded. "Well, maybe

that's because she's got a brain in her head. Maybe it's because she wouldn't disgrace me the way you seem so intent on doing. I'm in Europe, and I hear that my son has gone mad in New York, resigning from his firm so he can embarrass Lydia Billings, which is nothing to the fact that he's been publicly humiliating his wife with some young woman, who—"

"Father," William cut in, "the young woman's name is Miss Curtis."

"Is it indeed?"

"Yes, one of Henry Billings's victims."

"Henry Billings's what?"

"One of the children he preyed upon."

"I don't know what you're talking about," said his father with some conviction.

"No? Do you not remember the time I was alone with Billings at Bagatelle, and you came running to find us? Why?"

His father didn't respond.

"Miss Curtis didn't have anyone to protect her."

Charles Dysart cleared his throat. "Well, I'm sorry for that, I'm sure." He sipped his drink and was quiet for a moment. "But now I gather she has taken Lydia's offer anyway, no doubt having pushed for a higher price than she would have gotten without your involvement. And where is—Miss Curtis—today?"

William glanced away from his father.

"I thought so." His father put down his drink.

"This has all been a mistake, William, but it doesn't have to be a disaster. We can repair the damage that's been done." He got up and sat next to William. "I have talked to Lydia and she's ready to forget the whole thing."

William looked at his father.

"Yes. She was marvelous," Charles confided. "Phil Havering also said he would be willing to take you back at the firm, though not right away, of course—perhaps in a year or so. In the meantime, I thought you and Arabella should go away somewhere. Although all this has been kept relatively quiet, people do talk. I think it would be best if the two of you went abroad until it has been completely forgotten. Arabella told me you had asked for a divorce, but she has agreed to overlook that, as well as everything else, to try to salvage your marriage, which I think is pretty damn splendid of her."

His father paused, waiting, it seemed, to allow William to acknowledge Arabella's valor under difficult circumstances. But when William said nothing, Charles sighed quietly and continued.

"The *Columbia* sails for Southampton in two weeks. You can stay with the Lyalls in London. I spoke to Albert Hamilton today, and he said they would be delighted to have you. I've wired the Slocums in Biarritz. They said you can have the use of their place from late summer into the fall. Not exactly the height of the season, but I think it's best that you avoid seeing people we know for now."

William gazed at the carpet in silence.

"There is no other way, William. You must realize that. Everything will be all right, you'll see." His father stood. "Well, there it is. Come to the drawing room when you're ready and we'll toast to a new beginning." He left the room.

William sat a short while longer, then rose and went into the drawing room. Cady was reading by the fire. She looked up when he entered. Arabella was sitting in a chair in a far corner of the room with Charles. William could hear only the low hum of his father's whispered words as he approached. Arabella flashed a look to his father when she saw William, and his father turned to him with such grace that for an instant William doubted the obviously conspiratorial attitude in which he had found them.

"William, I'm glad you're here," Charles said. "There is something I want to say to the two of you. I am thinking of putting half my holdings in a trust in your name."

William looked at his father, then at Arabella, whose face was as fixed and impenetrable as a mask. He looked back at his father, and although he heard the sound of his voice, he could not hear the words he spoke. He realized that whatever his father truly thought or felt was hidden forever behind those hard blue eyes. He was imprisoned there, and William wondered at the power of the demons that imprisoned him.

"I'm sorry, Father," William said. "I am not going to Europe, and I'm not going back to the firm." He turned to Arabella. "I'll send someone around tomorrow to pick up my things. The divorce will be as quiet or as sensational as you care to make it."

"I warn you, William," Arabella declared with chilling imperturbability, "I will have Miss Curtis subpoenaed."

"If you so much as utter her name to anyone, I will have Lydia Billings down on you so hard and so fast that the doors slamming to you on Fifth Avenue will sound like an earthquake. And if you doubt what I'm saying, you need only ask my father."

"You listen to me, William." Charles stood and took him by the arm. "I'm not going to let you do this."

His father's fingers pressed into the sleeve of his jacket. William was startled by the gesture. So long as he could remember, his father had never touched him.

"I'm afraid, Father," he said, "there is nothing you can do to stop me."

"You are very mistaken if you think that."

"The only thing you could possibly do, Arabella has already done." He turned to his wife. "I can only imagine what you said to Miss Curtis."

Arabella looked away with seeming indifference, slowly turning a bright platinum and diamond bracelet over and over on her wrist. "You are so ridiculous, William. If you only knew what a fool you are making of yourself."

"Which, of course, I wasn't doing all the years I was married to you." William turned to his father. "Perhaps I'll see you again?" He waited a moment for some kind of response, but when his father only looked away, he walked over to his stepmother.

She took his hand. "No, William. Not good-bye. Not to me," she said tearfully.

"No, Cady." He bent over and kissed her. "Never." He squeezed her hand, then walked out of the room.

"William," his father called to him as he stood in the hall getting his coat and hat from Rogers. Charles dismissed his butler with a wave of his hand. "I want you to know that if you leave here tonight under these circumstances, you will get nothing from me. Nothing. I won't even acknowledge you as my son. Do you understand?"

"Yes," said William.

"You can't have much. Only what your mother left you."

"I don't need much."

"Easy to say. You'll come to regret this one day." His father moved toward the drawing room.

"Father," William called, and his father turned

back with a look of triumph he could scarcely conceal. "I don't want to hurt you, but I need to know. Might things have been different between us if you had truly been my father?"

For an instant, there was a flash in his father's leaden eyes, and his lips trembled as if he were going to say something, but no sound came. He turned, but William took his arm. "Father," he said with feeling, "there may come a day when your money and all the rest are not enough. If that day should come, and you need me for any reason, please don't be too proud to call. I'll come."

Wrenching his arm away from William, his father strode back into the drawing room.

"Your poor father," said Aunt Edith over dinner when William told her what had occurred the previous evening.

"Perhaps I shouldn't have said anything," William ventured.

"Of course you should. What a terrible burden for Charles—to be so proud." Aunt Edith slowly pushed the roasted carrots to the side of her plate. "You know," she continued, "I have got to have the most atrocious cook in all New York."

"Is she new?"

"New! Forty years she has been with me. Forty years of heartburn." His aunt speared a bit of potato with her fork and eyed it coldly before putting it down. "The problem is she's so sweet, I just can't fire her. But you have cleaned your plate."

"I thought it was excellent."

"It must be the gravy. The only decent thing she makes. I'm convinced men will eat anything if the gravy is good and there is enough of it. Well . . ." His aunt pushed her chair from the table. "I think it's time we had that talk. Shall we adjourn to the parlor?" She took a bottle of brandy from a tray on the sideboard. "Do you drink brandy, William?"

"Whiskey."

She picked up a bottle of whiskey. "Here," she said, and handed him the bottles, "I think we'll need these." She took two glasses from the table and they went to her parlor. Edith sat in a chair by the fire as William poured her a brandy.

"All three of them suffered," she said, taking the brandy from him, "perhaps your father most of all." She sighed and was quiet for a moment. "Suffering sometimes makes people better, but it made your father hateful and cruel."

William sat on the floor near the fireplace with a whiskey in his hand as his aunt leaned forward in her chair, the firelight flickering over her lined, still beautiful face.

"After her fiancé died, she was pursued by so many men. She should have been left by herself to grieve for a time. But we were worried about her, she was so young and desolate. We thought the best thing was to keep her in society as much as possible. Your father was charming and very persistent. She thought he was a good man. He seemed to be. But after they married, all he wanted to do was to change her, to make a great lady of her. He wanted a woman all feathers, jewels, and perfume. That was never her way."

Aunt Edith sipped her brandy and then continued with some difficulty. "He . . . your natural father's name was Andrew Greenough . . . an artist." As his aunt spoke, William noticed how she fell easily into calling Greenough by his given name, Andrew. "Andrew had done this painting, you see . . ." She sighed, took another sip of brandy, and continued as William listened.

Chapter 38

Elizabeth Dysart was rushing to meet her aunt for lunch at the Café Brunswick on Fifth Avenue when a painting in the window of the Coleman-Bethge Gallery arrested her attention. And although she was late, she could not help stopping to stare at the small seascape, a parched yellow shore shot through with brown blurring into the blue distance of a roiling sea, the sun unseen but felt through a swirling mass of gray-white clouds. Elizabeth thought it was one of the most beautiful paintings she had ever seen. She studied it for a moment, then hurried off to meet her aunt.

After lunch, she and her aunt returned to the gallery window.

"How extraordinary," said Aunt Edith. "It's the shore as you carry it in your mind."

Elizabeth stared at the painting.

"Let's have a closer look." Aunt Edith took Elizabeth's arm.

"No, we'll only be wasting their time."

"Nonsense." Aunt Edith marched Elizabeth toward the gallery door. "If you like it, I'll buy it for you."

"Aunt Edith, no, I couldn't."

"Never mind that. Think of it as a loan. You can leave it to me in your will."

Both women laughed at so unlikely a prospect as they entered the gallery, where a young man sitting behind a desk near the door rose to greet them.

"It's remarkable, isn't it?" said Elizabeth to the young man as he handed her the painting. "So finely done." She held it carefully, examining it closely. "Who is the artist? I can't quite make out the name. Andrew something."

Aunt Edith squinted at the painting. "Looks like Greenly."

"Greenough," the young man volunteered.

"Andrew Greenough." Elizabeth looked up from the painting. "It can't be."

"Who is Andrew Greenough?" Aunt Edith asked.

"You remember him, Aunt. He gave me drawing lessons when I was a girl. Always so serious. Does he still live in New York?" Elizabeth asked, handing the painting back to the young man.

"Boston," the clerk answered as he began to wrap the painting in brown paper and twine. "He will be in New York later this month. He's doing some work on commission."

"If I give you my card," Elizabeth said, and opened the small silk bag hanging from her wrist, "will you make sure that he gets it?"

"Certainly, madam," he replied, exchanging the neatly wrapped painting for her card.

Elizabeth Dysart thought little more about the artist after leaving the gallery, but one morning more than a week later she was pleasantly surprised when it was announced that a Mr. Greenough waited downstairs to see her. The distance between their ages when she had been his student, sixteen to his twenty-four, was much greater than that between twenty-seven and thirty-five, and Elizabeth Dysart entered her drawing room expecting a much older man. She could scarcely hide her surprise when she saw the youthful artist.

"It can't be Mr. Greenough." She held out her hand to him. "Why, I thought you'd have white hair and a cane, but you have hardly changed at all."

"I can't say the same for you, Miss Bradford, or

rather Mrs. Dysart—all grown up and so elegant."

"Not elegant, surely."

"And mistress of so grand a house. Who would have thought it? I always believed you'd end up as an actress, or—"

"Circus clown."

"Something like that, yes."

"But never an artist."

"Frankly . . ." Greenough smiled and shook his head.

"You made me so nervous. You were far too stern." She laughed. "It's no wonder I expected you'd be a decrepit old thing."

They sat and talked with such ease that when Greenough finally checked his watch, they were both surprised to find that more than two hours had passed.

"I really must be going." He stood. "I have an appointment downtown at three."

"It was lovely seeing you again." She walked him to the door.

He stared at her, but in a curious way, so that he seemed not to be looking at her at all.

"What is it?" she inquired.

"I was just thinking how perfect you would be for a painting I'm starting. King Lear. I've been looking everywhere for the right model for Cordelia."

"I'm flattered, but I think there's no greater

torture on earth than sitting for an artist. I did so only once, and swore I would never do it again."

"Of course." Greenough tried to hide his disappointment. "Well, this has been one of the most pleasant—"

"No, wait," she said. "I've changed my mind. What I just said about sitting being a torture sounded like something only a spoiled, rich woman would say."

He smiled. "Well, isn't that what you—"

"Don't you dare, Mr. Greenough, or you can find yourself another Cordelia. I will ask my husband's permission tonight."

Charles Dysart, after checking and finding that Greenough was considered by many to be a genius in the manner of the English painter John Everett Millais, gave his ready assent. Elizabeth Dysart made plans to meet Greenough the following week at his studio in the mews behind the mansions of Washington Square. The studio had been provided to Greenough by Hyram MacCourey, a wealthy industrialist who had commissioned him to do a series of paintings based on scenes from Shakespeare. It was actually an old carriage house. On the ground floor, where the wide doors to the stalls had once been, a large window had been installed, filling the room with northern light. Upstairs was a small apartment where Greenough lived.

On that first day, Greenough had hired an

elderly woman from the neighborhood, a Mrs. DeAngelis, to function as a chaperone while she did her knitting. Mrs. DeAngelis assisted Elizabeth Dysart in letting down her hair and in donning the simple toga Greenough had provided. She was a delightful old woman, although she seemed on the whole to do more snoring than knitting. Not that a keen chaperone was necessary. Greenough was so intent on what he was about that when he moved Elizabeth's naked arm a certain way, or gently raised her chin with the tips of his fingers to study her face, the only sensation she experienced was comparable to that of being examined by a competent physician. And when he told her she had a beautiful profile, he said it in such a detached, appraising way that she failed to acknowledge the compliment, if that indeed was what it was.

A great deal was accomplished the first day. Andrew thanked Elizabeth for being patient and for never once complaining about the contorted position she was obliged to hold. Everything proceeded without incident for the three weeks she sat for him. He was charming, very funny, and incredibly thoughtful. He would do anything for her comfort and that of Mrs. DeAngelis. He always had lunch brought in, and they broke again for tea in the afternoon. Each day, they would talk for hours as he worked.

On the last day of her sitting, Elizabeth had just

finished dressing back into her street clothes. As she emerged from the small room she used to change, she saw Mrs. DeAngelis standing in front of the painting, looking at the finished figure of Cordelia for the first time. There was an excited expression on her face.

"Do you like it, Mrs. DeAngelis?" Elizabeth asked, smoothing down her collar.

"Bellissimo. This man"—she pointed emphatically to Greenough—"is an Italian."

"Is that true, Mr. Greenough?" asked Elizabeth.

"In my heart, yes."

"May I see it?" she asked.

"My heart?" he asked slyly.

Elizabeth smiled and went to look at the painting for the first time. She stared at it for a moment before saying anything. She looked finally to Mrs. DeAngelis and whispered, "Bellissimo."

"I told you!" Mrs. DeAngelis clasped her hands.

Andrew smiled broadly.

"It's so beautiful, Andrew." Elizabeth looked at him with undisguised admiration. "Truly."

"I'm glad you like it."

"My only criticism is that you've made me far prettier than I am."

"No." Mrs. DeAngelis would not hear it. "This is not true."

"That would hardly be possible," said Andrew Greenough.

"Did you hear that, Mrs. DeAngelis? What he says to all his models."

Soon after, Mrs. DeAngelis kissed them both good-bye and left. Elizabeth picked up her bag to leave. She turned to Greenough. "Thank you, Andrew, for these past few weeks."

"Thank you."

"I hope it won't be another ten years before I see you again."

"No," he answered.

How sad he looked, Elizabeth thought. He seemed to read her mind, and smiled to hide his look of unhappiness, but only succeeded in making himself look more bereft. It occurred to Elizabeth Dysart then that perhaps Andrew Greenough was a little in love with her. The thought made her feel very uneasy, and at that moment she was thankful that her sitting for him was at an end.

It was not until the following Monday, when she would normally have gone to sit for him, that she realized that perhaps she, too, was a bit in love with Andrew Greenough. She tried to ignore her feelings, but by that very evening she was miserable. The next day, the sensation was worse. By the following Monday, she could bear it no longer. She decided to go to visit Greenough, if only to free herself of the longing—a strange kind of madness—which she thought seeing him in the cold light of day would cure.

Andrew was amazed when he looked up from his canvas and saw her standing outside his studio.

"Elizabeth!" He opened the door to let her in.

"I feel perfectly ridiculous about all this. If I had my way, I would walk away from here and never return. But it seems"—she began to cry—"I've lost my way."

Andrew led her to a chair. "What is it?" he asked with concern.

"I feel I have to tell you something," she said, sitting down. "But how can I, when I know I'll only appear foolish in your eyes if I do?"

Still, she was a woman totally incapable of pretense. She told Greenough exactly how she felt, and was astonished when he confessed to having been in love with her from the time she was his student. They became lovers that afternoon. After two months she could not bear to be apart from him, and asked her husband for a divorce.

She and Charles Dysart had been married for five years, and for most of that time he had treated her with little more than indifference, caring, it seemed to her, far more for his many business interests. His initial reaction was outrage, which she took merely for wounded pride. Soon, however, it became clear that his pride hid far deeper feelings for her than she had ever suspected. He pleaded with her not to leave him, promising her anything if she would stay. For weeks she was torn between her duty to her

319

husband and her love for Andrew Greenough. In the end, she could not justify leaving her husband, no matter her feelings for the artist.

On the day that Andrew Greenough left New York to return home to Boston, Elizabeth Dysart became deeply depressed and was unable to get up from her bed. Charles Dysart was never more tender toward her. She soon became physically ill as well, and a physician was sent for. She would be fine, Dr. Sayres announced to the much-relieved Charles Dysart, then congratulated him. His wife was pregnant.

Charles Dysart stared at Dr. Sayres and walked out of the room. The baby was not his, he knew; he and his wife had been estranged for too many months for that to be the case.

He tried desperately to rise above his feelings of betrayal, but when his wife's body began to swell with the life within her, there were times when the very sight of her could make him physically ill. He had never allowed himself to think of her physical infidelity to him, but the proof of it now was always before him, distorting her body and growing every day more obvious. When he could tolerate it no longer, he sailed for Europe, and did not return until after the baby was born. He was by then a far different man. Where before he might have been merely unkind, he was now cruel, and what once had been simmering anger against his wife grew to a kind of hatred.

Six years after William was born, his mother met Andrew Greenough at the home of a friend whose portrait he had painted. It was then that Greenough learned of the existence of his son and of Elizabeth's wretched life. They met again after that, and decided to leave together for London. On the day they were to depart, William, who was to have been taken to the waiting couple by Elizabeth's maid Anna, was locked in his room. Apparently the plan had been uncovered by one of the house maids, who made a habit of reading her mistress's mail. She had alerted her employer to the plot, so that when Anna went to get the boy, she found his door locked and a Pinkerton guard waiting to intercept her. Charles Dysart told his wife that she would never again enter his house or see her son. Elizabeth Dysart engaged a lawyer to fight her husband, but distraught at the loss of her son and worn down by years of her husband's vindictiveness, she grew seriously ill. Her condition quickly worsened, and she died of pneumonia less than three months after leaving her husband's house.

Chapter 39

Three days after dinner with his aunt, William was sitting at a desk at the St. Regis Hotel, where he had taken a room until he could find an apartment, going over what little information he had been able to find about Andrew Greenough. Rays from the sun setting over the Hudson River cut through the Venetian blinds at the window, filling the room with an amber glow that split the floor and walls into crisscrossing lines of shadow and light.

William opened the desk drawer to get a pen and saw the letter he had sent to Sybil Curtis. It had been returned to him from Long Island unopened. He glanced at his handwriting—a name and an address written by a more hopeful person. He began to make notes about Andrew Greenough in a small copybook. *Andrew Greenough*, he wrote at the top of the first page. He looked at the name, then wrote *father* in parentheses.

There was a knock at the door.

"Yes?" William called distractedly.

"A letter for you, sir," said a voice through the door.

William signed for the letter and tipped the porter. The name "H. MacCourey" was written on the envelope. He quickly tore it open. He had managed to find MacCourey, who lived in Brooklyn Heights, through a friend of his aunt's. MacCourey wrote that he remembered Andrew Greenough well. Greenough had painted four pictures for him, based on scenes from Shakespeare, which MacCourey was sorry to relate he could not show William as they hung at his summer house in Maine. He ended by inviting William to call anytime he liked.

William put the letter in his desk drawer, then rushed to bathe. He wanted to see Lydia Billings that evening; her secretary, Olivia, had said Lydia would only be able to meet with him for a short while around eight o'clock.

She was magnificently gracious when she entered her drawing room later that evening. Apparently his father had not yet spoken to her.

"So, William, is our little *contretemps* at an end? No one could be happier than I. Truly." She moved across the room in a slim black evening dress and around her shoulders was a shawl of some filmy material. Rubies surrounded by small clusters of diamonds sparkled at her ears, matching a diamond and ruby necklace at her throat. She checked suddenly for something in the small, beaded bag she carried. "Had you come a moment later," she said, "you would have missed me entirely." She closed the bag and looked up with a smile. "I am attending a crush at the Montgomerys'. Yes, I know. Frightful bore. But Alfie and Gloria Glendinning will be there, and they are always such fun. In fact"—she paused, a happy thought occurring to her—"why don't you join me? Yes. I'll make you a drink. We'll send for your evening clothes, and you can be my escort. Arabella will forgive me. After all, I have forgiven her for being so beautiful. Well"—she pouted flirtatiously—"not entirely. When, by the way, are the two of you leaving for Europe?"

"We're not going to Europe."

"Oh?" Lydia's voice lost much of its music.

"No, Lydia."

She looked at William for a long moment. "I see." She turned toward her drawing room door. "Hammond will see you out, William. As I said, I'm running a bit late."

"Please sit down, Lydia. I'll be brief."

She continued toward the door.

"Lydia, unless you want me to go to the newspapers with everything I know about Mr. Billings, you will talk to me."

"Don't threaten me, William." She held the drawing room door open for him. "Good-bye."

"Very well." William went to the door.

"She is a liar, of course." Lydia's eyes burned through him. "Everything she says is a lie."

"You mean like being a shop girl in Burford?"

"Oh, William." Lydia smiled indulgently. "I have neither the time nor the inclination to play

324

these games with you. Please give the young lady my regards the next time you see her. I understand the two of you are quite friendly."

"As you wish." William turned to leave.

"She is sick. I feel sorry for her."

"Is that why you brought her books and candies when he kept her at the Union Square Hotel?"

Their eyes met. Lydia turned and walked away.

William closed the drawing room door and went to her.

She sat on the sofa, her shawl slipping from her shoulders. "He wasn't doing what they said."

"What about Dr. Keating, Lydia?"

For a moment her face froze in a look of horror. Her lips trembled. Her shoulders began to shake, but she uttered hardly a sound. She reached into her bag for a handkerchief. "What are you going to do?"

"It's what you're going to do, Lydia."

She nodded. "What do you want?"

"I want you to telephone Philipse Havering tomorrow morning and have him draw up a letter to Miss Curtis, telling her that she may keep her property, or go through with the original offer of sale, as she decides. And I want your word that you will not, under any circumstances, trouble her ever again."

"Very well." Lydia raised the handkerchief to her eyes.

"With the letter from Philipse Havering, I want

you to include a handwritten letter of apology to Miss Curtis."

"How can I, William?" she pleaded, looking up at him. "If anyone should see it . . ."

"Lydia, I'm sure you can find a way to write something that will be understood only by the two of you."

She nodded. "Anything else?"

"No."

"Money?"

"How much do you think would be enough?" She sighed.

"The letters are to be delivered to Miss Curtis by no later than tomorrow evening."

"Of course."

William was about to leave.

"Please don't go."

"I'm sorry," he said abruptly.

She looked at him with her red-rimmed eyes, nodded, and tried to smile. How small and frail she looked on the sofa. Her shoulders drooped and her shawl gathered around the soft, protruding roundness of her abdomen, something normally hidden by her warlike posture. For the first time Lydia looked to William like an old woman. He thought of the books and chocolates— unforgivable and pathetic at once.

"I suppose I could use a drink," he said.

"Really?" She brightened. "I'll ring for Hammond."

By the time Lydia set off for the party at the Montgomerys', her shawl was thrown rakishly over her shoulder. William heard later from people attending the party that she had laughed uproariously at the shenanigans of Alfie and Gloria Glendinning, and had even insisted, to the delight of all present, that stuffy old Alden Montgomery do a Turkey Trot with her. Philipse Havering, who was also at the party that evening, was astonished, he later told William, to be awakened at six thirty the following morning by a telephone call from an icy-voiced and rather frightening Lydia Billings. She dictated word for word the terms of a letter to be sent to Miss Curtis, offering her several very generous options in regard to the disposition of her property. The letter, typed on the firm's letterhead and signed by Havering, was, Lydia insisted, to be at her door no later than four o'clock that afternoon. It arrived as directed, and was driven out, along with Lydia's personal note to Sybil Curtis by Lydia's chauffeur that same afternoon.

Chapter 40

Two weeks later, William saw Philipse Havering pushing his way toward him through a crowd of men at a bachelor dinner in the Red Room at Delmonico's.

Havering said something, but William could not

hear the words over the din of a minstrel band playing. They walked out into the hall.

"I met Miss Curtis yesterday," Havering said.

"In New York?"

Havering nodded as William tried to hide his profound disappointment. So she had been in New York, but had not contacted him.

"She came in to sign papers," said Havering. "Lydia insisted on paying her the full ten thousand dollars she originally offered. *Lydia,*" Havering intoned, "a great lady of the old school. Well, I think I'll freshen my drink." Havering turned, then paused. "I must say Miss Curtis is a lovely young woman. I was very impressed. Apparently she's leaving for London."

As Havering walked away, William felt suddenly desolate. Putting down his glass, he walked out of Delmonico's to the thumping sounds of banjoes, violins, and tambourines.

Although his mood didn't improve, William followed through with his plans to meet the MacCoureys the next afternoon. He drove across the Brooklyn Bridge to their red brick and brownstone home on Garden Street in Brooklyn Heights.

"Thank you so much for agreeing to see me," William said as he sat across from the MacCoureys, a handsome couple in their early seventies, in the parlor of their house. Hyram MacCourey was once a major partner in United

Petroleum of Ohio, but here he lived modestly with his wife, Florence. He had accumulated a vast amount of money, but his needs were simple, and he hoped to use the bulk of his fortune to establish a library dedicated to Shakespeare, a passion he shared with his wife.

MacCourey had taken out some scrapbooks to show William. He was sure he had a picture of Greenough, he just wasn't certain where. "So, what sparked your interest in Andrew Greenough? Have you one of his paintings?" MacCourey asked as he stood over a scrapbook, looking through it carefully with a magnifying glass.

"No, I haven't. My aunt told me about him. Perhaps someday I'll buy something of his."

Hyram MacCourey nodded without lifting his eyes from the scrapbook.

"Well, they've become quite valuable," said Florence MacCourey, "especially since he died."

"When did he die?"

"Around 1889, I would say." Hyram MacCourey glanced up at William.

"That's right. Hard to believe. Almost twenty-five years now," Mrs. MacCourey added. "Such a dear man, wasn't he, Mr. MacCourey?"

"Yes," MacCourey agreed, fingering the leather cover of the photo album. "Rather a sad case. He was doing a painting for me. Lady Macbeth. Said he just couldn't finish it. I think he had a nervous shock of some kind. A year or so later, I heard from his agent that he had died. In Boston, I believe."

"Poor man," said Mrs. MacCourey.

"Oh, look!" exclaimed Hyram MacCourey. "I found him. Two pictures, in fact."

William went to look at the scrapbook.

"Here." MacCourey pointed to two sepia-toned albumen prints. "You see?" One was a side view of a man sitting in a wicker chair on a sun porch. There was too much natural light, and it was difficult for William to get a real impression of his father's features. But he could see that they had the same build.

"That was taken at our house in Maine," said MacCourey. "He had stopped up from Boston to see us. This one was taken in his studio near Washington Square. He's standing by a painting of Lear and Cordelia he did for me."

"That's my mother," said William. "Cordelia." He looked at the artist standing proudly by his finished canvas. The face in the print was quite clear, and in it he saw he had his father's brow and nose. The eyes were different, it was true, and his father was fairer than he. But despite those differences, William felt as if he were looking at a version of himself.

"Your mother posed for Cordelia?" William heard Florence MacCourey ask. "But that can't be Cady Dysart."

"No." William turned to her. "Cady is my

stepmother. My mother was my father's first wife. She died quite young."

"Oh, I am sorry, I didn't know." Mrs. MacCourey looked closely at the painting in the photograph, then at William. "Yes, of course, it's the eyes. Why, you look just like her."

"And I was just going to say," said MacCourey, "how much he reminds me of Greenough. I mean, the way you talk and move. Don't you think so, Flo?"

Mrs. MacCourey turned a smiling face to William.

"I mean . . ." Hyram MacCourey paused.

Mrs. MacCourey's smile faded.

"No," MacCourey stammered, "on second thought . . . not really."

All at once, his wife's smile reappeared in all its brilliance. "As I recall, Mr. Dysart, we invited you to lunch. Well," she said, taking William's arm and walking with him toward the dining room, "I believe lunch is now being served."

Later, when he was leaving, Mrs. MacCourey handed him a small envelope. "Mr. MacCourey and I want you to have this," she said.

Once outside, William opened the envelope. In it was the albumen print of his father in his studio, standing by the painting of his Cordelia.

Chapter 41

The next day William decided to drive out to Sybil's cottage. He felt he had to see her, if only to say good-bye. Pulling into her driveway around noon, he saw that the porch had been removed and the windows boarded up. William felt as if he were looking at the mutilated body of a dear friend. He wondered where she could be, and his heart sank as he thought she might already have sailed for England. He looked out and saw the old maple tree. That at least remained.

The supple grass of spring bent easily underfoot as he set off across the broad field to the old tree, now a lime haze of soft green on the horizon. Honeysuckle sprouted here and there in improbable mounds as bees hovered over white and brown flowers blooming in bunches above deep green patches of clover. The sun, high in the sky overhead, filled the air with warmth and an almost palpable optimism, but William felt miserable as he approached the sheltering old tree.

"Oh," was all he could think to say when he found Sybil reading there.

"Mr. Dysart." She rose from the bench.

"I'm glad to find you here. I mean after seeing the cottage the way it is. Sad."

"Yes."

"When do you leave?"

"In three days." Sybil sat down again.

"Would you mind if I stayed for a moment?"

She shook her head and made room for him on the bench.

William put his hat on the ground. He leaned forward and tapped the tips of his fingers on his knees. He had planned to say so many things to her, but now it seemed that all that was left to him were scraps and bits of a once beautiful piece of cloth.

A mild breeze made the branches of the old tree sway overhead. "It's so clear you can see all the way to Connecticut," he said finally.

She leaned away from him. He looked out again at the water. "Sybil, what did my wife tell you when she came to see you?"

There was a long silence. "I can't say," she answered finally.

"Let me guess then. That I was making a fool of myself. That I had been, until I met you, a devoted husband, she a devoted wife, and my father devoted to us both. Or something like that?" He turned to her. "Three very unhappy people for all that devotion. And I imagine she spoke of my ruination, damnation, and all the rest." William paused. "I suppose," he continued, looking out again at the water, "in the end it doesn't matter what she said." He rubbed his hands together. "I have made mistakes in my life. I've been vain and arrogant and proud. And I have gotten the life I deserve." He turned. Sybil's eyes scanned his face. "I'm still vain and arrogant, but not nearly so proud."

A lovely half smile lit up her face.

"It's hard to live life with any real dignity, isn't it? Day in, day out. I never truly realized that until I met you."

"Me?"

He nodded. "I don't believe I've ever met anyone quite like you. No," he said to himself, glancing away. "You have a light—a light that nothing can darken." William heard the water splashing in small waves against the beach below. "Sybil"—he looked down—"please don't go. Please stay."

"I'm sorry."

"Why?"

She shook her head.

William took a deep breath. He turned around to say something, and saw her gazing at him intently. She stood then, and moved a short distance away.

"What is it?"

"I think you should go now."

"Is that what you want? What you really want?"

She nodded but wouldn't meet his eyes.

He walked over and stood behind her. "I . . ." He reached for her hand and held it. "I will never stop loving you. Never," he repeated, releasing her hand. He went to pick up his hat. The sounds of his steps rustling the ground cover barely broke the stillness. It ceased for a moment as he stopped to look at her one last time. He turned finally and left.

Returning to New York that afternoon, William lived like a recluse in his hotel room at the St. Regis, venturing out only at night to walk the city for hours. On the day she left for England, he went to Grand Central Station and caught an express train to New Haven, Connecticut, to prevent himself from rushing to the West Side piers to see her one last time. When the train made one of its few stops in Stamford, a half hour out of New York City, he got up impulsively to get off, but forced himself back to his seat. Arriving back at his hotel room that night, he brought a bottle of whiskey with him.

He poured himself a drink and raised the Venetian blinds at the window, where he watched the flow of people, motorcars, and omnibuses moving up and down Fifth Avenue far below, gray shadows flitting in the night, white lights, the din and laughter. He sat with his feet up on the desk and poured himself another drink. Suddenly a thought occurred to him. He took several sheets of hotel stationery and began to write. *Dear Sybil.* He mused for a moment, trying to organize his thoughts. He sipped his drink then crossed it out. *Dearest Sybil*, he began again and wrote furiously, drinking all the while, as he tried to convey in a letter the depth of his feelings—to use just the right words—that she might reconsider and return to New York.

William awakened the next afternoon on the floor, still dressed in his clothes. He pressed his hands to his throbbing temples. He had a crushing headache and a queasy sensation in his stomach. Pages and pages of the letter were spread all around him. He read what little of it he could decipher and was embarrassed and depressed by it. He poured the remainder of the whiskey down the sink, got into bed, and stayed there until early the next morning.

He then shaved and bathed, walked uptown, and got his car. Without hesitation—almost without conscious thought—he drove straight to the Adirondacks, hours and hours north of the city, where his father, Andrew Greenough, had left him a small cabin. He arrived late at night in the town of Saranac Lake, and took a room in a small hotel there.

"Can you tell me how to get to Moody Pond?" William asked the waiter at breakfast the next day.

"Not far from here," the man said, pouring William's coffee, "just take Route 3 out of town to Pine."

He arrived at his father's cabin at eleven o'clock that morning. The property was completely overgrown, but the log cabin standing upon it, with a peaked-roof porch and matching peaked dormers—grander than what William had expected—was in surprisingly good shape. He tried the two rusted keys that had been with the deed from Andrew Greenough's lawyers, but neither worked. Finally, he broke a small window to get inside. The cabin was empty. He had been hoping to find furniture or books, something that might give him a sense of who his father had been, but the man eluded him. He slept on the floor that night and the next morning went into Saranac Lake to buy furniture and provisions.

The next few weeks William spent cleaning up the cabin, clearing away vines and trees, moving rocks and cutting wood, so that by the end of each day he was so exhausted that all he could do was fall into bed. In the mornings he would fish and swim naked in the frigid waters of the pond. After six weeks there, he returned to New York and found a flat in a small apartment house on West Twelfth Street. He had been in the flat for two weeks when he heard that Theodore Parrish had finally returned home.

It was a sunny afternoon in mid-June. William stood on the front stoop of Theodore and Lucie's red brick town house on East Tenth Street with a bottle of champagne in one hand and a bunch of roses and tulips in the other.

Their maid, Dymphna, answered the door.

"Good afternoon, Dymphna, I was wondering if Mr. or Mrs.—"

At that moment Theodore strode into the hallway. He stared at William.

William looked past Dymphna. "Do you think you might forgive a bad-tempered old sod?"

Theodore went to the door. He looked at William, then took the bottle of champagne and examined it. "This is cheap champagne."

"The hell it is," said William.

Theodore laughed and threw an arm around William's shoulder. "Come on in, you old jackass. Lucie, come see who's here."

Lucie stepped into the hall. "William!" She ran to William and threw her arms around him.

He handed her the flowers. "From the fighting Orton sisters, proprietors of the florist shop around the corner."

"Aren't they the dearest old things?"

"I suppose, if by dear you mean conning every customer who comes through their door into mediating their battles?"

William sat with the Parrishes in their front parlor and drank champagne, then stayed to dinner. Dymphna made her specialty, terrapin cooked in Madeira wine. After dinner, they sat around the dining room table, talking. William proposed his plan to Theodore for opening their own legal practice. Theodore was intrigued but cautious. Lucie was all for the idea immediately. Then William told them he had left Arabella.

"Is that why you're blue?" asked Lucie.

"He's not blue," said Theodore. "Are you, Will? Women."

"It's called sensitivity, darling. Men usually have it beaten out of them by the time they're five years old."

"If I am blue, it's not because of Arabella."

"Someone else?" asked Lucie.

William hesitated. "Yes," he said finally.

"The woman who was with Albert Penniman the night of the ball?" asked Theodore.

"Yes, it is, in fact."

"I thought it was you."

William looked at him curiously.

"You didn't see it? The blind item in *Town Topics*?" Theodore went to the drawing room. He returned with a copy of the magazine and began to read:

A rumor has begun to circulate around the precincts of Fifth Avenue that on a recent evening the dark-haired scion of one of New York's oldest families went to see the fair-haired son of an even older one. When our dark-haired friend arrived at the home of the fair, he was told by Mr. Fair's butler that Mr. Fair was not at home. Whereupon Mr. Dark pushed his way into the house of Mr. Fair and cornered him in his library. The butler and housemaid, hearing much moving of furniture and breaking of glass, called the police.

"William." Lucie looked at him, astonished. "You didn't."

"Don't believe everything you read."

"No, not everything, Mr. Dark. There's more." Theodore continued:

No charges have been filed. Mr. Fair, much battered and bruised the next day, claimed merely to have fallen from the ladder in his library. And people knowing his fondness for drink, if not the farther reaches of his library, are inclined to believe him. But why does Mr. Fair now drop always into doorways, cross streets, and turn corners whenever he sees Mr. Dark? Some say Mr. Fair was having an assignation with Mr. Dark's wife. But this idea has been roundly dismissed, based on the impeccable reputation of that most estimable and, if we might be allowed, staggeringly beautiful young lady.

Theodore put down *Town Topics*. "Arabella can't be seeing Bertie Penniman."

William looked down and shook his head. He glanced up to see Lucie giving her husband a wide-eyed reproving look and he was thankful to her that there would be no further talk of Arabella or Albert Penniman. But he was wrong.

"Frankly, Will"—Theodore frowned—"I think they deserve each other. I never really cared for

Arabella. And Lucie—well, she's always said she doesn't think Arabella has an honest bone in her body."

"Teddy! Honestly. I am so sorry, William."

"It's all right." William took a sip of wine.

"She is beautiful." Theodore poured himself more wine. "Perfect, in fact."

"Perfect! The very idea," said Lucie. "Men are so . . ."

"Yes, I know," said Theodore with resignation, "foolish."

"Ridiculous."

"Right. Women are foolish."

"They must be, or they would have had the vote years ago."

"Is there anything—anything at all—you can't relate back to the vote?"

"All right." Lucie laughed.

Theodore leaned forward, took his wife's hand, and kissed it. "Is Arabella seeing anyone?"

"Darling, you don't ask questions like that," said Lucie.

"It's all right," William answered. "I don't think so, but I don't think she'll be alone for long."

"No?" asked Lucie.

"No!" said Theodore.

"Why do you say 'no' like that?" Lucie asked. "It's always the sex thing with men, isn't it?"

"Oh, Mrs. Parrish," said Theodore. "The sex thing. Did you hear that, Will?"

Lucie frowned at her husband. "I thank God women are too sensible to be blinded by things like physical beauty."

"But I thought you were blinded by my beauty." Theodore kissed his wife's hand again.

"Be sensible, dear. It is true, William," said Lucie, "I didn't like her."

"It certainly didn't stop you from trying to get her to join one of your committees," said Theodore.

"Of course. Who better to swing the men to our side?" Lucie reached over and ran her fingers through her husband's hair. "Honestly, darling, sometimes I think I did marry you for your beauty."

Chapter 42

As word of his impending divorce from Arabella spread, William found it more and more difficult to stay in New York, and considered leaving for the summer. He was thinking of several possible alternatives as he crossed Forty-fourth Street on Fifth Avenue, when he heard a woman's voice calling to him. He looked around and realized finally it was coming from an open window at Delmonico's restaurant. Alice Bourden was waving to him from a table just inside the window. She was having lunch with Eugenia Beckwith.

"Mr. Dysart, please come and join us. Do. If only for a moment."

Not having a ready excuse, William decided the easiest thing would be to just sit with the two women for a few minutes. As he entered the restaurant, he thought how happy they must be to have spotted him—better than dessert, the latest news on a scandal from one of the principal participants.

"Here we are, William." Alice Bourden waved to him with her napkin.

He walked through the crowded dining room toward the two women. Wearing boldly patterned dresses, their faces hidden by large hats pinned at precipitously stylish angles, they might easily have been mistaken for two rather large, comfortable chairs. They held out their hands to him. A mild breeze lifted the gauzy curtains at a nearby window.

"Please sit." Eugenia Beckwith patted the chair next to her. "Have some pastry?" She pushed a small ornate silver tray with various pastries toward him.

"I'm sorry, I can only stay a moment," said William, sitting down.

Alice Bourden gazed at him, then sighed dramatically. "Mr. Dysart, is it true you are starting your own law practice with the Parrish boy?"

"We have been discussing it," said William.

"Mind me." Eugenia Beckwith tapped the table with her finger. "If Lucie has her way, you'll find yourselves knee-deep in every manner of unpleasantness. Labor. Women's rights."

"Anarchists of every stripe." Alice frowned.

William shrugged.

"You'll see." Eugenia Beckwith's finger took to the air. "You will have very few of the right sort of people as clients, and those you do have will be the usual cranks."

"But Mrs. Beckwith," said William, "I'm one of the usual cranks."

Eugenia Beckwith flashed a look of wonder to Alice Bourden. "And do I understand," she resumed after a short silence, "one of your partners is a Mr. Isaacsman?"

"Isaacson."

"William, really!" said Alice Bourden.

"Pardon me?"

Eugenia looked to Alice and sighed. "This sort of insouciance is all the rage now with the young. Don't pretend, Mr. Dysart, you don't know that the Hebrews are taking over New York."

"And they will ruin it," Alice joined in, "just as certainly as the Irish have ruined Boston." She picked up the last raspberry tartin and finished it off. "I really must steal Delmo's pastry chef. Do you think they would mind, Eugenia?"

"Henri told me they scoured all of France for Yves."

"Yves. How romantic! His pastry is heavenly. William, you must have some. Please."

"Actually, I have to—"

"Try the prune whip." Eugenia slid the silver tray across the snow-white tablecloth toward him. "Now let's get down to the matter at hand."

"Yes," said Alice. "What is all this nonsense we hear about you and your lovely wife?"

"That depends on what nonsense you've heard."

Alice Bourden dove for the last prune whip.

"D-I-V-O-R-C-E," spelled Eugenia. "Is there nothing that can be done, William?" she asked as she unceremoniously pulled the pastry tray to her side of the table. "How could you think of leaving so lovely a wife? She is an angel."

"I adore her," said Alice.

"Your mother must be livid," Eugenia added. "I can't believe for a minute she would approve such a thing."

"Actually," said Alice, "I believe Cady is William's stepmother."

"Yes, of course," said Eugenia, "your mother was . . ."

"Elizabeth Bradford."

"Any relation to Edith Bradford?"

"Her niece." William stood. "Good day, ladies."

"That explains everything," he heard Eugenia whisper loudly to Alice.

In the end, William decided to stay in New York for the summer after all. He found offices for the new firm of Dysart, Isaacson & Parrish in the Flatiron Building on Twenty-third Street, with views from its sixth-floor windows of Madison Square Park. David Isaacson was the first to join him, with Theodore coming on a few weeks later. For a short while they made do with a temporary secretary, then Theodore suggested they should ask Miss Leary if she might be interested in working for them. William called her. She would be happy to join them, she said, if they would agree to an increase in her salary.

"After all, Mr. Dysart, I'll be working for three men instead of one," she pointed out, then added briskly: "One a flirt, one who's moody, and one who is far too grave. I'll certainly have my work cut out for me."

William was surprised at Miss Leary's new assertiveness and wondered which of the three she thought him. He agreed to the increase, and Miss Leary came to work for them in August. She set up her desk and had the entire office running efficiently within two weeks of her arrival. She hired someone to clean the place once a week and on the Wednesday of her second week there, William came in to find workmen taking down the curtains at the windows and replacing them with Venetian blinds.

"Blinds?" said William. "I had no idea."

"I could hardly wait until the three of you got around to approving them, Mr. Dysart. Really!

Those curtains." She turned back to her typing. "Your coffee and roll are on your desk."

For the first few weeks there was little work, then things began to improve. David Isaacson was asked to represent the family of one of the victims of the Triangle Shirtwaist Factory fire. One hundred and forty-eight victims, mostly poor working girls, had died the year before when the exit on the top floor of the building where they worked was locked during a horrific fire, forcing many of them to jump to their deaths from the ninth floor. Soon other victims' families came to him until he represented ten families in a civil suit filed after the owners of the factory had been acquitted in a criminal trial.

Theodore Parrish handled trusts and estates, and the eight clients who came at first, family and friends, were quickly joined by others on the basis of his skill and personable manner. William's first important case came in early September. Eleonora Paxman, a very pretty young woman from a well-to-do Upper West Side family, came into his office. Phil Havering had recommended that she see William. William was amazed when Mrs. Paxman told him she had just been released from prison on bail and was about to stand trial for the murder of her husband.

"Can you tell me how it happened?" asked William, getting up to close the door. "Everything."

"My husband beat me," Mrs. Paxman began. "Often. One night he was drunk. He held a knife to my throat, saying he was going to kill me. I managed to get away and struck him with a baseball bat."

"Where did you strike him?"

She raised her hand to the back of her head.

"Once?"

Mrs. Paxman nodded. "I hated him, but I didn't mean to kill him." She started to cry.

William interviewed her servants, none of whom had a kind word to say about the late Mr. Paxman, and all of whom were willing to testify on Mrs. Paxman's behalf. The baseball bat, of course, suggested premeditation, but Mrs. Paxman said she had only bought it to defend herself. William was certain he could win an acquittal for her.

The first few days of the trial were unremarkable and attracted little press attention. Then it was learned that Eleonora Paxman's mother was a colored woman. Suddenly photographers and reporters appeared at the courthouse steps. Mrs. Paxman became an "African temptress" and William her "socialite lawyer." News of his impending divorce from Arabella—the facts distorted or simply fabricated—fed the madness. Speculation that William and his client, now a "Namibian princess," were having an affair ran rampant.

"How was your night at Lula's?" Theodore walked into William's office one morning with a copy of the *New York World*.

"Where?" William looked up from his desk.

Theodore opened the paper and read: "Attorney William Dysart was reported seen leaving Lula's, the notorious Harlem cathouse, early this morning with client Eleonora Paxman on his arm. No doubt the swanky lawyer spent the night there interrogating the sable Cleopatra."

"They have no shame," said William.

"You should talk," David Isaacson called into the room. "Today's *Journal* says you and Mrs. Paxman ravished each other under a lamppost on Mott Street after getting stoned at a nearby opium den."

"You really ought to slow down, Will," said Theodore.

The next day there was even an allusion to William's involvement with Sybil Curtis, appearing as a blind item in the *Sun*, but that was quickly quashed (by Lydia Billings, William later learned). William managed to ignore the insanity during the four-week run of the trial and in the end Mrs. Paxman was found not guilty. She left for Paris the next day, swearing never to return to the United States.

One benefit of the trial was the notoriety it bought Dysart, Isaacson & Parrish. For William, it was exciting to come to work each day. He loved the sense of camaraderie with Theodore, David, and Miss Leary. But at the end of each day, he could not completely shake his sense of loss at a life that might have been.

Miss Leary hired an assistant and soon began to dress and do her hair in a more sophisticated way. Once a sweet-looking young woman, she blossomed into a very pretty one. William's only worry was that she didn't seem to care for David Isaacson. She would banter with Theodore and William, but never David, and when he spoke to her, her manner grew cold to the point of rudeness. William wondered if it was because Isaacson was Jewish. He considered talking to her about it, but as Isaacson never mentioned it, he decided to let the matter stand. Then one day in November, she came into his office in tears.

"What is it?" asked William. Miss Leary had never impressed him as a woman who cried easily.

"David," she said.

"Isaacson?"

"Yes." She sobbed.

"What did he do?"

David Isaacson walked in. "I asked her to marry me and she has accepted."

Miss Leary jumped up and hugged him.

"We have been seeing each other secretly," he said over her shoulder.

They planned to be married either at her church, Saint Cecilia's in Greenpoint, or at Temple

Emanuel, but when both church and temple—abetted by family and friends—raised insurmountable barriers to their being together, they married at City Hall. William was Isaacson's best man, and Miss Leary's friend Kitty her maid of honor.

His divorce from Arabella was granted in December. His father, who had not spoken to him since William left his house, put the still unfinished mansion he was having built for William and Arabella on the market. Cady met William for dinner one evening at the Palm Room of the Waldorf-Astoria.

"I insisted he sell it," said Cady, cutting into her lemon sole. "Arabella—divorce or no—was trying to talk him into leasing it to her for nothing. Nothing!" Cady set down her knife and fork. "Have you heard anything at all from that young woman, Miss Curtis?"

William took a sip of his wine. "No," he said finally.

A waiter came to clear the table. Another waiter placed silver dishes of sorbet before them.

"I'm sorry." Cady placed her hand on his arm.

They were quiet for a moment, then William spoke: "Someone told me that Arabella is engaged. It's odd; I have no feelings about her at all."

"She's not engaged, not yet." Cady picked up a small silver spoon and dipped into her sorbet. "But she will be soon. She wants that house."

Arabella's name was linked with both that of an English lord and that of a phenomenally wealthy railroad magnate, Earl Carpenter. The newspapers vied with one another with stories about which earl the lady would choose, accompanied by stunning photographs of Arabella. The papers pushed enthusiastically for the "self-made American aristocrat," "a real man," as opposed to the English "feather duster," "Lord Ponce," who was in fact a vigorous sportsman.

In the end Arabella chose the American Earl simply because he was staggeringly rich and the English earl was not. Unfortunately, Earl Carpenter was also incredibly coarse, and although Arabella thought she could remake him into a gentleman, he proved beyond even her considerable powers to control and manipulate. She did finally get her magnificent house, purchasing it from William's father, but by the time she moved in, she had already begun to drift, despite her best efforts, to the outer fringes of society. Most people could not abide the boorish, hard-drinking Earl Carpenter, and Lydia Billings, suspecting it was Arabella who had fed the blind item to the *Sun* about Sybil Curtis during the Paxman trial, worked actively for her exclusion. Arabella tried to enlist Cady as her champion, but Cady firmly closed her door to her.

In March, Thomas Holborn died. William went to the funeral, held at Grace Church, then to the

Green-Wood Cemetery in Brooklyn with Marian Meade. They stood together there beneath umbrellas in the snow and freezing rain.

"Miserable day," said William after the service in the cemetery had come to an end.

"A happy one for Thomas. All he ever wanted was to be with Charlotte again."

"And you think he is?"

Marian glanced back at Charlotte and Thomas Holborn's headstone. She nodded.

"Not just their bones, Marian. Do you think he is with her?"

Marian took William's arm. They walked down the side of a hill to a line of motorcars waiting for them on the drive. "Yes. And they're dancing."

"A polka, no doubt."

"I was thinking more a tango. Tell me, William," she said, "do you know what has become of Miss Curtis?"

William stopped. "She is in England. Why do you ask?"

"Thomas left her some money—actually, quite a bit of money—and his lawyers are wondering how they are going to find her."

"She sailed to England. Burford, England. In the Cotswolds. If she's not there, her family is, and they'll know where to find her." William heaved a sigh.

"Is something wrong?" Marian asked.

"No," he said as they continued down the hill to

the waiting cars. "I'm happy for her. And happy to know that Thomas wanted to make some kind of amends to her." William looked away.

William went to his Aunt Edith's house that night for dinner. He saw her now at least two or three times a month, and was always grateful for her company. She had made him her lawyer, which involved more work than he had imagined. Twice he had had to get her out of jail in the early morning hours after a suffragettes' rally. And there was the time she was held for kicking a young prosecutor outside a courtroom after a trial.

"I did not kick him, William. I swear to you. I merely raised my foot."

"Raised your foot?"

"Yes. And he ran into it—like a charging bull— I shouldn't wonder he was black and blue." She thought a moment then added: "Poor thing."

William chose not to have her testify in her own defense.

When his lease was up on his apartment, he bought a small federal town house on Bedford Street in Greenwich Village. He took two weeks off from work in May and spent the time painting and repairing the house himself.

On the Friday of his first week back at work, Miss Leary walked into his office.

"Yes, Miss Leary?" William looked up from his work.

She frowned.

"I'm sorry." William slapped his forehead. "I'll get it right yet, Mrs. Isaacson, I promise I will."

"At least you don't call me Leary the way Mr. Parrish does. There's a young woman here to see you."

"A young woman? But I'm not expecting anyone."

"A Miss Curtis."

"What?"

"Yes." She looked at him curiously.

He nodded distractedly. "I'll be out in a moment."

When he walked into the front room, she was sitting in one of the Windsor chairs by the office's front door. She rose when she saw him. She was wearing a pale green dress, gathered high at the waist then again at her knees, before falling in a straight line over her shoes. On her head she wore a wide-brimmed hat with a green ribbon. She looked absolutely beautiful. She gave him a half smile.

He felt himself at a loss for words. "Miss Curtis," he heard himself say. He opened the gate separating Mrs. Isaacson's desk from the waiting area and took her hand. "How . . . how wonderful to see you."

"I'm leaving again for England tomorrow," she said, "and I wanted to say hello before I left."

"Oh," he said, trying to hide his disappointment.

She wanted to say hello—when she was leaving tomorrow? A good-bye, really, a last-minute good-bye as to some fondly remembered acquaintance. He drew back. "Well, I wish you a safe journey and—"

"Mr. Dysart, have you a moment we might talk?" she asked, surprising him again.

"Yes . . . I suppose." He glanced at Mrs. Isaacson, who seemed so purposefully engaged in work at her desk that he guessed she was listening to every word. "Why don't we go for a walk," he said, and turned to Mrs. Isaacson, who was holding a file in midair as she stared intently at Sybil. "Mrs. Isaacson." She did not respond. "Mrs. Isaacson."

"Oh." She threw the file in a drawer and slammed it shut.

"I'm out for a short while."

"Of course, sir."

William opened the door and out of the corner of his eye saw Mrs. Isaacson leaning forward to catch a last glimpse of Sybil.

When they reached the street, they turned down Fifth Avenue toward Greenwich Village. It was a beautiful spring day, with the sun shining brilliantly overhead.

"How have you been since your return to England?" he asked.

"It was a bit difficult at first. I missed so many people here."

William nodded, wondering if he was one of them.

"Caroline Jameson. The children."

Apparently not. They walked a little farther in silence.

"Not your old friend Mr. Dysart?" he asked at last, trying for a jaunty tone.

She seemed uncomfortable with his question.

How stupid of him to ask, he thought, embarrassing really. "How is everything in Burford?"

"I was very lucky. I found my mother's two sisters. One a widow, one never married. Lovely women. Virginia and Katharine."

"Do they know?"

She nodded.

"It must have been difficult."

"Yes. For us all."

They walked along in silence. They were crossing Fourteenth Street when a motorcar sped up, its driver anonymous behind his driving goggles, honking furiously for them to get out of the way. William shook his head.

"There are some things I don't miss about New York," she said.

"I am sure." William smiled. "You look well."

"My mother's younger brother, Simon, lives not far from Burford in a village called Charney Bassett. I have two young cousins there—boys, whom I adore."

William tried not to stare at her. "I heard of your good fortune."

"Yes. I returned to sign papers, and . . ." She took a deep breath. "I wanted to apologize to you for the way I behaved in the end. I had to get away. I'm sorry. Can you forgive me?"

"Of course."

They came to Eighth Street, and a few doors in from Fifth Avenue was a lunchroom, Flemming's Fountain. "Have you had lunch?" William asked.

"No." She glanced toward Washington Square Park. "It's such a lovely day, perhaps we could get something and eat in the park?"

They went into the lunchroom and ordered sandwiches. William asked for a bottle of ginger ale.

"Not a sarsaparilla?" asked Sybil as they waited at the curved mahogany and marble counter, while a woman in a crisp white apron prepared their sandwiches before a great beveled mirror.

He looked at her curiously.

"That day I gave you one—I thought you would die."

"Oh, horrible. Sickeningly sweet."

"Yet you drank it all. How kind you were. I should have said something, but you made me so nervous."

"Did I? Why?"

"Perhaps because you were so kind."

They took their sandwiches to Washington

Square Park and sat on a bench by some azalea bushes, a riot of pink and white flowers.

"I submitted two poems to *The London Magazine*," she told him as she unwrapped her sandwich, "and they're going to publish one."

"Really? That is such wonderful news."

"And you with your firm. Congratulations."

"Funny how things change," he said. "I was just thinking, I sat on this exact bench less than two years ago and thought my life was over. I was miserable. Unhappily married and thought I would be for the rest of my life. Now less than two years later, my wife is married to someone else and I am living a completely different life."

"Are you happy?"

William hesitated. "As happy as I can be, I suppose."

"Have you married again?"

William took a deep breath. "No." He put down his sandwich.

"Is something wrong?"

"Miss Curtis . . ." He paused. "Sybil. The last time I saw you, I told you . . ." He stopped.

"What?"

He sighed and looked away. "Never mind. You have obviously forgotten."

"No. I haven't."

"Then how can you ask me if I'm married?"

"To some people 'never' means six months, a year."

"Not to me."

"No?"

"No. I haven't stopped . . ." He turned and stared across the park and sighed. "I haven't stopped thinking about you a moment since you left."

"I see," she said, and looked down.

"But you came to see me today, when you are leaving tomorrow, like I'm an old friend of the family. Which is fine, of course, if that's how you feel. But it is difficult." He tossed the remainder of his half sandwich to some pigeons gathered nearby. "Frankly, I wish you hadn't come at all."

She nodded and raised her sandwich to her lips, then set it down again.

"I'm sorry. I don't mean to be so harsh," said William. "I'm glad you came. I won't forget this, not one moment of it—ever."

"I waited until the last minute, because I was afraid you might have forgotten me."

"Forgotten you! I damn near forgot everything else."

She raised her fingers to her lips and started to laugh despite her tears.

"Why are you laughing?"

"You—you're so cantankerous."

"Cantankerous?"

"Yes. I know you don't think you are, but you are."

He laughed.

She reached into her bag and took out a folded piece of paper and handed it to him. "I wrote this for you."

"For me?"

"Yes."

William opened the paper and read:

Incognito

Unknown and unknowing
I assumed that disguise
till love lifted the veil
and I could see with your eyes

He tried to say something, but all he could manage was to shake his head. There was a long silence. "Thank you," he said at last.

Two little girls wandered over, giggling shyly; they joined hands and began to sing "Ring Around the Rosie," lisping and stumbling to the end of the rhyme. Sybil leaned forward. "That was lovely!" The girls raised their hands to their faces, then ran laughing back to their mother, sitting on a nearby bench.

"Friends of yours?" William mustered a smile. He turned and looked into the distance. "Ashes, ashes, we all fall down," he repeated quietly. He looked at her. "Are you really going to leave tomorrow?"

She was silent.

"Can you stay a few days more?"

She looked at him intently.

"Not forever. Just long enough to marry me."

"I'm still so frightened." She began to cry. "I don't know that I can ever make any man a good wife."

"Not any man. Me."

A sudden blush illuminated her face.

"I know something about demons—fear—dread," he said. "Let me face them with you. I can face anything but losing you again."

She reached up and touched his cheek. "How I missed you."

"Cantankerous old me?"

"So I could scarcely stand it," she whispered, her fingers tracing the outline of his jaw.

He leaned down and kissed her and she laid her head on his shoulder. Resting his cheek against the top of her head, he looked out at all the people, trees, buildings—everything within his sight—and felt part of it in a way he never had before. She took his hand and he smiled, as the soft rays of the spring sun seemed to muffle the sound of everything but the music in his soul for and because of her.

Readers Guide

Representing the widow of a wealthy Wall Street financier, lawyer William Dysart travels to a small Long Island town with a generous offer to buy a cottage and five acres of land from a woman he assumes is a stubborn old farmer's wife looking for a bargain. Instead he finds Miss Sybil Curtis, a beautiful young woman with a quiet demeanor. But when Sybil still refuses to sell, the widow threatens to use her influence with the State to seize the property.

Intrigued by Sybil's defiance and afflicted by a growing affection for her, William develops a desire to help her. His good intentions quickly turn into an obsession he cannot define—one that tears away the facade of his marriage and presents him with the truths of his own family. But it's not until he finds out the truth about Sybil's life that William begins to push the boundaries between what society wants, what his family expects—and what his heart desires.

1. When we first meet William and his wife, Arabella, they quickly enter into a disagreement about their living situation— William is content with their unpretentious house, while Arabella dreams of a sprawling mansion complete with an upgraded social

status. Are there other signs that their marriage isn't the most stable? Do you think that William is happy at the beginning of the novel?

2. When he first introduces himself to Sybil Curtis, William lies and says that he is interested in buying her property for himself. When he returns to the cottage a second time to ask her to reconsider, he admits that Lydia Billings is the interested buyer. Why does William lie at first? Conversely, why do you think he admits the truth? Do you think he realizes something is amiss with Lydia's offer?

3. William is taken aback when he spies Sybil with Albert Penniman. Why do you think their relationship bothers him? What do you think William's opinion of Sybil was before he learned of her relationship? Does her interaction with Albert change his opinion?

4. Arabella seems especially close to William's father, Charles Dysart. In fact, she tries to sway William in her favor by using his father's opinions to her advantage—first with building a bigger house and then with staying married. What do you think is the extent of

Arabella and Charles's relationship? How do you think Cady, Charles's wife, feels about their relationship?

5. Arabella and Sybil are both described as exceptionally beautiful women. Discuss the differences in their beauty. What do you think defines a beautiful person?

6. After learning the truth about what Henry Billings did to Sybil, William returns to her cottage to apologize for his previous behavior. Is that the only reason he visits? Do you think if he had not come to see her, Sybil would not have broken down? Would her breakdown have happened if they had never met?

7. When Sybil has recovered, William makes a habit of visiting her, and they grow much closer. Discuss the night that William sleeps on her couch and their relationship suddenly becomes physical. Why does Sybil break away when William admits his love for her? What do you think Sybil is hoping for in her impromptu seduction? Does she succeed?

8. There are three people that are aware of Henry Billings's deplorable behavior: Lydia Billings, Thomas Holborn, and Dr. Keating.

How does each of these characters react to the truth? Why do you think Lydia brought Sybil books and chocolates while she was being kept by Henry? Why didn't Dr. Keating report the abuse? Do you think that Billings's behavior would be as ignored today as it was then?

9. At a suffrage meeting William attends he is surprised to see Edith Bradford, his estranged aunt, stand up and explain why so many women—including William's wife, Arabella—are resistant to having the right to vote: "We're only asking men to give up some power—unpleasant, I'm sure—but we are asking women to take real power into their own hands for the first time *ever* and it terrifies them." How is this pivotal time period in women's history important to the story? How is Sybil taking power into her own hands throughout the book? Why do you think Arabella declines to be part of the suffrage movement?

10. As the story unfolds, the mystery behind William's mother's abandonment and subsequent death unravels. Were you surprised by Aunt Edith's story? How do you think William feels after learning the truth about his mother?

11. Charles Dysart appears to be a rather harsh man. While it is apparent that he was never overly affectionate with his son, why do you think he is so rigid and unyielding? Do you think that he was different before William's mother's death? Do you think that he will reach out to William in the future?

12. At the very end of the book Sybil presents William with a poem, entitled "Incognito":

> Unknown and unknowing,
> I assumed that disguise,
> till love lifted the veil,
> and I could see with your eyes

What is Sybil trying to tell William? Do you think that Sybil would have been all right if William had not entered her life? How did these two characters change each other?

Center Point Publishing
600 Brooks Road ● PO Box 1
Thorndike ME 04986-0001 USA

(207) 568-3717

US & Canada:
1 800 929-9108
www.centerpointlargeprint.com